Lizelle let her eyes half close and called to her horse, Darkwind. *Yo, fleet one! Yo, star-brow! Yo, rather dense and thick-witted one!*

She felt a faint reply, as if shouted from far away. *Does one of poor legs and wit need assistance?*

No. Thanks just the same, mount that only fools should ride.

Sometimes one thinks that only fools—

Don't say it. You escaped Guire?

Of course.

Good. See you tomorrow.

Beware the captain.

And a few others. I'll have a tale to tell.

One's done nothing rash?

Nothing more than I've had to....

Cats Have No Lord

WILL SHETTERLY

ACE FANTASY BOOKS
NEW YORK

CATS HAVE NO LORD

An Ace Fantasy Book/published by arrangement with
the author and the author's agent, Valerie Smith

PRINTING HISTORY
Ace Original/April 1985

ISBN: 0-441-09493-7

Ace Fantasy Books are published by The Berkley Publishing Group,
200 Madison Avenue, New York, New York 10016.
PRINTED IN THE UNITED STATES OF AMERICA

For my mother and father,
with love.

Acknowledgments

The influences in writing this book include William Goldman's *The Princess Bride;* Tanith Lee's tales of Azharn, Night's Master; Fritz Leiber's saga of Fafhrd and the Gray Mouser; Michael Moorcock's *Gloriana;* and Roger Zelazny's *Jack of Shadows*—though none of these books' authors should be blamed for my infelicities. Further, this book would be a far more painful thing to read if Emma Bull and Terri Windling were not such clever, helpful, and infinitely patient people.

Contents

prologue

Of Loss and Gain
in City Gordia

LIZELLE LINGERED IN Lord Noring's bed. The autumn night was cold and he, curled against her beneath many embroidered quilts, was warm and comforting. She listened to the gentle rasp of his breathing and thought, *Maybe I'm wrong. Maybe I love him. Maybe he loves me. Maybe—*

Darkwind's voice came like a whisper in her skull. *Maybe that one will decide before this one dies of old age?*

You interrupt a matter of the heart!

Oh. This one may die of boredom, then.

Very funny. You'll never understand simple human emotions.

True. This one is grateful.

"That one" is a pain.

This one has been very patient.

You're . . . right. I apologize.

Shall these two depart, then?

Lizelle glanced at Noring. He had been kind to her, and she liked his quiet manners, the rare display of his subtle wit. Yet she heard herself answer, and knew she answered without regret, *Yes. We go, Darkwind.*

Good. Hurry.

She dressed silently in red woolen riding skirts and a black jacket with gold braid that Noring had given her soon after they'd met. Her low black boots, her only possession from her circus days, had been kept in good repair by his sneering servants. Lizelle tied back her dark hair with a bit of crimson cord, then carried her boots to the tapestry that hung in the doorway and peeked out. No one walked the quiet hall. Lizelle set down her boots and padded back into

1

the sleeping room in her stockings.

The coals in the open fireplace still glowed, and some moonlight slipped through the milky glass shutters, but Lizelle did not need to see to move in this room she knew so well. Several lacquered boxes of Noring's jewelry, inherited from relatives and a wife who had died in childbirth, sat on his dresser. Lizelle emptied them into a saddlebag. *Ah, Noring. You'll be less trusting if you take another lover from the lower castes.* A miststone on a silver chain lay in one box. Struck by the necklace's beauty, Lizelle fastened it around her throat and tucked its gem under her shirt.

She stopped by the door, picked up her boots, and looked back. Noring's blankets had slid down, baring his lean, familiar torso and the pale scars from his duels. *I'm sorry,* she thought. *If I was different, or—*

Were that one different, Darkwind said, *these two would've fled Gordia hours ago.*

You could pretend to give me some privacy. Or, at least, sympathy.

Certainly. Shall this one conjure the sounds of restrained sobbing?

I cared for him.

And the expression of that care is midnight theft and hasty departure?

He wouldn't let me go, otherwise.

Or one would not be willing to go, otherwise?

Lizelle glanced back at Noring. *Perhaps.* She returned to the bed to pull the quilts over his shoulders. Then she slipped out the door, leaving Noring and her doubt behind her.

Ree climbed the dark tower stairs. The Hooded Man had said there were no guards waiting above, but the girl was afraid. Sweat dampened the leather-bound hilt of her knife until it felt as soft as her resolution. Her tunic seemed clammy beneath her arms, and she shivered in her dirty beggar's rags. Her wish for comfort only reminded her of her family's death—and of her own accidental survival when a broken carriage wheel had kept her from returning home on the night when the Empress's agents came to call.

Ree touched the vial in her sash to be sure she had not

lost it. She thought, *The Hooded Man uses me. Why do I believe his potion does anything at all?* The Hooded Man had said that Ree could avenge her family and free all Gordia, if she had the courage to act. The girl told herself that she must trust him, wiped her palm against her stained tunic, and climbed on.

When she heard distant conversation, she became a statue on the steps. After a moment, she could distinguish two speakers. The first was a woman, surely Glynaldis of Gordia. The other was more difficult to hear. Ree waited. When no new voices added themselves to the murmurings, she uncorked the Hooded Man's vial and drank.

The taste was so bitter that she almost coughed. Ree raised her hand to cover her mouth and could not see her arm, not even its shadow against the darkness. Smiling, she hurried on.

As she drew near, she heard part of a question asked by the woman: ". . . chooses not to answer?"

The other said, "There's no choice. If I conjure well, he'll come. If not, he won't."

"Then conjure well."

"Or?"

"Damn you, Thelog Ar—"

The stairway filled with an eerie mimicry of human laughter. "You've already damned me. And you know I always do well. What choice have I?"

"There are times when I would silence you."

"Ah! Do you threaten me, or promise?"

"Thelog Ar . . ."

"Yes?"

"Don't oppose me."

"Of course not, most treasured one."

Ree peeked over the top of the stairs. The room was almost bare, and though the large mullioned windows at each compass point were open, the chamber was warmer than any natural means could explain. The walls were the same pink-veined marble that composed most of Castle Cloud. The floor was a mosaic of green, black, and white tile. Near the center of the chamber, a tripod of grimacing brass snakes cradled an embossed bowl in which flames writhed, offering dim, flickering illumination. Beside this lamp, set into the floor, lay an obsidian slab, its diameter the length of a tall man's body. Its surface was slick and reflective, like oil on water.

The spectral voice came from a shrouded figure seated at the far wall. White robes covered the man's body, and a cowl hid his head. The woman stood near him with her back to the stairs. Ree first noticed her strong shoulders and rock-grey hair that cascaded in waves to slim hips sheathed in a scarlet silk gown. When the woman turned, Ree almost gasped, thinking someone so fair could never be evil. Then she mocked her notion as childish and gripped her dagger tighter. She noticed time's touch on the woman's features, a slight gauntness to her cheeks, a trace of weathering about her eyes. This was a much older woman than Ree had expected. Did Glynaldis appear publicly in paint and wig, and never near the people?

The woman said, "Please. Aid me, and I'll grant what you desire."

Again the laughter came. "How sweetly you promise. But never fear. This is in my power. You've forgotten none of your part?"

"Would I?" The woman drew her gown over her head and threw the wadded silk across the room. Clad solely in red slippers that laced up her calves, she ordered, "Begin." Her sudden nudity made her human and vulnerable. Ree stared. She had only thought to slay a symbol.

"Very well, my sister," said Thelog Ar.

Sister? Tales were told of Thessis Ar, an enchantress who also served Gordia's Empress. Had Glynaldis been called away, and Thessis Ar taken her role? This game of righting wrongs was more complex than Ree had thought. She wanted to surrender, to be punished and sent home, but she knew the only home she would find would be with Ralka, Lord of Wolves.

Thessis Ar took a dancer's stance beside the black floor-stone. The wizard spoke, neither chanting nor singing, yet somehow doing both. Hearing his words, Ree realized that she had waited too long. Now the sorcerers must finish what they began, for half-formed magics were the most dangerous of all. Ree wondered how long the Hooded Man's potion would protect her.

Stepping ever slower with high, stylized paces, Thessis Ar circled the black stone. Her body soon glistened with sweat, though her motions retained the illusion of ease. Eight times she stepped; then, when the ninth would close the circle, she looked beseechingly at Thelog Ar.

The mage remained still. Ree heard nothing, but she sensed the mystic words continuing like vibrations in her soul. Thessis Ar's breasts rose in a deep breath and, focusing on the spot at which she had begun, she leaped. In midair, her movement began to slow, almost as if she would be held aloft. Her eyes widened, eloquent in terror. She brought her arms before her in a warding gesture, Thelog Ar's voice rang out, and, with a look of exultation, the woman landed. Her slippers slapped against the tiles with the return of sound, and she laughed.

Motes of light shimmered in her wake. Inside the circle, tendrils of smoke wove themselves into the image of a slender man who hovered nude above the obsidian slab. His skin, as white and as luminescent as polished marble, glowed as though lit from within.

Thessis Ar said, almost bored, "You are the demon Asphoriel?"

"So may you think of me, if you wish." Its words hurt the girl's ears.

Thessis Ar said, "Can you make Gordia's Empress the ruler of this world?"

"Her legions will conquer all. You do not need me."

"And how long will they take?"

"That's what you would know?"

"No." The woman twined a lock of grey hair about her index finger, then said, "Her soldiers could succeed in a century or two. This I know. But Glynaldis is not so patient."

"Nor am I noted for patience!" Tiny flames rippled across the captive's pale skin. His eyes blazed, bathing Thessis Ar in a light brighter than that of day. "What would you have of me?"

The woman shrugged, then said calmly, "The key to ruling all of humanity."

Something in Ree suggested that losing her life in saving the world was a thing to be done, not debated. Someone else could slay Glynaldis, who would be hindered by the loss of her witches. The girl ran forward with her dagger ready to strike.

She had crossed half the floor when Thessis Ar said, "Excuse me," to the man in the cage of light. She asked Thelog Ar, "Someone comes?"

The sorcerer said, "Yes." He added a word from the magicians' tongue. Two paces from her goal, Ree fell, visible, immobile, terrified.

Thelog Ar told the woman, "Your perception has heightened. I didn't sense her."

"Nor did I, till she was close." With a shrug, Thessis Ar turned back to Asphoriel. "Well? Can you deliver what we wish?"

"The necklace of the Wisest One?"

The woman smiled as if the world were already won. "Exactly!"

"I can obtain it. Would you give me a third of the remaining years of your life in trade?"

Ree struggled to move, to scream, to somehow interrupt the pact about to be established. She could only blink and rock slightly in place.

"Are those your full terms?" the woman asked.

"They are the first part of them."

"You ask too much."

The demon stared. "If we cannot bargain, I'll have my price for attending you. Will you be it?"

"Oh, bother." Thessis Ar glanced at the girl. "Take her."

"Ah. I have no human pet." The cage of light parted, and Asphoriel reached out to Ree with a pale, blazing hand. "Come," he said.

Ree, abruptly free again, scrambled away, close to Thessis Ar. "P-please, Lady, spare me! I'll tell all I know of the Hooded Man's plans! I'll help—"

"Quiet," the woman said. "You know nothing useful, or he wouldn't have risked you." Then, with something like kindness, she added, "Go. Asphoriel will treat you better than I." She looked at the demon's naked form. "I almost envy you."

"No!" Ree darted back. The demon had stepped from

the black stone to block her access to the stairs. Still Asphoriel held out his hand, waiting for her to take it. Ree
raced to the shaded corner where Thelog Ar sat in his high-
backed chair. "Noble magician, aid me! Aid me, and I'll
render any service, do any—" At the sight of the wizard's
face, Ree cried out, and stumbled away, blind with horror.

A sad voice filled the room. "You see why I can't help
you, lass. I am sorry."

"Come," Asphoriel repeated.

"No!" The girl tripped and remained huddled on the floor.
"No! Please, gods, no! Aid me, someone. . . ."

Asphoriel's hand closed on Ree's wrist. His touch burned
without charring. Her dagger fell from her grip, and she
screamed then, in terror and fear and pain, knowing she
would spend eternity in that embrace.

Asphoriel and the girl and the shimmering cage of light
disappeared in an implosion of white smoke. Thelog Ar
said, "You gained nothing. You shouldn't toy with such
forces to test me."

Thessis Ar smiled. "You see so little, dear brother. Now
I know what we must find. If we can't win the Wisest One's
necklace through our own efforts, I'll call on Asphoriel
again. But only if we fail." She walked to her gown and
picked it up. "I retain a few scruples."

"Really?"

"Well, mostly to amuse myself, I admit. It's so satisfying
to be shocked."

"And the girl? Did consigning her to Asphoriel shock
you?"

Thessis Ar shrugged, then slipped on the gown. Smooth-
ing it about her hips, she said, "There was a price to be
paid."

"But a child?"

"My would-be assassin? You didn't recognize her?"

"No."

"That was the girl who escaped us earlier. Riawn, I
believe. Of the house of Oleth-ym-Arion. I suspect that
Glynaldis's reign will be less troubled now that the last of
those who might claim her throne are . . . absent."

"But to give the girl—"

"She was convenient, my mentor. And I'm sure she'll find some pleasure with her punishment. Indeed, I think this is just another case of Luck attending she who desired him least. Don't you?"

"I . . ." But the woman had already begun the descent to her chambers, and the sorcerer remained in his tower room, alone.

In a place outside of time, in what seemed a courtyard made all of turquoise, a man who resembled a wolf said, "She thinks to trick us!"

Asphoriel, seeming very naked without his garb of flame, answered, "And we, her. There is a balance." At his feet sat Ree, who leaned against his knees and watched with an expression of vacant contentment.

"You enjoy this," said the Wolf Lord.

Asphoriel nodded. "As you do, young Ralka. It's a pleasing game."

The Wolf Lord snarled. "What we do is no game!"

Ree cringed. Asphoriel stroked her shaven head to soothe her, then nodded to Ralka. "You wouldn't think so. Games are no part of your nature."

"Then how can you say I enjoy this?"

"Because plotting and winning are very much part of your nature. Else you'd never have called on me."

"You've complicated the Pattern."

"Of course. But I reinforce the future we wish to forge. Gordia's Empress has been given the clue she needs. She'll prove a useful ally."

The Wolf Lord bared his teeth in pleasure. "Especially as an unwitting one?"

"Especially." Asphoriel nodded. "And if we need to discard her for another pawn . . ."

"We do so!"

"Of course. And if nothing else, Gordia will divert the Questers' attention."

"You don't expect that band of complacent, mortal scholars to—"

"I try to expect everything. I intend to succeed, Wolf Lord."

"But the Questers! What can they do?"

"Dismiss no enemy as harmless."

"I don't. If they're a danger, let's destroy them. It'd be easy."

"It would be a declaration of war. We cannot."

"But—"

"We cannot."

"How'll we win, then?"

Asphoriel closed his eyes and sighed. "By letting our enemies win for us."

chapter one

A Lady Enters
Tyrwilka

LIZELLE LONGED TO race Darkwind up the Elf King's Road. Though many of the leaves around them were russet and gold and brown, the afternoon felt like one of summer rather than fall, perfect for mad darts and indulgent lingerings. Lizelle could have stopped to swim at any of several streams they had passed, then slept in the grass while the sun dried her skin. Instead, she rode slowly up the wooded valley to Tyrwilka with a troop of the Empress's soldiers, some thirty kilted pikemen wearing headbands of Gordian blue stamped with a white wolf's head.

The commanders were a middle-aged black-bearded captain in an indigo cloak and hat who said little, and his courteous blond lieutenant, a handsome young man who had either lost his wide-brimmed hat or who merely chose not to conceal his curly locks. The officers both rode geldings inured to the footsoldiers' pace, but Darkwind soon snorted his impatience.

Lizelle immediately fluttered her lashes at Captain Quentian—pretty Lieutenant Guire was more to her taste, but the dour captain had the power to hang her—and murmured, "Daddy said he'd be too much horse for me, but I insisted. Isn't he gorgeous?" Simultaneously, she flashed a thought to Darkwind: *Watch it, dumbass! Gordian noblewomen don't ride anything with spirit.*

Their loss. And this one is neither mute nor donkey.

Yeah, but sometimes you're godlings-be-damned obtuse. Try to act like a mare. A very old mare.

This one is a stallion. Stallions—

Needn't remain stallions.
One wouldn't!
Lizelle said nothing.
Would one?
Try me. If they suspect we're anything less than we ap-pear . . .
This one didn't decide that the best disguise for a circus performer was the dress of the First Caste.
It wasn't a bad idea. If we hadn't met Quentian's troop—
Others would have wondered why a gentlewoman trav-eled alone. For one who knows so much about the high castes—
Picky, picky. Sometimes I think you'd make a fine old nag.

Darkwind reared. Lizelle clamped her thighs together and leaned into his neck. *Hey! Anyone ever suggest you're a little touchy sometimes?*

Young Guire reached for Darkwind's reins as Darkwind twisted toward Captain Quentian, whose grey shied. The footsoldiers scattered, and one dropped his pike. Then Dark-wind settled, seemingly controlled.

Lizelle said, *I'm sorry I teased.*
One should be.

Quentian tugged at his beard with a gloved hand. "A more orthodox bridle might make that beast more docile. Something with a bit to yank. . . ."

"Oh, but Captain!" Lizelle giggled.
Don't overdo it.
Me? How unlikely. "Darkwind's such a silly horsie. He just likes to stand up once in a while so everyone can admire him. Isn't that so, you widdle horsie-worsie?" She stroked his neck.
Ugh.
Well, that's how young ladies talk.
The captain doesn't like it.
No. But he expects it.

Guire smiled, flashing perfect teeth. "Lady, if you'd care to take my horse, one of the men could lead yours."

"Why, Lieutenant! How kind! How very kind. But I won't have any more trouble with dear Darkwind." *Will I?*

Darkwind snorted, more tamely than before.

"An unusual name for a horse," Quentian said.

"Do you really think so? I was afraid it was too obvious. I mean, his color and his speed . . . You understand, Captain. Doesn't it sound positively romantic?"

Quentian grimaced and looked away. "Yes. I suppose so."

Guire said, "Most of the young ladies of my acquaintance have smaller animals with, well, friendlier names."

"I know what you mean, Lieutenant. I was going to call him 'Cupcake,' but then I just changed my mind. Silly me."

Cupcake?

I could call you that yet.

One would rather be gelded.

Really?

One would rather not decide.

"You ride very well," Quentian said.

"Oh, Captain! Is that a compliment?"

"Only an observation."

"And from such a fine horseman as yourself. My!" She gave the Gordian another glance from under her painted lids. *Perhaps I can turn his thoughts to other things.*

One is as subtle as rape.

I can be more blatant.

One does not doubt.

"Excuse me, Lady. I must see to my men." Quentian touched his fingers to his hat and rode to the rear of the column.

Did one succeed?

Not in seducing. But I bored him. That's just as good.

If one says so.

The only hint of mishap along the way occurred when Lizelle noticed the officers watching her and realized that she had been humming "The Way They Do It in Elflands." Her comment, "A pretty tune, hmm? The stablegirl used to whistle it as she worked. But when I asked her for the lyrics, she only tittered and changed the subject. Do you have any idea why, Captain?" had been received with embarrassed grunts from both men and laughter from a pikeman marching near.

* * *

They reached Tyrwilka at dusk. The woods had begun to thin, then suddenly ended as farmland began. Perhaps a mile beyond, the city walls rose out of the ground to cut off travel through Korz Valley. The fortifications seemed low and squat in the dying light, though they surely rose twenty feet high or more. A few torches burned in turret windows.

Ah, warmth at last, thought Lizelle.

If allowed in.

We'll get in. You fret too much. With a Gordian escort—Tyrwilkans hate Gordians.

Tyrwilka would fall quickly if the Empress ordered her legions this way. Tyrwilkans know that. Their customs officers won't halt Gordian troops, and we're with them. We'll get in.

One wonders.

Trust me. I know how men's minds work.

"Ah, city lights are inviting," Guire said wistfully.

"Indeed, Lieutenant. A warm room, a soft bed..."

The young man sighed. "I only have a cold barracks chamber and a soldier's pallet awaiting me, alas."

"Gordia has a fort in Tyrwilka?"

Guire shook his head, and his blond ringlets danced. "Hardly a fort. We're allowed our little garrison in return for, ah, favored trade status. And to help protect Tyrwilka from Faerie, of course."

"Oh? I'd always thought Tyrwilka was friendly with the Elflands."

"Well, they trade with them, but Tyrwilkans don't trust Elves any more than most folk do." Guire smiled as he changed the subject. "Will you stay in the city?"

Lizelle nodded. "Probably in an inn on Empire Avenue."

"They're quite good. I often dine at one."

"Oh? If I had someone to show me about..."

Quentian, riding slightly behind them, said, "I'd thought your aunt—"

"Oh, no." *Forgetting my own cover story. I ought to become a farmer's wife. And make you a plowhorse, eavesdropper.*

One could be content.

She had told the soldiers of journeying with her father to visit an ailing aunt. Then, this morning in the foothills, a messenger rode up and insisted her father return to Gordia for a business matter. Daddy could not bear to let his darling travel alone, yet she assured him she would be safe on fleet Darkwind. As they were only a few hours' ride from Tyrwilka, Daddy gave in. It was not a good story, but it was plausible. "Auntie's too ill, I fear, and her disease may be contagious. That's why I'll stay at an inn. Besides, I wouldn't consider disturbing her at this hour."

"I . . . see." Quentian dropped back to the rear of the column.

"Forgive him, Lady," Guire said. "He wasn't born to his position, but earned it through merit. He's a fine soldier. Many of our caste would resent serving under him, though I think I'm fortunate."

So Quentian isn't the formal, highborn fool I thought— no, hoped—him to be. Wonderful. How much does he suspect?

Ought these two to flee?

No. If he's lowcaste and at all wise, he won't voice his suspicions without more proof than we'll give him. "He did nothing to give offense."

"You're good to think so."

"Should I stay at The Red Griffin?" Lizelle touched Guire's sleeve. "Auntie says it's nice."

"Frankly, I prefer The Yarlwood Arms. It's newer, more comfortable, more private. . . ."

Lizelle nodded compliantly. "Then The Yarlwood Arms it'll be." *And has the young lieutenant made the most genteel of passes at me?* she wondered.

One wouldn't know. The mysteries of human sex are such that this one wonders how the race continues to continue itself.

You always say that.

One always thinks that.

"I'm sure you'll be pleased with the services," Guire said.

Services? Oh, the inn.

Guire added, blushing slightly, "I might free myself from this evening's duties, if you'd consider my company."

Lizelle smiled. "I would be pleased, Lieutenant."

Tyrwilka's gates had yet to be closed for the night. Four soldiers stood before them, each in white woolen trousers and the scarlet surcoat of King Milas's guard. Three bore spears; one had only a sword at his waist. This man, a stout fellow with traditional Tyrwilkan sideburns but with a plainsman's darker features, stepped forward, calling, "Identify yourselves!" A single plume on his steel helmet proclaimed him an officer.

Guire sat up in his saddle and answered, "Soldiers of the Empress, may she rule forever."

"Gordians, eh?"

"Yes, as you plainly see." Guire slapped dust from his blue riding kilt.

"Ah, yes. Such pretty clothes."

The sieve says the colander leaks, Lizelle thought.

What?

An analogy to kitchen utensils. Forget it.

Gladly. It seems somewhat strained.

"Anything to declare?" asked the guard.

"No," Quentian replied, indicating with a twist of his hand that Guire should remain quiet.

"The lady travels with you?"

Godlings, Lizelle prayed, *a gold royal to your priests if he says yes.*

Quentian looked at her.

He suspects, Darkwind said.

Two royals, Lizelle said.

"The lady joined us this morning," Quentian said.

"Oh?"

"I've nothing to declare," Lizelle stated quickly, striving for a highcaste Gordian's tone of mild annoyance.

The plainsman shook his head. "I must inspect your bags, Lady. It's a formality, nothing more."

"I've nothing to declare," Lizelle repeated. *Did Tyrwilka sign an extradition treaty with Gordia?*

Yes.

I begin to consider atheism.

The plainsman reached out to help her dismount. Lizelle accepted his hand and leaped down. *If I had a sword, we could fight.*

The Gordians hem these two too closely in. Besides, several soldiers with crossbows watch from the wall.

Your eyes are keener than mine. Then our only hope lies in diversion?

Agreed.

Escape with the bags. I'll be distraught. Meet me tomorrow morning by the brook a mile back. Lizelle screamed as Darkwind bolted from her. The plainsman lunged for the stallion's reins, but Lizelle managed to stumble into him and they both fell. "Oh, Lieutenant Guire!" she cried from the ground. "My horse! You must catch my horse!"

Guire grinned agreeably and, slapping his chestnut, raced after Darkwind. He would never overtake him. The plainsman helped Lizelle to her feet. "Don't worry, Lady. If the Gordian doesn't fetch your mount, we'll send Tyrwilkan riders out tomorrow. It won't go far. I know skittish animals."

"Thank you." She adjusted her clothing and brushed off dust. Her necklace had fallen out of her black jacket. As her hand closed on it to tuck it back into her blouse, she remembered that it was part of her gains in City Gordia. *Godlings you'll have your two royals. I promise a third if—*

Quentian spoke. "A beautiful gem on that chain, Lady."

"Thank you, Captain. It's really quite common. An ordinary miststone."

"Oh, something more than common, I'm sure. May I see it?"

A fourth, godlings. Four royals, eh? "If you wish."

Quentian weighed it in his palm. "Interesting," he said as though it were not. "Lord Noring's mother wore a similar necklace at the Empress's birthday ball."

Lizelle covered a gasp with her hand. "And my jeweler swore it was an original!"

Quentian cocked an eyebrow at her, then turned to the plainsman. "Sergeant, we have a slight difficulty here."

"Yes?"

"Yes. A message came by pigeon to the border post at Winterberry, where we barracked last night. Lord Noring reported some jewelry stolen. This woman's necklace greatly resembles one of the missing items. We'll take her into custody until the matter is resolved."

"I protest!" Lizelle exclaimed. "Sirs, this is no way to treat—"

The officers ignored her. The Tyrwilkan said, "Can't allow that, sir. She's in Tyrwilka now, so this becomes a Tyrwilkan concern."

"When our local minister petitions your king, she'll be back in our hands."

"Until then, I must insist that she's ours."

"I'm no one's!" Lizelle shouted. "There's been a mistake. Can't you see that? I bought this necklace!" She found it too easy to let herself cry.

"There, there, missy," said the plainsman. "We'll get this straightened out, one way or another. Never you fret, now." Then he coughed politely and said, "The necklace should stay with us. Until the matter's resolved."

Quentian frowned. "You think so?"

"I must insist."

"Very well." Quentian tossed it to the sergeant. "See that it's safe." Quentian bowed stiffly to Lizelle, nodded to the sergeant, and kicked his heels into his grey's flanks. "Forward!" he cried. The troop marched into Tyrwilka.

"You can't leave me!" Lizelle cried after them. "Daddy'll be furious! You can't leave me! You can't!"

"I'm afraid they just did, missy. Come along." The soldier's grip on her arm, though gentle, was firm.

"Where's Lieutenant Guire? Oh, Sergeant, he'll vouch for me."

"That pretty Gordian? He'll be chasing your horse all night, most like. Don't worry, though. We'll find a nice place for you to sleep, and a bit of warm food as well. Nothing fancy, mind, but good." He turned to a fat, bearded soldier. "Jaeko, you're in charge till I return."

"Shall one of the men accompany you?"

"To guard this slip of a lass? No, best you all stay at the walls. Suppose a band of Hrota attacked, or we suddenly discovered we'd lost our friendship with Gordia?"

"Yes, sir. You know best."

The sergeant pocketed the necklace. "A pretty bauble, missy."

"A gift, Sergeant. You must understand."

"Oh, I understand very well."

Tyrwilka at dusk was the realm of shadow and silence. Few of its inhabitants remained out-of-doors, and those few scurried by, hurrying home. Two-story structures of wood and stone and thatch loomed overhead, making a canyon of the narrow cobblestone street. All the shutters on the many small windows along the way were shut tight for the evening.

"Come along, missy. Don't want to dally here. Gutter dogs'd get us both." The sergeant kept one hand near his sword, thumb hooked in his belt as though he were at ease. "My name's Salamon. I won't harm you, and you needn't worry about the boys at the castle. King Milas is strict about the treatment of prisoners. Some say too strict, though I'm not one. Spent a little time in a Gordian cell, once." He spat. "Wouldn't care to repeat that, I tell you."

"I'm the Lady Lizelle. You'd better—"

Salamon laughed. "You might be Lizelle, but I doubt you're a lady, miss. Not even a Gordian'd be fool enough to treat you as that captain did, if he wasn't sure of your status." They turned onto a branching street beyond the sight of the guards at the gate.

"Excuse me, Sergeant. There's something in my boot." Lizelle stooped, slipping free of Salamon's grip, adjusted her stocking, and stood again. When the plainsman reached for her wrist, she knocked his arm aside with her left hand and raised her right to display the dagger plucked from her left sleeve. Placing its point against Salamon's throat, Lizelle said, "You seem a good sort, Sergeant. Don't make me kill you." Her voice quavered slightly. She hoped he would think it was from rage.

"I . . . I won't."

"Thank you." *Truly,* she thought, *thank you.* With her free hand, she felt in his tunic for the miststone necklace, then drew it out and slipped it over her head. Jerking his sword from its sheath, she said, "Unfasten your belt and cinch it about my waist."

"Ma'am?"

"You heard."

Salamon obeyed, moving with exaggerated caution.

"Tighter." When the belt felt secure, Lizelle said, "Lie down," and sheathed the sword, keeping the dagger at his neck.

"Here?"

"Yes. On your back."

"As you say."

They knelt together like partners in a courtly dance. Then Salamon lay back on the cobblestones. "Now," Lizelle said, "if you're smart, you'll wait until I'm far gone before you rise or yell." She ran. At ten paces, she heard the sergeant begin to stand. *Brave man.* She knew he would not follow. He would go to the gate to alert the guards. With luck, she had half an hour before they searched the city for her. How fast could Salamon run, she wondered, clutching his pants with one hand?

Lizelle angled toward the inner wall. If help was to be found, it would be in the quarters of the poor. Turning a corner, she almost collided with an immense hillman in a bearskin vest. She doubted an outlander could help her, but she asked, "Do you know the way to Moonrise Lane?"

"Moonrise Lane?"

She nodded.

"No."

She ran on.

A few blocks farther, she spotted a boy, perhaps fourteen years old, in a large coat of many bright patches. "You!" she called. "Do you know the way to Moonrise Lane?"

The boy looked up and smiled. "Do *I* know the way to Moonrise Lane?"

Lizelle said, "I haven't time for guessing games."

"Lady," he said, "I know these streets better than the First of Thieves. I can escort you to the homes of lords or lepers, artists or assassins, tradesmen or troubadours. I can show you sites of historical import, of religious wonder, of cultural—"

"Spare me the spiel. A royal if we reach The Wanderer's Roost in less than five minutes."

"Done!" With a grin, the boy darted into the growing darkness. Lizelle followed, thinking, *Five royals for your temple, godlings. How's five sound?*

In a room of many shadows where a single candle burned, a plump little man peered into a scry stone. "She passed the barbarian by," he said. "There's nothing more we can do."

The other, bald like the smaller man though with a beard full and white, turned his hands palms upward in his lap. "So it seems."

"I did my best."

"I'm sure you did."

"The barbarian was going the other way when she came near him. I arranged for a glint of light in the woman's direction, enough to catch his eye. Nothing was there when he went to investigate, but it kept him in the area for a few extra moments. And it still didn't help us."

"Perhaps," said the Elder. "Perhaps not."

"I didn't overstep our bounds?"

"No, Brother Merry. You did well."

"Thank you, Serenity."

"We dare not risk further mystic intervention. We can't call attention to our Order."

"I understand. A shame our part in this has to end now."

The Elder turned his head toward Merry. "Oh?"

Merry nodded sadly. "there's too much to do to bring them all together. I doubt that Luck will arrange it for us."

The Elder smiled. "As do I, unless we help him. You'll have to become one of the players."

The fat man's brows drew together and his jaw dropped agape. "I, Serenity? Surely you are mis—" He stopped for an instant, then began again. "I mean, I'm honored, but there must be one more capable, more . . ."

The Elder raised one hand to silence Merry's protests. "You, Brother Merry. Oh, I know that the cuisine beyond our walls is generally inferior to—"

"Serenity, I don't think of—"

"Not always," the Elder answered. Then, suddenly serious, he added, "I'd go myself, or send another of the Inner Circle, but we've all grown old. Not even Sister Felicity could hope to travel to World's Peak and back."

"But I—"

"You're the most adept of the Second Circle. Were it not for your fondness for worldly things... Well, you are our best choice. Say no more of your unworthiness. There's no honor in this, Merry. Only need."

Merry bowed his head. "Forgive me."

"That's not necessary." The Elder placed his fingers on Merry's forehead. "You go with our blessing, and our hopes."

chapter two

Adventures of a
Warrior-Apprentice

LIZELLE TRIED TO overtake her guide and failed. A year of
pampered life with Lord Noring had left its mark on her,
despite their many hours of swimming and fencing together.
She hoped that her wits had not also weakened, then grew
very frightened that they had: the Tyrwilkans would search
for a woman in red-and-black riding dress. "Boy!" she called.
"Wait!"

He halted near an alley. "I'm sorry, Lady, but if we're
to reach The Roost in five minutes..."

"You'll have your royal, never fear." She paused to
breathe deeply, then said, "Trade clothes with me."

"For another royal?"

Lizelle laughed, more to impress the boy with her manner
than from amusement. She had played at being highcaste
for months. Now, if she was to survive, she must remember
different rules. "You'll receive ten for the skirts alone from
any half-honest pawnbroker." She jerked her head toward
the alley. "Is there a better place to change?"

"Not near."

They entered. The cobblestones gave way to mud and a
carpet of rotting garbage. She searched for anyone or anything that might lurk in the shadows. A few rats scurried
away at her approach to burrow deeper among the trash
along either wall.

"Seems safe." She removed her jacket. She did not dare
to turn away from the boy for fear he would hit her from
behind to rob or rape her, so this was no place for modesty.
"Strip, lad," Lizelle said. "Quickly."

She tugged her silk blouse over her head. The boy's gaze traveled from her small breasts and the miststone that hung between them to the knife and sheath lashed on her wrist. "Hurry," she said. "I'm not paying you to admire me."

"Sorry, Lady." While the boy fumbled with the laces at his throat, Lizelle unbuckled her belt and placed it by her jacket on an empty beer barrel.

"Here, Lady." He gave her his shirt, a formless thing of unbleached cotton. It was clean, which surprised her, and fit fairly well.

She stepped out of her riding skirts but kept her silk underwear as something to remember Noring by. The boy's baggy green breeches were loose enough to pull over her low boots. Her jeweled earrings went into Salamon's belt pouch, and she wiped the paint from her eyelids with a lace handkerchief. Then she sliced the decorative gold cord and bangles from her jacket and held them out to the boy. "Here. You might sell these, too."

"Thank you."

He stood awkwardly in her blouse and skirts. Lizelle, rubbing dirt into her jacket to further disguise it, said, "You shouldn't fidget. You're a most attractive lass." Immediately regretting teasing him, she said, "Can you braid hair?"

"I had sisters, once."

"Then do mine. A single braid, like the warrior-apprentices of the forest folk wear."

Two minutes later, a young man from the eastern forests ran through Tyrwilka's narrow city streets with a short-haired city girl at his side. Lizelle's red skirts showed under her guide's many-colored coat, so she told him, "The guards'll search for someone in those clothes. Change them as soon as you can."

"Don't worry. I intend to."

A few blocks farther, after passing only two pedestrians who did not seem to care where foreigners ran, or why, the boy grabbed her arm and stopped. "We're here, Lady. Moonrise Lane."

They stood near a row of whitewashed buildings that rang with the sounds of Tyrwilkans laughing, singing, and, in at least one building, fighting. Signboards hung above the street, though Lizelle could not read their symbols in the dusk. Torchlight fell through the gaps in shutters and doors to lie like spears across the cobblestone street. "The Roost lies midway down the block, past The Dancing Goat," the boy said. "Its sign is a crowing cock."

"Thanks." Lizelle plucked two royals from Salamon's pouch and tossed them to the boy. "Go change."

He smiled as he caught the coins. "My thanks, Lady!" He gave her a stage actor's bow with a flourish to win the hearts of queens, and then ran, disappearing into the evening mist.

The Wanderer's Roost smelled of wine, sweat, burnt meat, mirthweed smoke, and cheap perfume. It sounded of loud chatter, clattering mugs, and the enthusiastic chords of a young lutenist whose instrument needed tuning. The first floor was an open common room, devoted to low white oak tables where drinkers sat on three-legged stools. A fire burned in a fieldstone hearth, and something simmered in a copper kettle set near it. Several lamps set in niches above the pine wainscotting flickered in the draft as Lizelle closed The Roost's door behind her.

The inn was crowded with townfolk in plain woolen ponchos, soldiers in scarlet vests and headbands, students in the yellow robes of the College of Thaumaturgy, prostitutes of both sexes in cloaks and short, garish tunics, and even several river people wearing bright kerchiefs tied about their heads and wide-bladed knives at their hips. The tavern owner, an old man with a few strands of grey hair clinging to his scalp, stood behind the rough-hewn bar, briskly serving his wares in blue-and-green ceramic cups. Lizelle nudged her way between a painted boy and a woman whose headband bore the wheel stamp of the merchant caste. When the tavernkeeper came Lizelle's way, she deepened her voice to say, "I'm looking for a tall, fair-haired man. He wears a patch over his right eye. His left is the color of amber."

The old man nodded knowingly. "Is he mustached?"

"Sometimes."

"A man like that has a room above."

"He's in?"

"No. He'll return soon."

"You're sure?"

"Maybe later."

"Thanks."

"Maybe tomorrow."

"I get the idea."

"Your name?"

"Why?"

The barkeep smiled, baring a few brown teeth. "Should he ask for you."

"Ah. I'm L'zar."

"I'm Tikolos. Some dinner while you wait, L'zar? A quarter-royal buys stew and bread and a pitcher of my best mead."

Her stomach rumbled its opinion, so Lizelle said, "Fine." She handed Tikolos a silver piece.

He dropped it into a pocket of his faded orange smock. "Find a seat. The lass'll bring your meal."

Lizelle spotted a vacant table near the rear of the crowded room and eased through a group of riverfolk and soldiers. As she reached for the stool beside the table, a heavyset sailor in high cuffed seaboots and a cape of ochre cloth rested his right foot upon it. His features were unremarkable, save for an intense cast to his brown eyes, which might have hinted at drunkenness, madness, or self-congratulating cunning.

"I arrived first," Lizelle said carefully, looking up and wondering if he was someone who disliked forest folk or merely someone who wished very much to sit.

The sailor sneered, and several of the people at nearby tables glanced their way. He said, "You have no manners, youth. Let your betters sit before you do." He wore a cutlass and a filleting knife, though he reached for neither. She decided he was just a drunk who wanted to fight with someone easy. Such men bored her, annoyed her, and, though Lizelle refused to acknowledge it, frightened her. "In the forests—" she began.

"You're not in your precious forests, outlander."

"In the forests," she repeated quietly, "we must kill three people in combat to win a warrior's earring. Would you be my third?"

The man said nothing, but his eyes narrowed. Thinking

he needed an excuse to back down, Lizelle added, "I've vowed never to begin a fight when the moon god shows his full face. Please, let me take this table." She felt herself in a subtle trap and wished the forest folk were known for pacifism. If she fled, people would notice that she acted oddly and might tell the guards to watch for a dark-haired forest man. Moreover, she knew nowhere else to go. If she stayed and fought, she would be given to the city guard as a brawler, and her present disguise would not survive close scrutiny. But the thought that troubled her most was the suspicion that this encounter, at this time, was more than could be credited to the gods of chance.

The sailor said, slightly louder than before, "I'm not afraid of you, moon worshipper."

Nearby drinkers again looked toward them. Lizelle said, "I never said you were."

"Louse-ridden forester."

As they stared at each other, a tall, plump, blond serving woman arrived with a wooden trencher full of lamb stew, a slender blue pitcher, and a small cup. "Here, love," she said to Lizelle. "Don't tell me there's trouble?"

"No," Lizelle said, praying there wasn't. "Not if I may sit and eat in peace."

The woman stared at the sailor, then cried, "Why, it's Daerko!" She set the trencher, cup, and pitcher on the table before Lizelle to clasp the man's sword arm. "I believed you'd sailed for the Dawn Isles!"

"Huh?" Daerko grunted in surprise and stepped back. "Me? Hardly."

The serving woman tugged him toward the bar. "Come, buy me an ale and tell me your adventures, Daerko. I've missed you." Over her shoulder, she gave Lizelle a wink. Lizelle smiled her thanks, glad that one danger had been averted. She wondered what else she would face before she could slip out of town with the next morning's traffic.

Her trencher was heaped high with thick cuts of lamb, potato, and carrot, with green beans and mushrooms generously mixed in. When Lizelle finished, she wiped her platter with a crust of dark bread and poured another mead. *A shame the fellow with the lute is tone-deaf,* she thought.

I'd appreciate a bit of peaceful music now. Well, the riverfolk seem to enjoy him.

Almost at peace, she let her eyes half close and called Darkwind. *Yo, fleet one! Yo, star-brow! Yo, rather dense and thick-witted one!*

She felt a faint reply, as if shouted from far away. *Does one of poor legs and wit need assistance?*

No. Thanks just the same, mount that only fools should ride.

Sometimes one thinks that only fools—

Don't say it. You escaped Guire?

Of course.

Good. See you tomorrow.

Beware the captain.

And a few others. I'll have a tale to tell.

One's done nothing rash?

Nothing more than I've had to.

These two shouldn't have separated. That one needs this one's advice.

A patronizing horse. What did I do to deserve such a companion?

The Roost's door swung wide on its leather hinges to admit a fat man no taller than a twelve-year-old boy. After an instant, Lizelle recognized his grey robe as that of a priest of the Second Circle in the Questers' Order. The man waited as most people did, blinking to adjust to light and smoke.

Lizelle looked away from the priest, then glanced back when she realized that his gaze had settled on her. The corners of his mouth drew up in a smile, and he dipped his head in a slight bow. The torchlight reflected from his bald pate like a halo.

Wondering whether the little priest had seen through her disguise or merely thought she was someone else, and not particularly caring which was true, Lizelle slid her hand to her stolen sword and looked for an exit. *If I make it past those farmers and out that window, what then? Avoid the guards, scale the walls, and sleep in the woods? Godlings, the situations you let me get into.*

She pushed against the table, preparing to stand. The

priest moved his lips and his fingers almost imperceptibly, and Lizelle's stomach clenched in abrupt nausea as the floor and the walls reeled about her. She fell back, gasping. The world steadied itself. Her neighbors seemed to have noticed nothing. *A vertigo spell,* she realized. *Discreet....*

The sailor, Daerko, watched her from the bar. She thought for a moment of horror that he and the short priest were allies who wanted ... Only her failure to suspect what they might want kept her from trying to stagger toward the door in spite of the Quester's dizziness spell. *The sailor is probably just a sailor,* she repeated to herself. *As for the Quester, if he wants to turn me in to the guards, he would not need to be this subtle. But what* does *he want?*

The priest jostled drinkers with placid nonchalance as he strolled through the crowd to Lizelle's table. One man turned angrily, then quieted on seeing the grey robe. The Quester raised his pale, pudgy hand, the man nodded, and the Quester walked on.

He stopped before Lizelle and said, "Greetings, my child."

She set her cup on the scarred table. "You knew my mother?"

"Would that I had!" the priest replied, laughing. "Would that I had. Had she your spirit?"

Lizelle shrugged.

"May I sit?"

"Can I stop you?" Lizelle picked up her cup. "The table's yours when I finish this mead." Perhaps she would not wait for the one-eyed man, who might not return this evening. She could risk taking a room in another inn, or she could wander the streets until she found a quiet place to await the dawn. She had few options left, but it comforted her to remember that she still had some.

The priest said, "Don't hurry on my account."

"I won't." *I'll try.*

He looked about, and a merchant surrendered his seat. "My thanks," the priest said, lifting his hand in blessing.

Lizelle drained her mead and observed, "Tyrwilkans like you."

The Quester blinked as though he had never considered the matter. His eyes were a startling blue. "My Order bothers none," he said. "We help those we can."

"Ah. You come on a mission of mercy?"

He smiled and shook his head. "No. I come to ask your help.

"*My* help?" Lizelle stared, wondering again whom he believed her to be. "How?"

The priest laughed. "Our conversation moves too quickly. Let's wait for one other, and then I'll explain."

"I think you'll explain now."

"There's gold to be gained," the priest said. "That should be worth a little patience."

There's also my freedom to be considered. That's not worth any risk. Lizelle braced her hands against the table and began to stand.

"Sit," the priest said calmly.

"Your dizziness spell won't stop me if I crawl, Quester. And I will if I have to."

The priest laughed. "Sit. Please. The crowd would hold you if I wished. And I might not be able to keep them from harming you. Besides, you'd look rather silly—and conspicuous—creeping along on the floor. Sit."

Feeling slightly foolish, Lizelle sat.

"What do you call yourself?"

"L'zar," she said.

"Ah. I'm Merry." He turned, waved his arm, and called, "Hessabeth!"

The serving woman hurried to their table. "Merry! I didn't see you enter!"

"That's understandable. A slip of a fellow like myself." The Quester patted his paunch and chortled.

Lizelle breathed deeply and tried to ignore their conversation. *Darkwind. Hear me, fleet one!*

His reply seemed a distant whisper that echoed in a cavern. *Flattery. One's in trouble?*

Yes. I'll come as soon as I can.

How might one aid?

There's nothing—

Hessabeth was asking her, "Are you thirsty?" Lizelle glanced at Merry, who nodded and said, "Another pitcher of mead and two more cups, if you please."

"At once."

As Hessabeth left, Lizelle said, "Whom are we waiting for?"

"A man called Catseye Yellow. Do you know him?"

She hid her surprise. "I recognize the name."

"He has a room here. He'll have to hear my tale."

"I hope he arrives soon, then."

The Quester sighed. "I'm sorry. I keep you because I must. Please, be patient."

When Hessabeth brought the cups and another pitcher, Lizelle poured herself more mead. Noticing that the sailor still watched them from his place by the bar, she said, "Who's—" Then the front doors swung open. While oil lamps fluttered in the sudden draft, guardsmen in red capes and coats filed into The Roost.

"Yes?" Merry asked.

"Later." Lizelle removed her jacket to hang it on the back of her chair. If Salamon accompanied these soldiers, he might recognize it, even with the decoration removed.

"Ah," said the priest. "Our valiant city guard. You're worried?"

She flinched, then tried to smile. "Of course not."

"You're safe with me."

"Say that again when the guards have gone."

The crowd had stilled on the soldiers' entrance. Salamon, the sixth and last, stepped in and said, "If any of you intend to leave unobtrusively, know that several men wait at the rear to greet the shy."

He scanned the room. Lizelle picked at her nose to cover part of her face with her hand. Salamon's gaze passed over her as he said, "Tonight we seek a young woman from City Gordia. She's dark-haired and dressed in a rich woman's riding clothes. She's a thief. There's a bounty: two hundred royals."

The reward was too much for her crime. Did that mean Noring truly loved her, as he so glibly professed? Or had she stolen more than she thought? She glanced at Merry, but the priest showed no interest in Salamon's offer.

"Has anyone seen her?"

No one spoke.

Salamon looked at the barkeep. "We'll search."

The old man shrugged in resignation. "So search. Don't break anything this time, eh?"

Two soldiers climbed the stairs to the sleeping rooms. A second pair entered the kitchen behind the bar. Salamon told the remaining guard, a southerner from Torgia or Bakh, "Check the crowd. Anyone suspicious bring to me."

The southerner grunted and moved slowly from table to table, studying each face. When he came to Lizelle, he said, "I've never seen you, outlander."

"I'll vouch for the lad," said Merry.

The southerner barked a laugh. "I know about priests and boys."

"Please! You have the Questers confused with the priests of the Nine," Merry said.

"And they prefer to be confused apart," Lizelle added quickly.

"Exactly." Merry smiled at her.

"Feh!" said the southerner, strolling on. "Drunks and wise-asses, everywhere. I should've become a sailor."

"He'd probably enjoy that life," Lizelle told Merry, "if he's so interested in priests and boys."

As the guards regrouped, Salamon asked, "Anything?"

"No," said the southerner. "The usual collection of tavern wits."

Merry was staring at a stocky soldier in an immense red coat. The priest frowned, whispered something, and two bottles fell from the man's coat to shatter on the floor.

The bartender sniffed loudly, then smiled. "Elvish brandy of '17. An excellent year. I commend your taste, Corporal. Four royals, please."

"What!" the guard cried.

"Jaeko . . ." said Salamon.

Looking shamefacedly at his feet, the man dropped several coins on the bar.

Salamon turned back to the crowd. "Remember! Two hundred royals reward!" With a last glance, he led his men out.

The tavern chatter resumed immediately. Merry said, "That wasn't so bad, was it?"

"No," Lizelle admitted, then added, "Thanks for protecting me."

"I have my motives."

"I'm sure. It would be nice to know them." She realized that her suspicions about the little priest had dwindled to curiosity and told herself that this could still prove to be a case of being rescued from dragons by demons. Then she noticed that a newcomer had slipped in behind the departing guards and indicated him with a twist of her chin. "By the door," she said. "In the sea-green cloak. Is that whom we've been waiting for?"

Merry looked over his shoulder. "Ah! So he is."

The stranger was a tall, darkly tanned man with high cheekbones, a shaggy, reddish-blond mustache, and a dark leather patch over his right eye. He wore soft moccasin boots tied below his knees with crisscrossing thongs, tan wool pants and a jacket buttoned with wooden pegs, and a battered black hat with a wide, drooping brim. Slung on his back over his cloak, he carried a narrow, elongated sword in a sheath of carved teak. The sword's leather-wrapped hilt, protruding above his right shoulder, was perhaps long enough for a hand and a half, as though it had not been meant for any human to wield. Its pommel appeared to be a tiny silver basilisk's skull.

As the man moved into the room, he took his hat in his right hand, revealing hair the color of fire in sunlight, brushed back from a widow's peak and caught in a tail with a silver band that matched his earring. His left eye, which skimmed and dismissed the crowd in an instant, was amber.

"He's handsome," Lizelle murmured to Merry. "But hardly worth being detained for."

The man spoke with the barkeep, and both of them glanced toward Lizelle's table. Merry smiled, lifting his cup in greeting. The one-eyed man twisted an end of his mustache between limber, manicured fingers, nodded to the priest, and passed a coin to Tikolos. Then he strode through the crowd to stand before Lizelle. "You asked after me?" His tone suggested that such practices were rarely wise, but his voice was pleasant and educated, with an accent Lizelle could not identify.

"I did," she said, "if you're a friend of a friend of mine. That can wait. This Quester has more urgent business, it seems."

He regarded the priest with obvious doubt. "Yes?"

"Yes," Merry replied. "A matter of great financial gain. Please join us."

"Ah!" One corner of the mustache twitched up into a smile. "As you wish."

A bargeman at a near table rose to stagger toward the bar, and the one-eyed man snatched his stool. "Hey!" the drunk shouted. "What the—"

"Might I borrow your seat?" the stranger said kindly. "If you've no more need of it, that is?"

"I, uh . . . Sure, Cat, sure. Didn't realize it was you. Take me chair, if you will."

"Thank you." The man swung his sheathed sword from his back to lean it against Lizelle's table, hung his hat on the sword's hilt, and sat. Behind him, the drunk muttered as he ambled away, "Arrogant bastard." The one-eyed man grinned contentedly, then looked from Merry to Lizelle. "So what's this about, then?"

"A moment for introductions," Merry said. "Are you still called Catseye Yellow?"

"I'm too well known by that name to change it now." The stranger smiled another of his easy grins. "Perhaps as well that I should change it, but it serves me."

The priest nodded. "I'm Merry, of the Second Circle of the Quest. This seeming warrior-apprentice is L'zar, at least for the evening."

Lizelle and Catseye eyed each other. "Well?" said Catseye, looking back at Merry.

The priest smiled and indicated the pitcher of mead. "Please, have a drink. Then let me tell you a story about the Lord of Cats."

Noring and the Empress lay in darkness, looking out on stars above them and the lights of City Gordia below. Naked in crimson sheets of moonthread, Glynaldis entwined a finger in the thick hair on Lord Noring's chest. "Lover?" she whispered.

"Yes, Majesty?"

She tugged the hair, hurting him. "Glynaldis."

"Forgive me. I find it hard to think of you as . . . Glynaldis."

"You must find it easier. Before the court, we may be
Noring and Gordia. Here we are merely Uyor and Glynaldis.
Here I am whatever you dare to have me be."

He did not dare to have her be anything. He wished she
did not want him to dare. "Yes, my . . . love."

"Ah, that sounds nice, doesn't it? You shouldn't be
frightened, Uyor. Not after this evening. You didn't seem
a man afraid."

"What we did was . . . something between a man and a
woman. Now we talk, and the voice I hear is Gordia's."

"Really?" She moved her hand lower and squeezed. "Does
Gordia touch you like this?"

He sighed. "No."

"Did Gordia cry out beneath you in her passion? Was it
Gordia who suggested . . . things . . . to you?" Her grip tightened.

"Why, no. Of course—"

Her fist clenched, and he screamed. She whispered, "Then
call me Glynaldis, sweet Uyor."

"Y-yes," he gasped. "Glynaldis. Sweet Glynaldis."

Her touch grew feather-light as she stroked him. "Did I
hurt you, darling Uyor?"

"No. How could my lover hurt me?" In the darkness, he
thought he could see her smile.

"Exactly. Ah, how you respond to my caress. . . ."

"Could any man fail to?"

"I like you, Uyor."

"I . . . like you, too, Glynaldis."

"I would show you how much."

"I wish that you would," he said as she slid lower. "Ah.
That's nice. That's very nice." He prayed she would not
bite.

She did not. After a bit, she said, "Now, you." Her
fingers moved on his head as if he were a pet. "You have
talents, Uyor." He did not attempt to reply. "You could rise
considerably in my court. Yes. And often. Ah, yes."

When he could, he said, "I would please you, Maj...
Glynaldis."

"You do."

"I'm glad." He cradled her in the crook of his arm as
though she were any woman.

"Tell me, sweet Uyor," she said in the stillness. "Do you
still have the gem your mother left you?"

"Gem? She left much jewelry. Some I gave to relatives...."

"You know of my wizard?"

"Thelog Ar?"

"The same."

"I've never seen him. I've heard of him, of course."

"He seeks a miststone, teardrop shaped, with setting and
chain of Elvish work. I remember your mother wearing such
a stone at my birthday ball."

"I..."

"Yes?"

"It was stolen."

"Aii! Noring, you..." The woman sat up, and her
breasts swung freely. Her voice came slow and rasping
from her throat.

"I know the thief, Gly...Maj—"

She laughed. "Do you?"

"Yes. A circus performer that I...befriended. I've spread
her description among the armies and offered a reward. Both
girl and stone will be returned. Soon. I'm sure."

"You are?"

"Yes. Very sure."

"Good." She rose from the bed, and starlight gilded her
body. Noring had heard rumors that Thelog Ar's sorcery
kept her young. He knew her form was not that of a woman
who had ruled for some thirty years.

A flame appeared at her fingertips. Noring gasped, and
Glynaldis smiled. "I've learned a bit of magic from my
wizard. It amuses me to do little tricks." She transferred
the spark to a candlewick. Under the flickering light, the
scarlet walls of the bedchamber pulsed like the interior of
a giant heart.

"So," she said. "Who was the girl?"

"No one. A performer. She called herself Lizelle."

"Pretty?"

"Scrawny, compared to you. I thought her attractive."

"Good?"

"Compared to—"

"Damn you, not compared to me! Was she good?"

"I . . . yes, she was good. She was very good."

"You didn't have to say she was *very* good."

"Sorry."

Glynaldis laughed. "Never apologize for small things when we're alone. Only for things that might mean your life. And I doubt apologies would save you then."

"I understand."

She nodded. "Yes. I think you do."

In the corner of the room, a gilt cage held a yellow songbird. The Empress walked to it and unlatched the door. The bird attempted to fly, but she seized it and nestled it to her breast, and smoothed the bird's feathers and made cooing sounds to it. It trembled frantically in her grasp. "You'll obtain this miststone for me."

"Of course."

"I should tell you that I've had other lovers, Uyor. Some of them failed me. I'm not tolerant of failure."

"I know that, Glynaldis."

"One I gave to Thelog Ar, who returned him to me as this." She lifted the bird to show it to him.

"I . . . see."

"And still he does not please me. He does not sing, he flies from me. . . ." She shook her head, and Noring could not see her face behind her auburn curls. "You won't fail me, will you, Uyor?"

"No."

"I'm glad." She held the songbird at arm's length. "Should I free him?"

"If you—"

She cast the bird into the air. Its flight for the open window began. Then the Empress spoke a word in the language of magicians, the old tongue of Faerie, and her fingers clutched. The bird hung motionless above the sill, and the woman reached out to return it to its cage. When she turned to Noring, her eyes, for one instant, seemed to have filled with sadness, but she blinked and said, "Come, sweet Uyor. Kiss me." Her arms opened to him.

And, despising himself, he obeyed.

chapter three

The Riddle
of Cats

SINCE THE LITTLE priest seemed to be waiting for a reaction, Lizelle said, "The Lord of Cats?"

Merry nodded.

The one-eyed man lifted an eyebrow. "I can't say I enjoy fables."

"The mead's free," said Merry, shrugging. "And there's more incentive than a drink and a story, I assure you."

"Speak on, then."

Merry refilled Lizelle's mug and poured one for the stranger. Lizelle glanced at Catseye, wondering what he made of all this. He seemed amused, as if he thought the priest a harmless, but possibly wealthy, madman.

Merry said, "Very well. In the realm of beasts, it's known that cats have no lord. Dogs serve Ralka the Wolf King, horses answer to an aging mare named Flowers, and ants obey Her Peerless and Exalted Majesty, Bzxxyl the Eighteen Hundredth and Forty-Second, Mistress of the Universe and Eater of Treats. Yet cats have no lord."

Merry squinted at them both, then continued. "Hawks serve Deathswoop the Daring, but all birds honor the Phoenix. Sharks only share with the Hungry One, while all fish swim at Tam Tuna's request. Cobras turn at the command of the Hood of All-Potent Poison. . . ." Merry sipped his whiskey. "Sometimes translated as 'omnipotent poison' by Byrgondians with pretensions to scholarship." He chuckled, and Lizelle wondered how long his story would take.

"Now, all snakes revere Nosey Groundsnake. And so on. Some wise folk claim there are creatures smaller than the eye can see. If so, they're ruled by a Supreme Atomie, for so the God ordered all things when She shaped the levels of existence."

The priest paused to drink again. "Even the fabled Sargoniom sorcerers failed to discover why cats have no lord. Triskaliom Myrdana *became* a cat, but when quizzed about the freedom of felines, she regarded her questioners gravely for a moment, licked her whiskers clean of milk, and lay down to sleep. Which may have been an answer."

Catseye, frowning, said, "What has this matter of cat lords, or the lack thereof, to do with us?"

"My Order"—Merry smiled with considerable pleasure—"will pay you each three thousand royals to climb World's Peak, discover whether the Wisest One lives there, and ask her for the answer to that old riddle."

Catseye whistled a long, low note. "A small fortune."

"But a fortune nonetheless," Merry said.

The one-eyed man drained his mead with a single draught, placed his cup on the table, and said, "That was an amusing tale, friend Quester. Did you hear about the Byrgondian wizard who decided he couldn't be too safe when conjuring demons? He drew a sixth point on his pentagram. Now, if you've finished, I'll go."

"I don't joke, Brother Yellow." Merry turned to Lizelle. "What do you say?"

She shrugged, not sure how to answer. "You offer me protection now and profit later. What can I say? I'll listen further." *Which does not mean I'll seriously consider your fool's quest.*

He smiled slightly, and Lizelle realized that this small, fat priest was not nearly as confident as he wished to appear. "And you, Brother Yellow? Do we offer too little?"

"You might offer more. Climb an unclimbable mountain, seek out a figure from myth, ask a question whose answer, if it exists, will profit no one. . . ." Catseye shook his head. "Offer all you will, priest. I won't go." He toyed with his cup, hesitating for reasons that Lizelle could not guess, though the discrepancy between his words and his deeds intrigued her.

"We think you will." Merry smiled with greater assurance. "You have a reputation among the adventurers of our city."

"Do I?" Catseye smiled skeptically.

"Oh, yes. They say you do things others won't. Things others can't."

"Perhaps. Not the impossible."

"In certain quarters, they say even that. The theft of the Sword of the Sargoniom Lords—"

"Enough." Catseye spoke coldly, glancing from Merry to Lizelle. "Nothing's been said here."

She nodded. "I'm as deaf as a vacationer gone a-gorgon gazing."

Catseye glanced at her, then laughed. "A fortuitous impairment."

Merry said quickly, "The Order can offer something more valuable to you than gold."

Catseye said, "Oh? And what's this?"

"Ah." Merry drank. "You're an interesting sort, Brother Yellow. No Tyrwilkan, we're sure. Your complexion suggests Hrotish savages for forebears, yet your height and the color of that eye—"

"I don't enjoy these surmises." Catseye set his left hand on the sheath of his sword, which still leaned against their table.

"I'm sorry," Merry said. "I'm only explaining how we chose the carrot to dangle before you."

"Nor do I enjoy being made an ass. If you have something to send me scaling World's Peak, speak of it."

"Very well. We have the Egg of Yrvann."

"The Egg?" Catseye's voice softened, and his hand fell from the sword to his lap.

"So. You know of it."

"A little."

"It was payment from a Gordian who helped sack Faerie during the last Great War. It had no value to him. None to us, either, but it was a pretty thing. A blue gem, fist-sized, with a stripe of white that runs—"

"I know what it looks like."

"We thought you might."

"Why?"

"Your mead isn't to your taste?" Merry quaffed his and beckoned to Hessabeth for another pitcher. Lizelle watched the two men and wondered what this gem was, and why it was important to Catseye, and what Merry might have said to her if she had seemed as reluctant as this tall woodsman.

"The mead's fine. Why do you offer a valueless egg to me?"

"Valueless to the Gordian," Merry corrected patiently. "Valueless to the Order, until now. That's the marvelous thing about value: it vanishes and appears like a gift from the gods." Hessabeth brought a third pitcher and took away the empty ones. "But I doubt the value of Master Tikolos's mead ever decreases," Merry added, beginning to drink.

Catseye covered Merry's raised cup with the palm of his hand and pressed down. The wood of the table and the thick base of the clay cup met with a sound like the careful closing of a well-made box. "Tell me," Catseye whispered.

Merry glanced at Lizelle and asked kindly, "Before others, Brother Yellow?"

"Tell me," Catseye repeated.

Merry freed his fingers and flexed them. "Very well. Our sources suggest—"

"I'd like to know these sources."

Merry smiled. "I imagine you would. They suggest you came to Tyrwilka on the Elf King's Road."

"So?"

"They say you came from the west, Brother Yellow. From Faerie."

Catseye threw back his head and laughed. "Oh? And are my ears clipped like some perfumed Elf's?"

Lizelle had noticed nothing unusual about Catseye's ears, but she looked at them again. They seemed as human as any she had seen.

Merry raised one finger and waggled it at Catseye. "Ah, if I was so far from the truth, I'd expect your jest to affirm my surmise."

Catseye squinted at him, then spread his hands wide and smiled. "Please yourself. I'm Elvish. I poisoned myself dining with iron cutlery and now inhabit the mad god's hell."

"You say more than you suspect. It's said—"

"Speak to the point," Catseye said.

"If you insist." The little priest sat forward on his stool. "We think you're part Elf. The Gordians raped when they pillaged the Elflands. The last War Against Faerie ended about the time of your birth, if you've the thirty-some years you appear to possess."

Catseye sneered. "And maybe I'm a vampire that's lived an undead life since Sargoniom days." He raised his mead in a mocking salute. "You know nothing about me."

"I admit as much. But I'm only proposing what's logical."

"Madman's logic."

"Maybe. Now, if you were exiled from Faerie—"

"What point is there to this?"

"You asked. I'll stop now, if you'll join us."

"Tell all your thoughts, priest. I want to know what you've surmised, what you've misunderstood. I listen for lies. Speak on."

"A moment for a drink." Merry lifted his cup and looked at Catseye for agreement.

Catseye slowly nodded. "You like to keep me waiting," he said as the priest drank.

"He loves to keep us both waiting," Lizelle noted.

"Forgive me," said Merry. "But at least you're now willing to wait."

"True," said Catseye. "I no longer think you mad, though I begin to wonder about myself."

"The birth of wisdom." Merry smiled with childlike satisfaction, and Lizelle realized that this duel between the priest and the one-eyed man was almost over. "As for the Egg of Yrvann, we believe it's important to the rulers of the Elflands. Every known portrait of a High Lord shows a blue gem, either in the subject's hands or worn as jewelry. If you undertake our little quest, we'll give you the Egg. If it's as important as we think, the present High Lord will reward you well."

"If I should want anything from him," Catseye said.

"If you should want anything from him," Merry agreed.

The matter almost seemed resolved, so Lizelle said, "Why

not offer this Egg directly to the High Lord?"

Merry shrugged. "Faerie holds nothing the Order needs."

"And no human desires the Egg?" Catseye said suspiciously.

"As a jewel, of course. But it speaks most eloquently to you alone."

Catseye stroked his mustache. "Why not have the Elflord send his legions up World's Peak? They might succeed. I'm no mountaineer."

"There's a legend. 'World's Peak is reached by one who is less than Man, and more.'"

"That's rather vague," Lizelle said.

Merry nodded. "That's a legend for you."

"Send an Elf, then," she suggested.

Merry shook his head. "An Elf is either more than Man, or less. Not both."

"Send a woman." Catseye nodded at Lizelle. "This one would do."

Lizelle glared at him and said in her deepest voice, "Listen, Catling! What makes you say—"

"My sense of smell is better than most."

She felt her cheeks redden. "I—"

Catseye laughed. "Why blush? You smell nice, something like a squirrel. Or like apples. Or . . ."

"Enough," she said, both pleased and annoyed and unsure whether to thank him or strike him.

"An Elf woman went long ago," said Merry. "The Wisest One. Now we hedge our bets with a human woman and a halfbreed. Either could be the answer."

Lizelle watched Catseye for his reaction to "halfbreed." He only asked, "Where's the Egg now?"

Merry smiled. "Safe. Bring our answer about the Cat Lord and you'll have the Egg."

"Where shall I bring it?"

"To me. I'll accompany you most of the way. If I'm . . . not available, come to the temple, and the Egg will be delivered to you shortly afterward. You have the word of the Order."

Catseye stroked one corner of his mustache, then said, "Very well."

"You'll do it?"

"I'll attempt it."

"We thought as much."

"For reasons of my own."

"Of course."

"Gold in advance?"

"Some. Enough for the journey."

"Fine. As for—"

Merry waved his hand slightly to stop him. "Let's haggle over details tomorrow, eh, Brother Yellow? Best to enjoy Master Tikolos's wares while we can. Another cup?"

"I . . ." Catseye paused and grinned. "Agree. Another cup."

"Say," Lizelle said after a moment, "I know another Byrgondian joke."

"Good," said Merry. "Don't tell it."

"What do you call a Byrgondian who commands five legions of footsoldiers, two troops of cavalry, and a dozen warships?"

"Your Majesty?" Merry suggested.

Lizelle shook her head. "No. Confused."

"I know one that's more appropriate," Catseye said. "Did you hear of the Byrgondian mariner who sought the waterfall at World's End?" Catseye's hand arced downward through the air. "He found it."

A morbid sense of humor, Lizelle thought.

Catseye grinned at her, and a few faint age lines about his eye deepened with his amusement.

But I might grow to appreciate it.

In the room of many shadows, the oldest Quester turned his face toward a single lit candle. His eyes were white, clouded like the surface of milk. "What do you see?"

The woman's robe was black, like his, and her skull was also bare. "Several are together," she said.

"Which?"

"The woman who fled from the Gordians and the one who may be part Elf. And Brother Merry, of course."

"Where are they?"

"A tavern. Probably on Moonrise Lane."

"You see clearly?"

"There's much smoke. Ah, Hessabeth serves them. They're in The Roost."

"And the large hillman?"

"He still wanders Tyrwilka's streets."

"Perhaps he will come into the game later."

The woman nodded. "Perhaps."

"Do you see trouble?"

"Not now. The halfbreed was on the verge of doing... something. Who can know his nature? Merry pacified him."

"Merry's more competent than he thinks."

"He's too fond of the world."

"Aren't we all, Felicity? The God's last and greatest creation, for which She gave Herself...."

"I meant the ways of the world, Serenity."

"I knew that," the Elder said sadly. "Forgive me. I quibble."

"These are trying times."

"Yes."

They sat in silence while the woman watched the scene in her stone.

"They appear to be in agreement."

"Good." The Elder leaned forward, seeming to peer at the woman through his blindness. "I have doubts, Felicity."

"As do all of the Inner Circle."

"Are we doing right?"

"As best we know," the woman said.

"That's just it. We can't know. We can barely suspect. If we knew the Pattern..."

She took his hand in hers. "We do what we can."

"But what of our means? We arm Brother Merry with half-truths, then instruct him to lie in turn...."

"Not to lie! Only to... withhold."

"As we withhold from him. Ah, I grow old, Felicity. I have doubts. I know that good and evil are not distinct, independent things, and yet..."

"Yes?"

"Perhaps we should live as though they were."

"We do."

"As witnessed by this?"

"We do—"

"What we must. I know. I cast my vote. For the sake of the God, I don't back down. But I—"

"Have doubts," she said. "I understand."

"We battle an adversary whose identity we don't know."

"Yes." She squeezed his hand.

"I grow old."

"So do we all, Serenity. So do we all."

"Lead me to my room, Felicity. I know the way too well, but I wouldn't be alone, just now. You understand?"

"Yes." She squeezed his hand again. "Yes. I understand."

Smyorin, First Among Dragons, flew in lazy spirals above Korz Valley. The night skies danced with gusts of wind, carrying her easily beneath surging clouds and a bright moon. She watched for something small, a deer or a cow, that would serve as a last tidbit before she slept through the winter.

A tiny voice suddenly whispered by her ear, "Beside the great falls, try."

Smyorin whirled furiously, almost losing the updraft that she rode. "What's that!" she cried.

The whisper returned. "In the lower valley, where the Fastwater falls. There try. Several sheep sleep in the grass."

"Who are you?" Smyorin demanded, but it did not answer. "Where are you, I say?" she insisted, frightened that she could not see, feel, or smell any presence.

She heard wry laughter, and then the other replied, "If you could tell me that, friend Smyorin, grateful would I be."

"Cat Lord?" she whispered, thinking of no one else who spoke in this fashion. "Are you playing some silly game with me?"

The voice seemed pleased. "That much I know. Yes. The Cat, am I, but no game do I play."

"Where *are* you?"

"And that you have asked. Lost I may be, or trapped, I do not know. A place this is that changes its form to my whim, and never allows me to escape."

Language had always been a mysterious toy to her friend, but Smyorin, famed for her knowledge, had many excuses to practice it. To guide him, she said, "I suppose you were investigating something you should not have? Curiosity is your—"

"No, I slept in my home, then woke here. My fault it is not, Smyorin. That much I know. An enemy, I suspect, whom you might also know hates me."

"And why do you whisper to me now?"

"Listen, Smyorin—"

"Do I have a choice?"

She heard his laughter, then his voice. "To my temple in Sargoniom's ruins one came some years ago, thinking me gone forever. A time it was like this time, when the Pattern had stretched and none knew what threads next would be woven. The fabric of this place where I am trapped will open tiny windows on our world, at such times. Then I talk and hear, as now, but hear me and talk to me few can. When the windows seal, alone I am again."

Smyorin said, "Why should I help you, even if I could?"

"Were we not friends, once? Are we not still?"

She wanted to feed quickly, return to her unguarded treasures, and sleep. Yet she said, "Yes, Cat Lord. I'll help you, if I can."

"I can see pieces of the Pattern, Smyorin. Help me you cannot, but help my agent you may yet, if any of certain threads join the true Pattern. This agent is named Kephias. Though our communication is imperfect, he is bound to me, for a small substitution I made when little did he expect it. If you can help Kephias, you will help me."

"I will," the dragon promised. Thinking again of sleep and her hoard, she added, "If I can."

"Thank you. Go now I must. Little time remains before this window closes, and others must I speak to, should different threads be woven into my future. Remember, several sheep by the falls, friend Smyorin."

She should be glad that the Cat Lord was leaving her to trouble someone else with his plight, but she called in the silence, "Wait!" and was afraid he had already directed his attention elsewhere.

The whisper returned, fainter than before. "Yes?"

"How will I know your agent, if I meet this Kephias?"

"Human he is," her friend answered. "Another name he sometimes wears, and it is Catseye Yellow."

chapter four

Cats' Play

YO, SPEEDY! YOU listening?
  Someone's been drinking.
  I'm in a tavern. I drink to be inconspicuous.
  Very wise.
  Look, smartass—
  As so often occurs, one is half-right.
  I just wanted to tell you that you needn't fret. Things are under control again.
  This one does not fret.
  That one worries like an old nag. And don't give me any of your stallion's pride, hmm? I only wanted you to know that everything's all right.
  After an instant's silence came, *This one is glad to hear that.*
  Good.
  But this one does not fret.
  Right. You don't fret. I'll speak with you later.
  Later. . . .
The noise in The Roost had grown steadily louder as friends and new acquaintances shouted gossip and lies at each other. A woman with lap drums had joined the lutenist, as had a boy with reed pipes, and their lack of familiarity with each other's repertoire did little to inhibit their enthusiasm. The air was so dense with smoke from tobacco and mirthweed and the open hearth that the serving woman opened a small window above the front door.
  Lizelle had discreetly watched the sailor in the ochre cape since their confrontation over who would sit at this

table. He continued to watch her, she noted, with as great an attempt at discretion. The more Lizelle drank, the more ominous the sailor's presence became. Finally, she tugged at Catseye's sleeve. "Friend Cat. See that fellow by the bar?"

"The one with the ring in his nose?"

"No. Next to 'im. The sailor."

"Yeah?"

"Yeah. You know 'im?"

"No."

Merry said, "Someone watches you?"

"Yeah. See that sailor?"

"With the—"

"No. Next to 'im. In the dark cape. His name's Daerko. He tried to pick a fight with me. I don't know why. The serving woman intervened; that's how I learned his name. He's been watching me."

Catseye said, "It may not mean anything."

Merry bit his upper lip, then said, "There's something I should tell you. Someone may try to keep us from reaching World's Peak."

Catseye laughed. "That's all you have to say? We knew as much. No one offers fortunes to go a-holidaying in the mountains."

"The sailor may be one of them," said Merry, and Lizelle thought she heard a trace of fear in his voice.

"Them?" she asked.

"Our opponents," Merry replied.

"And if he is?"

"I don't know," Merry said.

"I won't kill him for you," Catseye said. "Unless the fee is right."

The priest's eyes went wide. "No one asked you to!"

"That was a joke," Catseye said.

"Good."

"Of sorts." Grinning, Catseye looked at Lizelle. "So, what should we do, you who call yourself L'zar?"

The beauty of his yellowish eye held her for an instant. She wondered how he had lost the other. Looking away, Lizelle said, "Daerko may not be interested in *us*. He may only be interested in *me*."

"Why?" asked Merry.

"I don't know. Yet he continues to watch me." Perhaps the sailor was waiting for help before doing whatever he planned. Considering this, Lizelle noticed a moth sitting on an empty pitcher and suddenly understood one of the many things that had been gnawing at her sense of comfort. She said, "I've heard that wizards sometimes use insects and small animals and such to spy on people. True?"

"True." Merry glanced at her. "What's this got to do with the sailor?"

"Maybe nothing. But be still. I've been watching the moth on that pitcher for the last half hour, and I just realized what's odd about it. It hasn't flown to the lamps or the candles or anything. It hasn't moved at all."

In the resulting silence, Catseye said, "It may be dead," though he remained perfectly motionless in his seat.

Lizelle whispered to Merry, "You're the magician here. Can't you do something?"

"What do you suggest?"

"You could burn it."

"A rather flamboyant act in a tavern, that."

"Then make it dizzy so we can catch it."

"Those spells work best on higher forms of life."

"Well, what use are you, then?"

"At catching bugs?" He shrugged. "Little."

Catseye said, "We can't play statues all evening. Agreed?"

"Agreed," said Merry.

Catseye lunged forward, hand darting with feline speed. His fingers grazed the moth's soft wings as it fluttered up to The Roost's rafters and headed, high above the crowd, toward Daerko. Catseye snatched his sheathed sword in his right hand, dislodging the battered black hat that he had hung on its hilt, and gave chase. Confronted with the press of people, he jumped onto a table to leap from tabletop to tabletop. Drinkers cursed him, and bottles and pitchers crashed to the floor as he passed.

Impulsive sort, Lizelle thought. She pursued Catseye, weasling through the mob and upsetting several people who attempted to stand in his wake.

The moth dropped into Daerko's hand. The sailor whispered something to it, and it flew toward the small window

above the door that had been propped open to dispel smoke.
With a wary glance at Catseye, the moth's master followed
immediately behind it.

Catseye ran faster on the tabletops than Daerko could
move through the crowd. Only a few paces from the sailor,
Catseye sprang into the path that the man created as he
jostled people aside. Landing lightly on his moccasined feet,
Catseye grabbed Daerko's shoulder with his left hand to
spin the sailor backward, out of his way, then he drew his
sword with the same hand. The slim blade keened as it arced
through The Roost's smoky air, bisected the moth in mid-
flight, and returned to its wooden sheath in Catseye's right
fist before the insect's halved corpse had wafted halfway to
the floor.

Meanwhile, unnoticed in the uproar, Lizelle caught
Daerko before he fell. She whispered, "Don't do anything
you may later regret," while thinking, *An interesting man,
this Catseye. He fences left-handed, and quite well. How
would he fare against Noring?*

A drunken bargeman yelled, "What the twelve hells do
you think you're doing, Cat? You don't own the place!"

Several scowling mercenaries, a pale Tyrwilkan, a stocky,
darker Gordian, and a very tall, very dark southerner, muttered agreement. They looked surprisingly alike in their
mercenaries' garb of leather jerkins and wine-red headbands
stamped with a down-pointed dagger, though perhaps it was
their clenched fists that unified them. As they strode toward
Catseye, Lizelle shouted, "You're such a show-off, Cat!
What do you call that skinny sword of yours, anyway?
Flyswatter?"

Catseye's face grew crimson, though Lizelle could not
tell if this was from rage or embarrassment. "Why, you . . ."

The mercenaries halted and laughed. "Tikolos!" Lizelle
called quickly. "A pitcher of mead at every table!" She
tossed him two royals, glad that Salamon's purse had been
so well filled.

"At once!" said the old barkeep, catching the coins. The
crowd cheered. "Hey!" cried a red-haired man in a farmer's
green headband. "Cat! Whenever your friend's paying, you
can always dance on my table!"

Lizelle still gripped Daerko's arm. She said, "I'm sorry my companion bumped you. Come, join us for a drink."

"Uh, thanks. But—"

As the youth with the lute began a song that most of the tavern seemed to know, except for the boy who played pipes, Catseye took the sailor's other arm and told him, "I insist. I'm *so* embarrassed by my impetuosity."

"That's all right, man," Daerko grunted.

Lizelle adjusted the stolen sword that hung at her hip, moving it slightly as if for comfort. "Please. We insist."

"Very well!" Daerko said, baring stained teeth as he scowled at them. "I'll come. But by the nine true gods, you'll regret this."

"Ah," said Catseye. "So many regrets in a misspent life. Never to have sailed the Sunset Sea, nor to have eaten ice lollies in Torgia. . . ."

"I don't jest," the sailor said.

"And who suggested you had the wit to do so?" Then, to Lizelle, Catseye said, "By the way . . ."

"Yes?"

"My thanks."

His smile seemed too smug. "For what?" Lizelle said. "You owe me two royals."

Catseye laughed contentedly. Disgusted, Lizelle rolled her eyes up, and Catseye laughed again.

"So," said Merry as they approached, "you convinced the sailor to join us."

"Yes." Catseye pushed Daerko toward Lizelle's seat and sat in his own. Lizelle leaned against The Roost's rough wainscotting, folded her arms, and decided she should have let Catseye face the mercenaries alone.

He gestured at his black hat, which had fallen near where Lizelle stood. "Do you mind?" he asked.

"Not at all," she replied, lifting it with the toe of her boot and kicking it toward him.

Daerko stared at them both. "What do you want with me?" His voice grated unpleasantly in his throat.

"Information," said Merry.

"I know nothing," Daerko said.

"That's probably truer than you suspect," said Catseye,

still holding his sheathed sword.

"I needn't take this!" Daerko gripped the table's edge. The veins of his hands rippled under weather-battered skin.

"Try leaving," said Catseye. "I'll cry, 'How dare you!' and run you through before you rise. No one will care."

"Look," said Daerko less gruffly. "I've done nothing. Nothing at all. To any of you. You've got no reason to treat me this way."

"You've been watching me," Lizelle stated. "Why?"

"It's a free city. I needn't answer to any of you."

Merry snapped his fingers. The sailor looked at him, and the priest spoke one of the words of power while his fingers traced a quick pattern in mead on the tabletop. "Why?" Merry said.

The muscles in the sailor's face slackened, and his hands fell limply into his lap. "The wood grew warm when she passed."

"What wood?"

"The wood in my pocket."

"Put this 'wood' on the table."

Daerko placed something before him that had been carved to resemble a finger bone.

Merry glanced at the token, but did not touch it. "Who gave this to you?"

"Thessis Ar."

"Ah." Merry nodded.

"And who's Thessis Ar?" Lizelle asked.

"She's an enchantress," Merry answered. "Said to be related to the Empress's conjurer."

"Thelog Ar?"

"Yes." Merry asked Daerko. "Why did she give this wood to you?"

"To find the one who carried the miststone."

Noring's necklace suddenly felt heavy and cold between Lizelle's breasts. She glanced at Catseye and saw that he was studying her. Unable to interpret his gaze, she looked at Daerko.

"Many people wear miststones," Merry said.

Daerko, after a moment, said, "Yes."

"Did Thessis Ar seek any miststone?"

"No."

"She sought a special miststone?"

"Yes."

"And this person has it?" Merry nodded to Lizelle.

"Yes."

"What's the stone's importance?"

"I don't know."

Merry looked at Lizelle. "What do you know of this?"

"Nothing," Lizelle said truthfully. "When I was in Gordia, I heard of Thelog Ar, of course. I never knew he had relatives."

"And the miststone?"

She hesitated for a moment, but the necklace was the sort of thing a particularly naive forester might acquire and wear. And only Quentian or Salamon would be likely to recognize it. "It must be this." She tugged the stone out of her shirt.

"A very good specimen," Merry said. "Worth a bit, I'm sure. But it doesn't look at all special."

"No," Lizelle agreed. *Yet if magicians hunt it . . .*

"Where'd you get it?"

"I stole it."

Merry's brows raised as his eyes widened.

"Not from Thelog Ar. From a Gordian lord. Lord Noring. We were . . . friends, for a while."

"There's something familiar about this." Catseye reached out to hold the stone in his fingers. "The Sargoniom sorcerers . . . Didn't they have a use for miststones?"

"Maybe." Merry shook his head. "If so, the secret's lost."

"Hmm." Catseye released the gem, and Lizelle tucked it back in her jacket. "You could sell that," he told her.

"That's why I sought you," she said. "Zinjin Taleteller suggested I come here, if I ever needed assistance in Tyrwilka."

"Ah." Catseye eyed the others, then Lizelle. "Would you still sell the stone?"

"Not now." She grinned. "Zinjin said your percentage fell somewhere between exorbitance and theft."

"She would."

"Fascinating though this is," Merry said, "I think we

should concentrate on our friend here." He turned to Daerko. "Did Thessis Ar tell you to look for anyone in particular?"

"Yes."

"Who?"

"The person with the miststone."

Merry cleared his throat. "Ah, did she suggest that any particular person carried this miststone?"

"No."

"When did she give you the wooden piece?"

"Several days ago."

"Did she give such things to others?"

"I don't know." Daerko stopped as if he would say no more, then added, "Perhaps."

"And what of the moth?"

"She gave that when she gave the stick. She said to set it after the one who carried the stone, and then to speak a word to it."

"What word?"

Daerko uttered something from the First Language.

"What did she offer to pay for this?"

"Four hundred royals."

Catseye glanced at Lizelle and whistled. "Your value grows."

"L'zar travels with us," Merry said quickly.

"Of course," said Catseye. "It was only an observation."

Lizelle sipped her mead while eyeing the one-eyed man over the cup's brim. *I'll watch you, too, friend Cat. I wish there wasn't so much money chasing me, so we wouldn't have shadows on our understanding of each other.*

"Can either of you think of anything more to ask?" said Merry.

"Yes," said Lizelle. "Ask what else he knows about this."

"That's too general a question, I fear. The sailor answers like a drunk or a dreamer, from the part of the mind that knows no laws and understands only specifics. Should he tell everything he knows, or, if no man can ever 'know' anything, should he bother to answer us at all?"

"I don't know," Daerko said.

"You see?" said Merry.

"I see," said Daerko.

"I didn't know magic had such limits," Lizelle said.

"It does. That's why we Questers rarely use it." Merry tapped his finger on the table. "Daerko, leave the Roost and return to your present abode. You will remember nothing about this evening."

"Yes."

"Go, now."

The sailor rose and marched briskly into the street.

Catseye raised his cup. "Well, now that all that's resolved, we can enjoy the evening."

"Hardly," said Merry, standing. "We depart immediately."

"Why?"

"Because there are certainly others who search for our disguised friend. And Daerko's memory will return in a day or two. We must go while we can."

"The spell's not permanent?" Lizelle asked.

"The only permanent spells," Merry said, "are those that deal in death." And then, as abruptly as he had stood, the little priest sat, gasping in pain or surprise.

Thraas Thundersson had circled Tyrwilka's palace four times when a red-cloaked guard said kindly, "Sorry, outlander. No loitering here."

Thraas scratched his head. "But Thraas has discarded no small bits of paper."

The man, after a moment, said, "Er, loitering means to stay somewhere without a purpose."

"But Thraas always has a purpose. To be."

The guard smiled. "A philosopher, eh? I like that, but I doubt my sergeant would care to debate with you. Best move along, eh?"

Excepting the guard and a hurried woman who might have been lost, Thraas had encountered no one in Tyrwilka since sunset. He tried to enter several particularly interesting buildings, but they were all barred from within. When he noticed an old man by a door near him, Thraas waved his double-bladed axe, his only baggage, in a friendly way. The old man shrieked, poked a stick into a small hole by the door's handle, and ran inside.

Thraas tried the old man's door, only to find it barred like all the others. He had seen the old man's technique, though, so he had his first clue to opening this strange city. He began gathering twigs and fitting them into the tiny holes in each door.

After an hour or more, he had begun to grow discouraged when a horse's hooves clattered along the cobblestone street. "You there! What're you doing?"

Thraas looked to see a blond-bearded horseman in a blue jacket, kilt, and cape. "Thraas pokes small sticks into holes in doors. Magic is involved. Thraas does not understand."

"What?"

"You are man of army? That is"—Thraas fumbled for the right word—"uniform? Pretty."

The man sighed patiently. "Haven't you savages anything better to do than insult Gordians about their dress?"

"Gordians wear dresses?"

"No!" The soldier gripped his saber hilt.

"Not even Gordian women?"

The other stared, then said, "Well, uh, yes. But only the women. The men sometimes wear robes or kilts, but that's different."

Thraas nodded. "Different words." He groped for another twig.

"Say, are you locked out of your house?"

"No."

"Then what do you do here?"

"Thraas tries to open doors."

The Gordian paused, then said, "Are you drunk?"

"Thraas . . . drunk? No. Are you?"

"Look, I don't know what's considered good behavior where you come from, but . . . Where are you from, anyway?"

"From hills. Far from here. Wise woman says go to Tyrwilka. Thraas goes to Tyrwilka."

"Why?"

"Else wise woman have Thraas beheaded."

"Ah. Look . . ."

"Yes?"

"You can't go around opening doors. Not even in Tyrwilka."

"Thraas does not open doors. Thraas tries to open doors."

"Same thing."

"Not yet."

The blond man squinted at Thraas. "I don't want to argue semantics."

"Argue . . . what?"

"Semantics. Philosophy."

"Philosophy?"

"Word magic."

"All magic is word magic, for witches. Thraas knows this much. What witches say in Secret Tongue, is."

"No, Thraas—"

"What is your name?"

"I'm Lieutenant Guire, of Her Majesty's Tenth Legion."

Thraas struck his fist against his chest. "Thraas Thundersson. Of village called Fork In Stream. Far from here. In hills."

"Well, um, good. Any more questions before you head home?"

Thraas nodded. "What is the word"—he searched for all the syllables—"philosophy?"

Guire laughed. "You have a strange mind, Thraas. Why do you ask?"

"Guard used that word. No, a word like it. The guard called Thraas 'philosopher.' Was Thraas insulted by that man?"

"Some would say so," Guire replied, smiling.

"Oh." Thraas frowned.

"It's not an insult, though."

"Good!" Thraas said. "Thraas does not enjoy fighting."

"It means 'wise man.'"

"Magicker?"

"No. One who thinks much."

"Ah." Thraas nodded. "Thraas is philosopher. Thraas must find that guard."

"Why?"

"To thank him for telling Thraas what Thraas is. Maybe why wise woman sent Thraas to city. To learn what Thraas is."

"Maybe. I doubt it was to have you poking twigs in doors. Hasn't anyone objected?"

"At some doors, angry voices tell Thraas to go away."

"And what do you do?"

"Thraas goes away."

"That's very pragmatic of you."

Thraas stroked his braided beard. "Is pragma-tic like philosophi-tic?"

"Philosophical," Guire said. "Some people would say they were the same. Others would say they were opposites."

"Ah. Thraas thinks there are no words like these in Secret Tongue."

"Probably not. Say, are you done at that door?"

"Yes. There is something Thraas does not know."

"If I tell you, Thraas, will you leave? Then I'll be able to return to my barracks without feeling I should've called the city guard."

"City guard?"

"Yes. I realize that you're not afraid of them, either."

"Why call them?"

"Because you can't wander about attempting to enter houses."

"Thraas does not attempt to enter. Merely to open."

Guire sighed. "Someone should teach you the rules of civilization."

"Good." Thraas sat cross-legged in the street. "Do so."

"Not me!"

"Why not? Thraas thinks you wise man, Guire."

"Thank you, but . . . Look, I've got to return to the barracks."

Thraas stood. "Then Thraas come."

"No! It's only for the army."

"Maybe wise woman wanted Thraas to join army." To have found his nature and his purpose in the same evening . . .

The Gordian smiled. "I rather doubt that. Look, I'll tell you the secret, and then you'll go wherever you're staying. Agreed?"

"Agreed."

"Those holes are keyholes. A lock is inside. A special stick, called a key, fits into the hole. The key is made in a special way, so each key only opens its own lock. Turning the key opens the door. Understand?"

Thraas nodded. "Thraas must find keys."

"No!"

"But Thraas must see. How can Thraas know if—"

"Ask your innkeeper to demonstrate his lock. How's that?"

"Yes. What innkeeper?"

"You're staying at an inn, aren't you?"

"Ah. Ti-ko-los."

"What?"

"The innkeeper. He cares for Silky."

"Silky? No, don't tell me. I don't want—"

"Silky is best pony—"

"Right. Well, now that all that's taken care of, we might as well be going."

"Right," Thraas said reluctantly, deciding he liked Guire.

"Please," said someone behind them. "Not so soon."

Thraas spun about as Guire wheeled his gelding. A city person came so quietly that Thraas could not hear any approach?

Guire's chestnut gelding whinnied in fear, and Thraas tightened his hold on his axe. A grey-haired woman in a loose red dress waited in the middle of the street. Her complexion suggested that she had been dark-haired when younger, and the prominent bones of her face hinted at an earlier, regal beauty. She hovered several inches above the cobblestones and cast no shadow in the moonlight. "I would talk with you," she said. "My name is Thessis Ar."

A moment passed before Thraas could speak. "Flee, ghost. Thraas cannot touch you, but you cannot touch Thraas. And Thrass knows a chant to use against you."

"I'm no ghost," the woman said, obviously amused. "I'm only the spiritual projection of one whose physical form lies elsewhere."

Spiritual . . . Ah. The ghost of one who still lived. Thraas was not sure if this was less frightening. "What do you want with Thraas?"

"Actually, I don't seek you, outlander. I sought the bold young officer at your side."

Guire said, "M-me?"

"Yes," said Thessis Ar. "Y-you. You've spent some time in the company of a circus performer known as Lizelle."

"Performer?"

"You thought her a lady, I know. I'm sorry to disappoint you, dear boy."

"But why—"

"She has the misfortune to have stolen something desired by Thelog Ar. His agents now hunt her."

"And you . . . ?"

"I act for him, and for the Empress." She smiled like someone with a treasured secret. "Wait here. Your captain comes, with others." She turned to Thraas. "There's something interesting about you, outlander. That axe . . ."

"Father's grandmother won it in war," Thraas said proudly. "You fear it?"

"No. It isn't magical, though the workmanship's magnificent. But I sense something about you. . . . Do you value gold?"

"No."

"Then what do you do in a city?"

"Thraas sees sights. Pretty. Wise woman tell Thraas to come; Thraas come." These were unimportant things. The witch woman could not use them to hex him.

"She did? Why?"

"Thraas does not know."

Thessis Ar smiled. "Join the Gordians, Thraas. They're part of your fate. When they come to City Gordia, accompany them."

She addressed Guire. "Tell your captain what I've said. I won't visit him again for some time. The barbarian is to be paid and treated like any other mercenary. Understand, young handsome one?"

Guire nodded and said, "Yes!" Thraas suspected he shouted to keep from stammering again.

"Excellent," said Thessis Ar. She smiled at each of them, then faded into a shadow that dissolved in the texture of night.

"Easy there," said Guire to soothe his horse, spooked more by the enchantress's parting than it had been by her presence.

"Something odd," said Thraas. "Woman is what she is, yet is not."

"What do you mean?"

"Thraas doesn't know. Thraas only knows he knows this. Odd."

"You sense things?"

"Sometimes Thraas knows something and does not know why he knows it."

Guire peered about as though he expected Thessis Ar's return. "You should study with someone. You might have some power."

"Thraas went to wise woman. Wise woman hit Thraas on head with broom and laughed. If Thraas is witch, Thraas has little power. Only enough to make Thraas very confused."

He stopped, hearing men marching toward them. Without speaking, Thraas and Guire moved toward the clamor. The marchers carried torches, and, in the unsteady light, Thraas saw that most of them wore headbands of Gordian blue, Tyrwilkan scarlet, or the free soldier's blood red. Most were well dressed in leather or wool jackets dyed according to their allegiance, though some only wore such rags and cast-offs as could be found in alleys, snatched from bins, or stolen from corpses. At the front, a dark man all in indigo strode beside a heavier man in scarlet.

"Captain Quentian!" Guire called, hurrying his horse onward.

"Guire! Where've you been? Chasing the girl's runaway?"

"Yes, sir. Thessis Ar, ah, found me. There's to be some action tonight?" Guire glanced at the plainsman next to Quentian.

"Yes. You remember Sergeant Salamon of King Milas's Guard? Tonight we cooperate."

Guire and Salamon nodded curtly to each other.

"What were you told?" Quentian asked.

"Little. That Lizelle was a thief. That the Empress's magician wants something she has." While Guire spoke, Thraas wandered up beside them. "And that this man should join us as a soldier."

Quentian looked at Thraas, who wondered how a man could assess another so critically and yet reveal so little of his estimate of the other's worth. "If she says so," the captain said. "He'll be in your charge, Lieutenant."

"Yes, sir."

"What?" said Thraas.

"Stay by me," said Guire, "and be quiet."

Quentian said, "The sergeant thinks the girl is somewhere near Moonrise Lane."

Salamon nodded. "We looked there once, but only quickly. We thought we'd catch her before she discovered a hiding place, but she's either well hidden or well disguised, which suggests she had help. Help of that nature is most likely to be found around the taverns."

Quentian pulled riding gloves from his belt and slipped them over his hands. "We three should be able to recognize her, if she's disguised," he said. "And we have enough men to cordon the neighborhood, if she tries to slip away. She won't escape us again."

Girl? Thraas remembered the woman who ran with a sword in her hand. The same? It did not matter. The witch . . . Thessis something . . . had told him that this was part of his pattern, and he had felt that she spoke the truth. Now he was to set out on a great search. Civilization promised to be enjoyable after all.

chapter five

True Names,
Shadow Games

"WHAT IS IT?" said Lizelle as the little priest sat again.

"I don't know," he gasped. "Something I sensed. But..." He shook his head. "There's something wrong. The Pattern ... changes. If I were a seer..." Merry stood. Lizelle reached to steady him, but he said, "I'm fine. Let's go."

"Where?" said Catseye.

"To the temple. The Inner Circle will know more than I do."

Catseye lifted the carved wooden token that Daerko had left. "What of this?"

"Bring it." Merry strode to the bar to settle the bill.

Thinking their departure might be cause for wonder, Lizelle called, "So! Your credit's good at The Unicorn, friend Cat?"

Catseye raised an eyebrow. "My credit's as good as my sword, wherever I go," he said, slinging the weapon onto his back.

"Oh. It's fortunate I'm not very thirsty."

"You"—he hesitated in the midst of adjusting the brim of his hat—"add to an account that we must soon settle, eh?" Simultaneously, so quickly she barely saw it, so quickly that it was little more than a twitch or a blink, he winked his amber eye. "I look forward to that."

"Prove yourself as a drinker first, my friend." Lizelle clapped his shoulder. "Then as a bladesman."

"I," said Catseye with a smile, "might enjoy doing exactly that."

Lizelle prayed her reddening cheeks would seem a drunken flush. She resolved to end these little bouts of wit while she led, henceforth.

Merry paid Tikolos, tipped Hessabeth, and hurried into the cold night. Leaving The Roost, Catseye said, "Do you want this?" He held out Daerko's wooden finger bone.

"Ah, yes. Thank you," said Merry. He halted at a small stone bridge over a stream that was little more than an open sewer. "Does this flow into the Fastwater?"

"Yes," Catseye said, wrinkling his nose at the stench. "Why?"

Merry told Lizelle, "Take out the necklace."

She felt for it in her jacket. "Why?"

"Quickly. We've little time."

Lizelle drew forth the miststone, and Merry gripped it in one hand. In his other, he held Daerko's wooden token. Merry spoke several words that Lizelle could not later remember. The jewel and the chain vanished.

Lizelle inhaled deeply, then said, "But I still feel it. . . ."

Merry shook his head and added other words from the Secret Language. When he finished, Lizelle said, "What've you done?"

"A simple precaution, in case another uncovers you as the sailor did. I've transferred the essence of the gem into that bit of wood. Anyone searching mystically will discover Thessis Ar's talisman, not your necklace. And to protect the necklace from physical discovery, I've made it invisible. A shame I couldn't make it intangible as well." He sighed. "Put it back in your shirt, but handle the chain, not the stone, or you'll break my spell. Understand?"

"I think so."

"Good." Merry grinned, seeming a happy, fat, malevolent idol in the moonlight. "There's a secondary effect," he said, tossing the wooden finger bone into the stream.

Lizelle gasped. Something cold and slimy dangled between her breasts. She reached to remove it, but Merry ordered, "No!" She dropped her hand, understanding before he explained, "The wood and the stone are linked." He pointed toward Daerko's token, already lost in the water. "That bit of wood is warm and dry. The stone, however, feels exactly as it would if it floated down there."

Catseye peered into the murky stream. "I trust it's more comfortable than wearing a toad on a string."

"Barely," Lizelle said, cringing within her jacket.

"It'll be better in a week or two," Merry noted, "when the wood reaches warmer waters."

"That," said Lizelle, "is hardly reassuring."

"You can end the spell now, if you wish."

"No. I'll endure it."

"Good. We'll all be safer."

They continued up Moonrise Lane. Catseye exhaled as the fetid stream was left behind. "Just out of curiosity," he asked, "might some enemy already seek us? Friends of Daerko, perhaps?"

"I don't know," Merry said.

"You could lie," Catseye suggested. "If you thought it better for our morale."

"Better you stay alert."

"Don't worry. We might be trapped, but we won't be surprised."

"Oh?" said Lizelle. "You're sure?"

"I'm always sure."

"That must be nice for you."

Catseye gave her a crooked grin. "I'm just not always right."

"Ah." *I think I'm in love. At least for the evening. What will Darkwind think of him?* She dismissed the thought and called to Merry, "How much farther to your temple?"

"Not far. Another ten minutes."

Catseye cocked his head to one side. "Wait!"

All was still in the hour before midnight, as though the three of them were the only people alive within Tyrwilka's walls. Lizelle shivered and buttoned the top of her jacket about her throat. That only pressed the cold stone more firmly against her skin. *If I enclosed it in a leather bag . . . there'd be no advantage to having it invisible. Any more brilliant ideas?* A mountain bird called to its mate, then silence resettled about them.

"I don't hear a thing," Merry said.

Catseye snapped his head, demanding quiet.

Several blocks away, someone began singing: "The gypsy

came on the Elf Lord's daughter, swimming naked in the water. . . ."

"That's nothing," said Merry. "Midnight revelers, too drunk to be afraid to walk these streets at night."

"When he asked if she was cold, she replied with answer bold. . . ." The song faded as its singers wandered farther away.

"Not the drunks." Catseye nodded in the opposite direction. "There. A good number of marchers. They don't speak, but judging from the tramping of their boots . . ."

"I still don't hear anything," Merry said.

"It'll be too late when you do," said Catseye. "Might they be those who seek us?"

"Any might seek us," Merry said. "But I think we'll take another route, just in case." He angled toward an alley.

If the street was like a canyon, the narrow alley seemed a cave. Lizelle moved blindly at first, and Catseye caught her wrist to direct her around a crate. His fingers were strong, but his skin was smooth. "Thanks," she said when he released her. She wished she could see his expression.

The alley intersected another, momentarily widening. Moonlight illuminated rags and refuse and created odd shadows at the angles where buildings met. Mud squelched underfoot, too loudly for Lizelle's comfort.

They passed through blackness again. Lizelle thought something may have died nearby and, grateful she could not see what it was, tried to breathe shallowly as she hurried on. She almost bumped into Merry, who waited at the edge of moonlight at the next branching of alleys.

"Which way?" she asked him.

"I'm not sure." He glanced in either direction. "I think—" He gulped as a dark arrow buried itself in the decaying planks of the wall before him.

Lizelle dropped into the muck and rolled to one side of the alley. Catseye leaped to the other, pressing himself against a stack of cut firewood. Merry remained motionless in the open. "Down!" Lizelle hissed at him.

The priest began to stoop. A second black arrow splashed mud onto his robe when it appeared between his sandals. Merry froze, half-squatting. He seemed befuddled, not afraid, as a faint, keening laughter began. It came from all about them as though the sky were amused.

Someone has a lousy sense of humor. Lizelle slid her hand to her sword. A third arrow broke against the bricks behind her head. *Trapped! Godlings....*

The fourth arrow struck a log beside Catseye. Its initial vibration slapped the dark shaft against his cheek. He jerked his head away, saying nothing. A line crossed the side of his face, and it was not cast by shadow.

The laughter ceased. A figure stepped into moonlight, bearing a black bow with an arrow nocked and ready. An inky cloak covered its form from shoulders to black-booted feet, and the hands that held the arrow and bow were gloved. In the shrouded mystery of its hood, two small red embers glowed where eyes might be. "Greetings," the apparition said in a voice that sounded like wind. "I am the Thief in Shadow, and you have something I want."

Habit made Lizelle try to bluff. "What do you mean?"

The spectral laughter began again, sounding from all sides.

"What, damn it!"

The laughter heightened, then died. "The jewel, of course."

So much for the efficiency of Merry's magic. "What jewel?"

"Come, girl."

She was amazed her disguise had fooled anyone. "You can search. We have no jewels."

"The miststone, girl. I know where it is, I know what you've done. Give it to me."

"Miststone?"

The mocking laughter echoed along the alleyway. "I admire your persistence, but only the night lords know more than I of what transpires between darkness and light. I know what the priest did by the stream, for I heard every word. And I must have the bounty that Thessis Ar will pay, so give the stone to me."

"I..."

"I've nothing to gain from your death, girl, but if you make that the fee for acquiring the gem..."

"All right. It's yours." Surely there were easier ways to grow rich.

"That's certainly the more reasonable choice."

"No," said Catseye, stepping out into the alley. He placed his hand on Merry's shoulder to move the priest aside.

The hood turned toward Catseye, and the twin cinders flared for an instant. "What affair is this of yours?"

"Perhaps none. But I so hate to see another profit when I might."

Again Lizelle heard the ghostly laughter. "An admirable attitude, stranger, but you've no hope of gain here."

"Do you know who I am?" Catseye said softly.

"Who *you* are? *I* am the Thief in Shadow, sometimes called Master of the Master Thieves. Why should I care who you are?"

"So you've not heard my name, eh, Sneakshadow?"

"They call you Catseye Yellow, but that name will not be remembered." The wraith released its jet-black arrow.

Catseye skipped forward, drawing his strange, slim sword from its sheath on his back. The blade enscribed a circle that intersected the arrow's flight to bat it aside. The shaft of the arrow dissolved into powder. The head struck the brick wall near Lizelle and shattered like glass.

"What is that sword?" asked the Thief in Shadow. His words wavered like notes in a distant wind.

Catseye smiled sardonically, raising his weapon in salute. "You ask the wrong question, Knave of Night." The blade whisked back into its teak sheath. "Who am I?"

The second arrow was nocked, but the string had yet to be drawn. "Let your true name be known, then. Who are you, Catseye Yellow?"

Catseye stepped forward. None of the others could see his face. "If you would leave now, you need not hear it."

"I leave with the bauble kept by the girl, Lizelle."

She let the dagger drop from its wrist sheath into her waiting hand. Did everyone know her name and what she carried?

"Then you will never leave." Catseye stepped closer.

The apparition drew the arrow's fletching back to its hood. "Halt there, Catseye Yellow."

"Are you afraid, Master of Cutpurses?" In spite of his words, Catseye stopped.

"If you would be remembered," said the whispering wind, "identify yourself now."

Catseye whispered, "Perhaps you've heard of Kephias Flame-haired?"

"Doomed Kephias?"

Catseye's voice was sad. "Yes."

"You can't be . . ."

Catseye raised his hand to his face. "Perhaps this will identify—"

"No!" screamed the shadow. Its arrow lunged from the bow, and then Lizelle could only see an all-encompassing light, as if the moon had exploded.

When her sight returned, Catseye stood in the middle of the alley with his hands open at his sides. Merry had moved past him to pick up an empty black cloak. As he shook it, particles like dry mold sprang from the cloth.

Lizelle walked over to Catseye, who did not seem to see her. She noticed the welt on his cheek where the wraith's arrow had snapped against him and resisted an impulse to stroke it tenderly with her fingertips. "Some trick," she said. "How did you do it, Kephias-called-Catseye?"

Catseye's left fist went to his right shoulder, ready to backhand her. Lizelle stepped away, very aware of the dagger still in her grip. Catseye held her gaze for long seconds, then let his hand open and fall. He shrugged and looked away. "Kephias was a fool who died. Sometimes I act like him, but rarely. You can sheathe your knife now." His lips curled up in a rueful smile.

Lizelle looked at her dagger and then at him. She nodded, slipping her weapon back into her sleeve. *I should smile to show that it's all right. But it isn't.*

Merry said, "There's much about you that we don't know, Brother Yellow."

"That's some relief, at least," said Catseye. "Let's go. People come the way we came, and more approach from the right." He pointed down the smallest of the intersecting alleys. "So this is the only route still open."

"Not quite," said Merry. "It's a dead end."

"What of the rooftops?" asked Lizelle.

"If we can get up there," said Merry.

"We'll get up there," Catseye stated.

Merry said, "I'm not particularly agile."

Catseye said, "Right now, you're eminently disposable."

"On the other hand," said Merry, "I know how we might climb." He began to tear strips from the Thief in Shadow's cloak.

Catseye smiled. "As I said, priest, you're indispensable."

"In some lands, this is called the rope trick."

Catseye said, "You might save the patter for later."

While Merry knotted together the last fragments of the cloak, Lizelle heard the searchers' footsteps. Startled, she sought Catseye's glance. He nodded grimly.

"Faster!" Lizelle whispered to Merry. *I'll never again complain of being bored,* she promised herself. *Never....*

Lord Noring slept restlessly in the Empress's soft bed. He turned from side to side, swatting at nameless things swarming about his face and mumbling sounds of warning into his pillow. When at last he woke, he sat up, crying, "Sih!" Catching the sound in his throat, he felt suddenly foolish. He ran his fingers through his hair, massaging his skull. What had he been about to say? Sit? Sister? Cistern? He remembered nothing of his dream. Silver? That seemed closer.

Silly, he thought, and he laughed when he realized he had made a small joke. Definitely silly. He rolled onto his hip to see if he had wakened Glynaldis. She was not in the bed, not in the room.

That was some relief. He doubted she would be tolerant of the fears that show themselves in sleep. He did not care to imagine what cures she might find for a restless bed partner. He lay back. Moist sheets clung to his skin, so he rolled over, seeking a dry spot and finding one not so damp. He thought he might sleep again, but, lying still, he grew uneasy about the Empress's absence. Though her presence increased danger, it lessened surprise.

Did she expect him to stay or to leave? He had heard no hints and would listen more carefully henceforth. Seeing the songbird's cage, he shuddered.

The Empress's chambers were in the uppermost part of Castle Cloud, which squatted upon a hilltop like a toad. The city, ancient suppliant, crouched below. This image of servitude touched him too closely and, he rationalized, the night chill promised an early winter. He rose and began to shut the heavy glass shutters.

"Uyor!" the Empress said behind him.

Noring started in midstep, almost falling. The gardens were far, far below him. He caught his balance and, wondering if she had waited for this moment to return, forced a wan smile. "Glynaldis. I . . ." Should he claim to be departing? "Was about to shut the window." When she said nothing, he added, "It's . . . cold."

"My love!" she cried. "You're so gaunt!"

"I—" He did not like to think of being fattened.

"But I swoon when I see your strong shoulders, your cheeks so rosy red . . ."

Praise embarrassed him. He should have draped a blanket about himself.

". . . and I like your face, too." She stepped closer, smiling up at him.

She never said whether she noticed a moment's hesitation. He had sense enough to guffaw in mock outrage as he picked her up and threw her onto the warm and rumpled bed. At one instant, he thought he would be willing to die for lesser things than this. Her cry of "Yes!" seemed to answer that, and more.

Afterward, she said, "You grow bolder, sweet Uyor."

"My passion grows stronger."

She pulled away. "You feigned interest before?"

"No!" He drew her to him. Her fingernails raked his shoulders, and he shook her fiercely. "No! I wouldn't have thought I could've desired you more. But now . . ."

She peered at him through tangled hair. "Now?"

"Now . . . You'll laugh."

Without humor, she said, "I like to laugh."

"Now, I find that having you to end wanting you is like quenching a blaze with lamp oil."

"Ha!" She spun away, presenting her naked back to him.

He stroked her arm, then massaged her neck, then pressed himself against her. "Ah," she purred in forgiveness. Pressing more firmly, he thought, *And now, a fourth time? No wonder she takes so many lovers*.

When she spoke, she said, "You have a youth's strength."

"I hope he never asks it back."

She giggled. "I, too."

"You inspire me, Glynaldis."

"Do I?"

"Yes," he said, with more truth than he hoped she knew.

"I'm glad." Resting above him on her arms, she slowly turned. One breast slid along his chest, the nipple tracing a line in sweat and matted hair.

"Where were you?" he asked, hoping to distract her.

"Hmm?"

"Earlier."

"Out." She moved farther, and the second nipple followed the first.

"Walking?"

"Yes."

"Alone?"

She settled sleepily on his chest. "Where I go, none disturb me."

"I was surprised to wake by myself."

She snuggled up, nestling her head at his neck, rubbing her face against his beard. "Poor babe. It won't happen again."

"I was surprised to be sleeping, in fact. I'd been completely awake, and..."

"Yes?"

He heard a warning in her voice that told him she must have cast some drowsing spell on him. "But I suppose I was more tired than I knew," he finished. "The rest did me good."

"Mmm-hmm." She nodded her chin on the pillow of his chest.

He put an arm around her. "Glynaldis?"

"Yes?"

"If you'd wanted company, you could've awakened me. I would've gladly attended you."

She slid farther up to kiss his nose. "I'll remember, my sweet. But I had messages to deliver where you couldn't have gone."

"Oh."

"Would you know more of where I go and what I do?"

He answered cautiously, "I would know more of you, Glynaldis."

"Hmm." She lifted her head high. Her auburn locks fell around his face like a trap. "What would you know, my Uyor?"

"Anything," he said. "I know much of Gordia, how she appears in court and in conference. I know nothing of Glynaldis."

"Nothing?"

"Well, I—"

She laughed. "Very well. As you've satisfied me, I'll try to satisfy you. Fair?"

"I didn't mean to make a bargain."

"I make no bargain," she said. "I give what I will and I take what I will."

"I—"

"Would you know of the men in my life?"

"Or the women. What you will."

"There are no important women in my tale, sweet Uyor. My mother died when I was nine, I had no sisters, no female friends. . . ." She laughed. "So it's to be the men, but I promise you won't be jealous."

He kissed her, thinking he would rather not hear this. "I'm glad."

"My father, then. May he rot in the mad god's hell."

"He . . ."

"Yes?"

"He was a good king?"

"So? Aren't I a wonderful Empress?"

"Of course."

"See?" She laughed again, then said, "Best you don't comment, my Uyor. I like you too much to want to know what you think, and I'd rather not hear you lie, just now."

"As you wish." He hugged her tighter.

"I never saw my father until I was fourteen. Perhaps that

was natural. My elder brother, whom I never met, would
inherit, so I was unimportant. I rarely saw my mother. When
I did, she wept. At least, that's how I remember her. On
several of my few visits to her quarters, I heard a servant
announce that the king came to call. Then she'd weep more,
and I'd be sent away in the company of my latest nurse.
Though I'd try to linger, I was never able to stay long enough
to glimpse this man who was my father. Once I heard his
footsteps, ringing on the stone, and I decided he must be a
giant or a god." She hesitated. "Do I bore you?"

"Never."

"Good. My nurses were always ancient, withered, and
irritable. I had a new one every month—undoubtedly so
none need poison the royal brat to free herself of her charge.
They were recruited from the Sisterhood of the Snake and
wore the scratchiest green robes. One gave me candy once,
I remember. She was sent away the next morning."

Glynaldis was quiet so long that Noring thought she
would speak no more. Then she said, "I was playing in my
mother's room one day when the nurse ran in, cried, 'The
king!' and snatched my hand to drag me out another door.
As she pulled me away, I heard the footsteps I'd heard
before, and then I heard blows, like, like . . ." She shook
her head. "My mother was screaming, and I, for some
reason, was crying. She was only a very pale woman who
wept often, but she was one of the few people in my world,
then." Glynaldis shook her head again. "The next day, it
was announced that the queen had fallen down a flight of
stairs and died."

The Empress's right hand was at her mouth, and she
chewed at the side of her little finger. Noring wanted to
take her hand and pull it away. If he knew how she would
react . . . She continued to speak, her apparent calm only
belied by the gnawing at her flesh. "I was never allowed
to see my father. Not in court, not on parade. I thought he
didn't know I existed, that I was kept hidden from him. I
used to plan ways to sneak away from my nurses to find
him. I'd dream of how he'd recognize me, honor me, and
love me. I didn't blame him for my mother's death. I thought
she'd done something wrong—I understood punishment,

thanks to my nurses. So I ran away often, though I never found him. The guards and nurses knew the castle better than I. I didn't even know where his chambers lay.

"On birthdays, I'd receive a present, a ring or a dress that I was told was from 'him.' There was never a letter or a note enclosed. I thought my nurses lied to pacify me, so I found ways to lose or ruin those false gifts. But on my thirteenth birthday, no presents came. And then, after dinner, my nurse had me bathe. She dressed me in a simple white gown and arranged my hair about my head as my mother's had always been. Then she took me to my father's chambers. To this very room. He was here with a woman I had never seen before, and together they . . ." She moved her hand from her mouth to Noring's face, tapping the end of his nose with the tip of the finger she had chewed. "How should I say this, my sweet? They introduced me to love's many delights? Is that how I should say it? They taught me the fine distinctions between pleasure and pain while they laughed and drank and sang the birthday songs and, and . . ." She gasped, then said, "Would you know all they did? I remember clearly."

"No," he whispered, stroking her hair.

"Are you sure?"

"Yes."

"Quite sure? It's a stimulating story, my lord, sure to please any man."

Softly, he said, "Glynaldis . . ."

"Never reproach me, Noring!"

"I do not."

"Nor pity me, either!"

"I—"

"Would you hear my tale?"

"If . . . if you must tell it."

She stopped to study him. "Ah, Uyor. You'd have too much kindness to survive at court, if you hadn't so much fear."

"I'm no—"

"I mean no insult. In truth, a compliment, my lord. Nor do I mean you fear as many do. You kill quickly and well when you duel."

"Glynaldis . . ."

"Though that," she said, "hardly exonerates you of cow-
ardice, now that I think on it. Why should you fear, being
the best pupil of our nation's greatest swordsman, and he
retired abroad with rheumatism to play at tavernkeep?"

"I never claimed to be brave."

She smiled. "I wouldn't care if you were. I prefer you
with your fear. It makes you careful."

He said nothing.

"Like now." She laughed. "Well! On with my happy
history! When next I was aware, as Book the Second should
begin, I'd been bathed and bandaged and dressed, and trun-
dled off in a carriage to one of the Sisterhood's nunneries.
Do you know anything of life in service to the Snake?"

"A little."

"All prayer and meditation. Little sleep. For the king's
daughter, tutoring in languages, history, and philosophy,
as well. I didn't like living there. Perhaps I should've been
glad to have escaped Castle Cloud, but the Sisterhood places
great value on virginity, and I suffered over what I thought
was my sin. I think that was why my father entrusted me
to their care. Do you like this story so far?"

"Glynaldis, you needn't—"

"Ah, don't think there were no happy times! Oh, no.
We'd all gather in the chapel, huddled together and singing,
thinking thoughts of virginity while gazing at the great jade
snake. . . .

"I stayed there for two years. Compared with my earlier
life, it was neither worse nor better, I suppose. Merely
different. While I wasn't happy, I wasn't miserable. And
then a coach came, perhaps the same that had brought me.

"Here begins the Third Book. I was taken to Tyrwilka.
Yenzla the Fat still lived, though his son, Yenzla the Bald,
ruled. I was married to the grandson, Yenzla the Toad."

"I . . . have heard of that."

"It was my father's final joke, or possibly the final stage
in his education for me. The marriage was said to be of
political convenience, though Gordia had nothing to fear
from Tyrwilka, then as now. Nothing to gain, either. It did
free my father of responsibility for me, which must have

been a considerable relief. And if his spies told him tales of his daughter forced to . . . to entertain the Tyrwilkan court, he probably laughed and retired early to the bed of his latest concubine."

Her body was tense in Noring's embrace. He said gently, "I needn't hear any more."

"But the story's not over. I must tell of Book Four, Uyor, when the happy ending begins."

"Ah?"

"Yes. I met Tyrwilka's mage sometime after my husband had poisoned both his sire and his grandsire at his birthday feast—an impromptu present to himself, apparently. Yenzla had forgotten me by then. I lived secluded in a tower much as my mother had lived in one wing of this castle. But the magician saw me at my window once, and"—she smiled— "as old men are sometimes wont to do when, in their dotage, they meet a young woman, he became enamored of me. He used his magics so we could meet, and soon we plotted together. From afar, he arranged to slay my brother, and I was suddenly heir to Gordia. We intended to kill my father soon after. Isn't this a cheery tale?"

"I can see how you find it satisfying." He wondered how much of her story was true. He doubted that the wizard's infatuation had been left to chance.

"Our plans were upset when the Islander slew Yenzla and usurped Tyrwilka's throne. The mage and I, not caring what happened to that hated country, fled to Gordia. We thought to arrive as harmless outcasts seeking refuge, then to wait for the best moment to seize control. But Fate unveiled one of her surprises. My father had died in his sleep two nights before the barbarian took Tyrwilka. So justice was served, though vengeance was not, and now I live happily ever after. The end. You may applaud."

The last was told too quickly, but he was glad she had not reveled in detail. Perhaps the entire story was an embroidery to amuse herself during a sleepless hour. Still, he asked, "Who was the mage?"

"Oh. Thelog Ar, of course."

"What . . ." Too late, he realized that were any of this true, he should know no more.

"Yes?"

Cursing his curiosity, he said, "What of the woman? The one . . . with your father?"

"I found her."

"Ah."

"She's managed to kill herself three times. I've had Thelog Ar bring her back every time."

Noring closed his eyes.

"Well?" she asked. "Did you like my story?"

"No," he said.

"Careful, Uyor."

"If I'm too careful, I'll bore you."

"And so you're safer taking an occasional risk? A novel theory, my lord."

"Is it safe to sleep now?"

"I think not, my lord. I think I would have something besides the past to occupy my thoughts."

He understood that. Knowing his role, he said, "Gods! Are you insatiable, woman?"

"Why, I'm very satiable, lover." She slid against him. "But not for very long. . . ."

chapter six

The Price of
Survival

MERRY TOSSED HIS rope of knotted black cloth high into the air. As it uncoiled, almost disappearing in the darkness, he spoke a few words and gestured. The rope stood rigid before them.

Lizelle said, "I wish you knew another form of magic. Forgetting what you've said makes my head ache."

"Oh. I'm sorry," the priest said, and Lizelle believed him.

"Is it safe?" Catseye asked, indicating the rope with a twist of his chin.

"Yes," said Merry.

"Good." Catseye sprang, seized the cord with both hands, and raced up into the shadows.

"Show-off," Lizelle muttered. She followed Catseye with an acrobat's ease. The rope swayed like a drunken snake as Merry clambered after her. Lizelle's hand abruptly closed on air when she reached the top. Catseye stood with arms akimbo, watching from the roof's edge, some two feet away. Lizelle swung herself, released her hold, and fell forward, landing on cedar shingles on the balls of her feet.

"Nicely done," Catseye said.

"You might've helped."

"You needed none. Unlike him." He jerked his thumb downward. Merry, midway up the knotted cord, labored to climb higher. "The longer we linger here..."

Lizelle hesitated, reluctant to abandon Merry even though she knew that Catseye's instincts were right. "The priest's responsible for getting us this far," she said at last. "He may be useful again."

"He's also responsible for getting us into this, whatever it may be. We flee his enemies now, not ours."

She suspected that was not entirely true, at least in her own case, but only said, "We may not be fleeing anyone."

"Someone is searching the streets quite thoroughly," Catseye said. "I don't particularly want to ask one of them if they're looking for me. Do you?"

"My friends!" Merry whispered from where he hung helplessly on the cloth rope, unable to climb farther. "Please! Pull me up!"

Lizelle gripped the end of the cord, which writhed like a live thing in her hand. "Well?" she asked Catseye. "You think you've earned a rest?"

He laughed, and together they dragged the priest to the roof's edge. As Merry scrambled onto the shingles, Catseye said, "I don't suppose you've considered fasting?"

"May the God forbid!" Merry traced a circle over his chest.

Lizelle said, "A shame you're not one of the mad god's followers."

"I often suspect he is," said Catseye.

She glanced at him. "But they're all thin," she noted.

"I know," said Catseye. "It was a fairly slim joke."

Lizelle groaned.

Merry said haughtily, "Do you intend to remain here all night making bad puns?"

"Not necessarily. I can make bad puns anywhere."

"I thought you were in a hurry to leave."

"That was before we dragged you up with us. Now I think we might as well wait until the hunters pass, then continue on at our leisure." Catseye sat cross-legged on the shingled slope.

Merry squatted near him. "I'm not fond of heights. I think I like your plan." As Lizelle sat beside him, the priest whispered, "The Thief in Shadow called you Lizelle. That's your name?"

She nodded. "I'm thinking of having it tattooed on my forehead."

Catseye raised a finger for silence. "The searchers approach."

Lizelle listened. A faint scuffling came from far away and soon became the tramping of many marchers. Catseye gazed intently in the direction of the sound, while Merry sat huddled on the roof and poked at a loose shingle with a pudgy finger. Lizelle shivered in her jacket and turned up its hood. She was too aware of the cold, damp necklace on her chest, and she wished she had never taken Noring's jewelry. Caught and returned to City Gordia, she would have her hands cut off for stealing, then her ears and her nose for impersonating a member of the First Caste. If the Tyrwilkans kept her, they would be kinder. They would hang her.

Lizelle heard murmurs of conversation as the marchers came near. When one man spoke, the rest halted and fell silent. Though she had expected it, she grew more frightened when she recognized Quentian's deep, grim voice.

"Guire!" the captain called. "Take the mercenaries and search this passage! Salamon and his soldiers will investigate the other. The rest of us shall wait for you here."

"Agreed." That was the plainsman, the pleasant Salamon.

"Yes, sir." And that was pretty Guire, who had hoped to meet her elsewhere.

A small group detached itself from the larger and came toward them. Someone stumbled and cursed, advocating an imaginative arrangement of the nine gods and their animal companions. Someone else laughed. Then the first said, "Nine hells, man! Only drunks are out tonight. I think the Gordians expel their brains with their bowels."

Lieutenant Guire's melodious laugh was loudest. "You must've met my former captain," he said.

"Quentian?"

"No. Before him. Quentian's no fool, and better you never think he is. But you needn't worry whether we find the woman we're hunting. You'll still be paid in good Gordian gold."

"Which'll be bettered by becoming Tyrwilkan gold," another said.

The first man said, "Still, it's crazy to be poking around here. No one's passed this way since nightfall."

"Perhaps not true." The newest speaker's voice was pitched low, a rumbling reminiscent of waterfalls.

"What's that?" asked Guire. "You've seen something?"

"Bring torch. See?"

"Where?"

"Here. Footprints of those who last walked through here. Like prints at scuffling, earlier. Three people. One man or large woman. One small person, maybe child, who carries something heavy. Or who is fat. One woman or youth."

"Interesting," said Guire. "But they might've passed this way hours ago."

"Ah. But did not someone say this way leads to wall, not street? Tracks go in, not back."

"Bah!" a mercenary uttered. "Probably gypsies sleeping off a drunk."

"Well, we'll find out," Guire said, then asked, "You're sure of this?"

"Thraas is sure. And these are not gyp-sies. Little one wears boots that are not boots, like priest wears."

"Sandals?"

"Yes. Big one wears soft boots, like woodsman. Other one wears very good boots, that gyp-sies would sell for other things."

Lizelle noticed that she was pressing the back of her hand against her mouth. She moved it away. Catseye caught her glance and shrugged apologetically. The priest, who she expected to be the most nervous, seemed the calmest. When Lizelle suggested with a jerk of her head that they go, Merry raised his hand for patience. After a moment, Catseye seconded that with a nod.

The searchers were directly below when Lizelle heard, "Guire! Prints end here!"

"What?" said the lieutenant, and then, "Magic?"

"Thraas does not know. Like the witch woman, Thessis Ar? No. Witch woman left no footprints. Maybe up there. With a rope?"

One mercenary said, "This may be an ambush."

"No," Guire said. "They'd have attacked by now, if there were more than three. I wonder who her companions are?"

"They may've already gone," said another mercenary.

"We'll know soon enough," Guire declared.

Lizelle grimaced at Catseye. He held out his hand as if to say, "How could I know?" She pointed onward and mouthed, "Run?" Merry dipped his bald head in reluctant agreement.

"There must be stairs, somewhere," said Guire, below. "Or a ladder. You two search farther down the alley."

The roof sloped sharply to shed rain and snow, and the painted wooden shingles made for slippery footing. The trio moved slowly, striving for silence. Then Merry gasped as he fell to his knees.

Lizelle and Catseye halted where they stood. The one called Thraas said, "Something up there, Guire."

"Maybe a cat," said the skeptical mercenary.

Lizelle decided against attempting a meow.

"Big cat, then," said Thraas.

A shadow moved by a building ahead of them, and the quiet of the rooftops ceased. "Lieutenant! Someone's up here! Hurry!"

Catseye's sword was in his hand as he ran forward, but their discoverer dropped back into the alley to wait for reinforcements. "Run!" Catseye hissed, perhaps to his foe, perhaps to Lizelle and Merry, who had already begun to hurry.

Below them, Guire yelled, "Captain! Surround the block! Someone's on the rooftops!"

The buildings, all two-story structures with peaked shake roofs, were almost the same height and rarely farther than a handsbreadth apart. Crossing from one to the next was a matter of leaping down or scrambling up a foot or two.

Quentian's soldiers showed themselves on the roofs behind the fleeing trio, following cautiously for fear of falling, for fear of ambush, for fear of being first to confront the people they pursued. Several called, "Halt! You can't escape!"

Catseye stopped at the edge of the next building. "What..." Lizelle began to say, then saw. Empire Avenue crossed before them. They could go no farther.

Merry, puffing frantically, caught up with them. Catseye said, "Priest! Can your rope get us across?"

"No," Merry wheezed. "Too far. Only down."

The street below them was empty yet. "A chance," Lizelle murmured. She looked back to see if some miracle had rid them of their hunters. The soldiers still advanced, only a few buildings away. One raised a spear to throw it, but another caught his arm, saying, "A bonus if she's alive, remember?"

That did not cheer her. Lizelle waited in frustration while Catseye lashed the priest's rope to a cornice and slid down to the cobblestones. As Merry eased himself off the roof, Lizelle snatched the small eating knife from the priest's belt and glanced back over her shoulder. One man had reached the adjoining roof. Lizelle looked down. The street was still empty, save for Catseye, who waited by the rope. Merry was over halfway down. Lizelle sliced the cord, spun, and threw the knife, hearing Merry's cry as he fell, and then the scream of the approaching Tyrwilkan, who staggered back, clutching the knife in his belly. His companions scattered, lest they be her next target.

She stood poised at the edge of the roof, prayed she remembered her circus training, and then jumped. The ground rose too quickly to greet her. When her boots touched cobblestone, she tucked and rolled and, slightly dizzy and slightly proud, came up standing.

Catseye whistled. "Not bad." He jogged beside her as they hurried down Empire Avenue.

"I know." She tried not to pant. "I didn't think you'd wait for me."

"I sprained my ankle."

"Oh? Seems all right now."

"I heal quickly."

The soldiers, shouting and waving, emerged from the alley behind them. Lizelle checked to see how many followed and how far behind they were. She thought, *We'll lose them, if we've no new surprises. We may also lose Merry. No, he moves quickly when his life's at stake.*

The man who ran closest behind them was a huge hillman with a brown, many-braided beard. He wore a large bearskin vest and carried a crescent-bladed war axe in his left hand. With his right, he spun something on a string above his head. He threw it at Merry, and the priest fell with his legs snared. Lizelle, barely believing, realized, *A bola!*

When the hillman again reached into the pocket of his vest, she tried to run faster, though she already pushed herself to her utmost. *Nothing to do for Merry,* she thought. *He knew the risks....*

Something whirred behind her, and something wrapped itself about her feet. Lizelle rolled across the muddy cobblestones, snatching her wrist knife free and hacking at the bonds about her ankles. Catseye hesitated. "Go!" she said.

His strange sword whisked through the bola. Grabbing her wrist, he yanked her to her feet.

The pursuers were too close. She felt them behind her, as untiring as hounds. "Do your trick, Catseye!" she breathed. "Like you did with the shadow thing!"

"No good," Catseye gasped as they fled. "Sneakshadow's bane ... was bright light. That's all. Might blind a few. Not all. A last resort. Understand?"

The third bola looped about Lizelle's leg and she fell. Catseye somehow managed to sprint ahead, to no avail. The fourth bola brought him down, and he cried out like a jungle beast impaled on a trap where no trap should be. The mercenaries gathered around them, kicking their weapons away and laughing as they struggled to rise.

The soldiers parted for Captain Quentian. He kneeled and took Lizelle's chin in his gloved hand. "Didn't I say we'd meet again soon, Lady?"

She wanted to spit in his eye, to bite off one of his fingers, to scream her opinions of his ancestry. Instead, she smiled with the greatest gratitude she could feign and said, "Oh, Captain, you've saved me! If you'd known what these kidnappers intended..." Then, to hide from Merry's disbelieving stare, she cupped her hands about her face and wept.

The old Quester wondered what woke her. Perhaps it was only that, at her age, one woke sometimes, as her body's sense of time, like so many of her body's senses, had begun to fail. A wrongness crowded her mind that seemed the

precursor to a headache. Her right shoulder was stiff—and
had been stiff for fifteen years, she realized, coming more
fully awake. Her bladder demanded relief, her feet were
cold, and, somewhere, someone was crying. This last re-
alization made her wonder if she was the one who cried
and, if so, why. Then, fully awake, she turned and whispered, "Serenity? What is it?"

His sobs continued. She slid closer to him. "Serenity?"
The mat beneath her was poorly padded. Each lifting and
resettling of her hips hurt her in a long familiar way. "Can
you tell me?" Finding him in the darkness, she put her arm
about him, hugging him and huddling against him. "Can I
help?" She was ashamed of a thought that he might have
grown senile overnight.

"I love you." She squeezed him, shook him, and, finally,
frightened more than she knew, spoke to him as she had
not since they were novitiates in the Questers' Order thirty
years before. "Tival, it's Ilen. Please, Tival. Speak to me."

His crying changed to a harsh gurgle. Felicity gasped
before she realized that this was not the death breath. The
old man rocked forward, free of her arm, and flung himself
against her, knocking her back onto the mattress. Perhaps
she was right to fear madness. As he squeezed her so she
could not breathe, so her ribs threatened to give under a
pressure she would not have believed him capable of in his
youth, she decided that if she must rejoin the God, this was
neither the worst time nor place to rejoin Her, nor he the
worst person to aid her departure. She said his name fondly.
It came out a rasping whisper.

She thought she could see newer and richer darknesses
in the unlit room when his strength left his grip. He held
her gently, sobbing again. "Felicity, I . . ." He stroked her
cheek with awkward, feeble fingers.

"Shush." Air filled her lungs, hurting and thrilling her.
"It's all right." She sensed that it was, for now.

"No. It's not."

"You're fine. You are!"

"We were wrong."

"How?" She remembered their earlier conversation and

said, "We did what we could. And we do what we can."
She placed her palm against his hand, which rested on her
cheek. "What more dare we do?"

Still he did not answer directly. His role of First Speaker
seemed to settle on him as he said, "I thought I dreamed.
I thought I walked through dark halls. I knew they were
dark, because I could see, which I accepted as normal.
Something ahead was more important than the loss of my
blindness. Then I could see, truly see. A light, far in the
distance, grew brighter and brighter. I drew closer to it,
faster than a man should be able to walk. The light flickered
like fire, and I saw that I walked through walls carved with
representations of cats, as though I walked in a temple
dedicated to their kind. But I didn't feel as if I were in a
temple. I felt as if I were in a prison. That was when I
began to fear the end of my journey. I thought I knew who
the prisoner was."

She wanted to do something more to comfort him. He
sounded stronger now, so she only said, "It wasn't a dream."

"I think not."

"You visited—"

"Hush. Name no names. We don't know."

"But you—"

"We don't know," he said. "I'm old. Let it stay a dream,
for now."

"If you wish."

"I thought someone would be waiting at the light. And
then I thought someone might be the light. The idea of such
power frightened me. I tried to turn back, but I couldn't,
for something drew me. At last, I entered a chamber at the
end of the hall. The light was a pulsating red globe that
hovered in the air. Around me were bare obsidian flagstones
and high pillars of jade. Beyond, in shadow, were the marble
walls with their fresco of cats. I didn't dare study them. I
turned, searching the room, and saw no one.

"When I sighed my relief, something warm and heavy
settled on my shoulder. I didn't want to look down. When
I did, I saw a paw, twice the size of my hand, lying there. I
couldn't make myself look back to see what had such a
paw. It was orange, with long fur marked with flecks of

white and black. As I watched, pearly claws the size of daggers unsheathed themselves.

"'Kill me,' I said. 'You can't play with me.' But I didn't feel very brave.

"'Hmmm?' it growled.

"I didn't repeat myself. The paw pushed against my shoulder, and I spun as I fell.

"'Hmmm?' it growled again. I saw it then as I picked myself up. It looked like a jungle cat, but it was larger than a wasteland bear. Its left eye was amber. Where the other should have been was only darkness.

"It growled, 'Slay you I can. Yes. In this place, I can.'

"'Then do so,' I said. 'Why else have you brought me here?'

"'Brought you? No. Came you, yes, of your own accord. Slay you I can. If I will. Serve me you can. If you will. Choose.'

"'I serve all,' I replied, 'as best I can.'

"Its growl was like laughter. 'Different you are from others who came before. Yes.' It turned my head with its paw, studying me. 'Yes. Into my eye you shall look.'

"I looked and only saw my reflection. The cat purred and said, 'Know you now I do. Yes. Different you are. Yes. Slay you I will not, and serve me you will not. Yet serve me you shall, and slay you I shall, for many choices there are, but choices there are none. Slay you I will by serving you, and serve me you will by dying.'

"I stepped back, afraid that a quick death was the only service it offered. 'Fear you need not,' it said. 'Say did I not that choose you will? Into my other eye look.'

"I peered into the hole where its other eye should have been. I saw a city at night as seen from its roofs. It was Tyrwilka, little changed from its appearance in my youth. I saw figures that must've been those you saw in the scry stone. The woman, our own Brother Merry . . . they fled across the rooftops with soldiers in pursuit.

"'The present this is,' the great cat purred.

"'I must—' I began to say.

"'Patience have,' said the cat. 'The present this is until here you leave. Changed it cannot be. Look now. The future this is, if others act not.'

"Again came the swirling scene of falling through something other than space, and then..." The old man clenched the woman's hand. "And then he showed me scenes of... of our world, scenes worse than the worst of our expectations. I saw the deaths of our friends, the end of our Order. This temple fell in ruins. Gordia governed all, if the Empress's self-serving domination can be called 'governing.'" He spoke with difficulty. Felicity thought the words themselves seemed to pain him. "I saw you, too, dying, and children..." He halted. "And children... I think you can imagine it. That's kinder than seeing it."

She nodded.

He said, "I asked... the cat... what could be done to avoid that future. 'Anything,' it answered. 'But what will happen then?' I asked. 'Something else,' it answered. 'But what?' I insisted. The cat only shook its head, saying, 'If change things you would, act then you must.' And then I woke here."

Neither spoke for several minutes. She clung tightly to him as she thought about his tale. She said, "What'll you do?"

"I don't know."

She allowed herself a tiny laugh. "You still try to fool me."

He joined her, chuckling. "And still fail."

"You'll intervene," she said, suddenly feeling as if no emotion could ever again touch her to harm her. Yet she heard her voice carry quiet accusation.

"Yes," he answered.

"Serenity... wait for the Circle to join. Together—"

"I... dare not wait."

Becoming afraid and not knowing why, not knowing anything else to say, Felicity said, "This isn't our way."

"I know. And I fear the consequences. I..."

"Yes?"

"I love you, Ilen."

Before she could reply, he kissed her. And then he spoke a word, and her arms held only air, and the sobbing that she heard was her own.

chapter seven

A Soldier's Lot

At THE TOWER that lay outside of time, the sky was always a luminescent grey, as though day or night would arrive in another minute or two. The tower, a simple cylinder of turquoise blocks, stood upon a cliff that rose from a restless sea. A small walled garden of rocks and ferns and meandering streams adjoined the tower, and at the garden's center a fountain sprang up in the midst of a pool enclosed by a low stone wall.

Three watchers sat by this pool. Two of the watchers, a naked man whose skin was as pale as alabaster and a grey-furred being who might have been a wolf become a man or a man become a wolf, studied the rippling pool. The third, a girl with a shaven head, watched the naked man. Her eyes were moist with anger or love.

The wolfish one said, "A day has passed, and they do nothing but ride."

"It can't be all spectacle," the naked man answered. "The silences in a song may be as important as the sounds. Maybe more."

"This bores me." He turned suddenly, and the girl gasped in fear.

The naked man put his hand on her shoulder to comfort her, then said, "This is important, dear Ralka."

"Of course. I'm still bored."

"Watch. Something may yet happen that even you can appreciate."

"When?"

"Soon, I fear."

"As we measure time, or as they do?"

"As you do."

"Good."

The second day ended. The girl lay curled at the naked man's feet with her eyes closed. Ralka clenched his clawed hand and snarled, "They sleep! I've waited for this?"

"No," the other said calmly.

"I think we've won."

"Really?"

"Yes. I could tell you why I think so."

"If you wish."

"If you ask!"

"Do you want to tell me?"

Ralka bared his teeth in something that resembled a smile. "Yes, Demon Lord. I want to tell you."

"Ah," Asphoriel said. "Then I ask."

"Thank you."

Asphoriel shrugged. "I notice that you become sarcastic, now."

"That's because you frustrate me so."

"That's because I have had ages more practice than you. Yet you have some talent of your own, Wolf Lord."

Ralka grinned and bowed. "Thank you, Demon Lord."

Several hours passed. Within the pool, a distant moon began to set.

Asphoriel sighed. "Congratulations, youth. You've succeeded. I am curious. Why do you believe the end is certain?"

"Not certain. But little more can happen now."

"Oh?"

"Two of the three are in chains. The third is tied with silk and watched constantly. All are being transported to Gordia under heavy guard, and they haven't been allowed to communicate with each other."

"They aren't the only ones who might act."

"The Order won't call attention to itself for fear of being destroyed by the Empress's servants. The one called Guire has sympathy for the woman, Lizelle, but he won't betray his country to help her. The one called Noring has little sympathy for the Empress, but he's too frightened to defy her openly."

"And what of the prisoner in our tower?"

"Him? He has no power left."

"I wish I could be so sure." .

"I am."

"I wish that comforted me."

"No matter. Who else might intervene, Wolf Lord?"

"There's the renegade Quester."

"He's old and blind. And, like all of his Order, his vows constrain him."

"If he cast his vows aside?"

"I don't know. Would he?"

"You are the one so sure of all. Tell me, Ralka."

"He . . . would lose his power."

"You are sure?"

"Yes. Though I realize that doesn't comfort you."

"What of the Empress?"

"Our ends don't exclude hers. She won't seek a conflict where none is necessary. And, as you've said, if we can't use her, we'll use the Questers or their pawns."

"What of the Empress's sorcerer?"

"Thelog Ar's thread was knotted long ago. He'll never unravel it."

"What of Lizelle's horse?"

Ralka stared. "The horse?"

"Yes. It is no common beast."

"It's a horse. I'm amazed it's done what it has."

"What of happenstance, coincidence, luck?"

"Those would have to be great to alter what exists. And then we would act, eh?"

"Perhaps. Those are all the possibilities you see?"

"Yes. Do you agree with me?"

"You are thorough."

"Thank you."

"But young."

"And you're far too pretentious, Demon Lord, but that's irrelevant."

"I confess, I do enjoy your attempts at wit, Ralka. A

shame that wit is invariably the loser."

"You say that to silence me?"

"And that I dare not answer. Enough of this." Asphoriel turned slightly, careful not to disturb the girl sleeping at his feet, and gestured toward the pool. "Watch, Wolf Lord, if — you will. Learn, if you can."

Catseye's sword was easy to find, and Merry's pouch lay near it. The blind man, sensing these things better in the darkness than others might see them in light, took each from the Gordians' supply tent and went in search of the captives. Too little time remained. He hurried through the camp, silently cursing the spell of concealment that hid him from the soldiers and made him much too vulnerable to anyone who searched for magic.

He halted in the middle of the ring of canvas tents. The Pattern seemed tangible there, heavy and almost insupportable. Its branchings were a tangle that ended in many places, perhaps in only one; he could not know. He soothed his doubts with the hope that if there was only one goal, it might be shaped, however slightly, by the path one walked toward it.

There was no time for standing and thinking, he knew, just as there was never time for anything important. He shrugged the shroud of possibility from his shoulders and hurried to the tent where Catseye and Merry slept in their chains. If they could free the woman, so much the better. If not, Merry might yet find a way to success; neither the woman nor the halfbreed had sufficient knowledge or inclination to attempt anything more than escape. Whatever they might do, the old man knew his own role in the world game ended tonight. He could see his personal pattern before him. All its paths were short or dark ones.

Feeling profligate with power, he made the Gordian guards sleep at their post by the tent flap and stepped in, still wearing invisibility. Merry and Catseye both looked up from their blankets. Merry's look was curious; Catseye's, wary.

He extended his protection to include them. Merry, eyes wide as he suddenly saw his visitor, whispered, "Serenity!"

Catseye said, "Who?"

Merry answered, "My mentor."

Catseye smiled. "I didn't know fools needed tutors."

The old man smiled disparagingly and said, "Your scorn may be deserved, Catseye Yellow, but I hope my help will not be rejected."

"Help never is."

"Good." The old man gestured, and their chains fell away. Merry's mouth gaped wide. The Elder held out Catseye's sword and belt. "You may have use for this."

"Ah! My thanks." Catseye strapped it onto his back.

Merry squinted in puzzlement. "I thought you dared not interfere."

"So did I." Serenity handed him his pouch. "The situation's grown worse."

One corner of Catseye's lip curled into a thin smile. "That seems to be the way of situations."

Merry said, "But then the Empress's agents—"

The blind man nodded. "They'll come."

"What'll we do?"

"You needn't fear them. I have a plan. You two must go on, as though I never had a part in this."

"Will you be all right, Serenity?"

"No," said the Elder. "But I haven't time to answer questions. You must go. Immediately."

"What—" Merry began.

The old man reached out, hugged Merry quickly, then pushed him away. "Go, now. My spell will hide you both until you're beyond the camp. Do nothing foolish."

Catseye said, "I wish I'd heard that advice before I agreed to help you." He slashed the side of the tent with his sword and pulled Merry after him. "My thanks, old man, for your aid."

Merry stumbled after Catseye, looking back frequently. Serenity smiled and raised his hand in blessing. He thought, *Ah, Merry. You've been dearer than a son to me. I pray your fate will be kinder than mine.*

Guire walked the midnight rounds and wondered if he should have accepted Quentian's offer of a few soldiers to serve as his escort. He doubted company would make him

feel safer. Two guards had been found the night before with
their skulls crushed, and during the journey, menacing messages—FREE THREE, OR ONE SLAYS AGAIN!—
awaited their discovery, scrawled broadly in the dirt of the
road. Who took such an interest in the Empress's prisoners?
Surely not a large band, or they would have attacked by
now. This thought offered him little comfort. Though annoyed with his weakness, Guire started at every sound in
the night, at every twig that snapped underfoot.

The last tour of the camp was usually his favorite duty.
It was the final one of the day, when no one watched him.
He could stroll at his leisure from sentry to sentry and chat
for a moment with each about things seen or heard during
their watch, which often led to digressions on soldiering,
gaming, or love. He could detour where his fancy bid him,
since his job was best done when he investigated everything
that attracted his notice. If the noise in the dark was a
raccoon in search of food scraps and he happened to have
a crust of bread in his belt, and he then lingered, listening
for Hrotish marauders or Tyrwilkan outlaws while the raccoon ate, well, that was duty, and no one could complain.

The storm lords seemed restless. A strong wind whipped
at the pines and birches about the camp. Guire wished for
a hood instead of his wide-brimmed hat: if he had to walk
alone because his pride would not permit bodyguards, he
should at least walk in sufficient comfort to tell shivers of
chill from those of fear. That thought amused him, and he
laughed aloud. To his relief, his voice did not falter. When
no giants with great, skull-crushing clubs appeared, he
laughed again.

"What's funny, Guire?"

He whirled, one hand dropping to the hilt of his saber
and the other sweeping his cloak free so he could draw.
Then he recognized the gruff voice, the large stature, the
simple questioning. "Thraas! You shouldn't sneak up on
people that way!"

"Oh." The hillman scratched his head. "How should
Thraas sneak up on people?"

"Thraas..." Guire suspected that it ought to be more
difficult to be patient with him. "You... Was that a joke?"

"Yes." Thraas grinned. "Funny?"

"It might've been funnier some other time."

"Oh. Thraas will tell it again later."

Guire sighed patiently. "That's very considerate of you."

"Thraas thinks consider . . . ation?"

Who could say army life was dull? Where else could he give language lessons to barbarians in the middle of a cold night? "Yes."

"Thraas thinks consideration very important. Else Thraas spend half time fighting rude people, half time cleaning Speak-softly."

"Speak-softly?"

Thraas nodded at his axe. "From saying of wise woman. 'Speak softly. Others carry big sticks.'"

"An interesting philosophy." Thraas amused him, and he was glad for any distraction. Guire's own thoughts ran to murderous rebels or, more painfully, the young woman they now conveyed to City Gordia.

"Thraas thinks so. Thraas is not sure of all it means, but Thraas thinks it interesting. Many philoso-phies interest Thraas. So many have feel of truth."

"True."

"Yet so many say such different things that all can't be true."

"Also true."

Thraas guffawed. "Guire makes joke! Guire is funny! When Thraas returns to village, Guire must come, too. All people near Fork In Stream will come hear his jests, feed him dirt-apples and flying lizard's liver, offer him fattest daughters to bed!"

"That, um, sounds like fun, Thraas. But I have respon-sibilities here."

"Oh. Sad. Thraas understands responsibility. Else he would be home now, eating dirt-apples and flying lizard's liver, maybe enjoying month's marriage with Tikli." Thraas held his hands far apart. "Tikli is fattest woman in village. Tikli is fatter than mammoth pregnant with twins. Tikli is fatter—"

"Thraas?"

"Yes, Guire?"

"Perhaps you'd tell me about her some other time?"

"Thraas understands. Here, where only woman near is skinny Gordian ... Thraas understands."

"Good." Guire smiled. How could Thraas dismiss one so ... so delightfully slim as "skinny"? He wished their captive was what she pretended to be, highborn and wealthy and eminently courtable.

"Responsibility," Thraas said, "is lord worse than Ralka, Wolf King."

Guire started to suggest that Thraas speak more respectfully of Gordia's patron, then decided he was not up to speaking on mythology and religion. "True."

They shared a moment of silent sympathy. Then Thraas said, "One thing Thraas does not understand about Guire and responsibility. If you do not do as you must, who will cut off your head?"

Before Guire could decide whether to speak of conscience or the laws of the Empire, he heard the shrill blast of a guard's horn at the post he had just left. "Follow!" he ordered immediately. Wanting to run away, he darted toward the alarm.

Thraas passed him in a few strides. Guire ran as quickly as he could through the trees, but Thraas was already bending over the still form of a Gordian soldier when Guire entered the tiny clearing.

"What is it?" he asked the sentry who stood near with a horn in one hand and a pike in the other.

"An attack, Lieutenant! A nightmare wraith—"

"Where?" Guire peered into the darkness about them.

"Fled now. It came from nowhere and struck Akar down. I grazed it with my pike—more from luck than skill. It reared above me, kicking at me with its hooves! I had nowhere to retreat, so I stayed, braced the butt of my pike in the dirt, and managed to raise the horn to my lips with my free hand. It fled, then."

"What was it?"

"A creature of the night lords, Lieutenant, I'm sure! It attacked as a cloud passed across the moon. Perhaps some Hrotish shaman sent it—"

Guire, impatient, said, "You mentioned hooves. What form did it take?"

"That of a horse, sir. A great black horse, larger than

any I've ever seen. Hooves of obsidian, and a white star on its brow."

"A white star?" Lizelle's horse was marked . . . No. This must be coincidence.

"Yes, sir. Just above its eyes."

"I . . . see." Guire looked at Thraas. "How is he? Dead?"

The hillman's braided beard swung as he shook his head. "No. Scrape on skull makes him sleep. He'll hurt for days when he wakes. Arm is out of joint. That, Thraas can fix. Man will live. May not wish to, at first."

A clamor from the woods warned that others approached from their camp. Guire unsheathed his saber, and the sentry with the horn called, "Halt! Who's there?"

Quentian's voice, pitched low in anger or excitement, came from beneath the trees. "Your captain!"

"Sir!"

Quentian entered the clearing with eight or nine men. "What is it?"

Guire said, "The . . . being that killed last night has returned. It's gone, now."

"How?"

The sentry said, "I fought with it, Captain. When I sounded the alarm, it raced away like a creature of wind. Perhaps the horn is its nemesis."

"Perhaps not," Thraas said.

"What do you mean?" asked Guire.

Thraas pointed to the blade of the soldier's pike. "Blood."

Quentian eyed the sentry. "A creature of wind, hmm?"

"I saw it!" the man said. "I swear! A demon horse—"

"A horse," Quentian said softly. "Thirty of the Empress's finest, besieged by a horse. I see."

Thraas said, "Horse was here, recently. See print? Unshod horse, very large."

"Unshod? Hrota, then," the captain decided. "A couple of savages playing with the soldiers for a tale to tell when they return to their tribe."

"I saw no men," the sentry repeated firmly. "Only the horse that struck Akar down—"

"When we reach City Gordia," Quentian said, "you may speak your fancies in every tavern. I won't hear them. Lieutenant?"

"Sir?"

"Post another man at every watchpost. The Hrota aren't fools, usually, but if these are youths on their naming quest who've eaten the moon god's mushrooms—"

A second horn sounded from the heart of their camp. Quentian glanced at two of his soldiers. "Stay here. The rest of you, follow me!" With a wave of his hand, he ran toward the Gordian tents.

Guire said to Thraas, "Remain...." But the barbarian was already gone, already ahead of Quentian. With a sigh, Guire dashed after the others.

The camp was in chaos. Someone cried, "Sorcery!" while another screamed, "They escape! Beware!" and a third, "Flee! They attack! They attack!" The supply tent burned, casting light, harsh, and hellish, on a scene of naked and half-dressed men who scurried in confusion. Guire saw no attackers, no escaping prisoners.

In the center of the madness, an old blind man in a black robe stood patiently, as if this were his natural place. No one seemed to see him, yet all who ran near circled around him. When Quentian had organized enough men to drag down the blazing tent, Thraas tugged on Guire's shoulder. "Who is priest?"

"Priest? What—" Guire saw the old man then and knew that he had seen him for some time without realizing it. He walked toward the priest, dimly aware that Thraas followed him. "Excuse me, blessed one," Guire said. "I'm sorry to disturb you, but I must ask what you do here."

"Ah," said the blind man. "Never apologize, young man. If you have will enough to know that what you do is wrong, you have will enough to do otherwise."

"Perhaps." Guire began to wonder why they spoke so calmly amidst chaos. "Yet I must know. It is my duty."

"And soon you shall," the blind man answered. "But first I would ask for a favor, if I might."

"You..." A tiny voice, far away, screamed, *No! This is not right!* Guire noted that the voice was his own, then forgot it. "...may ask."

"Would you lend me your knife? For the briefest moment? There's something I must shorten."

"My knife?"

Thraas, nodding, said, "Priest said knife."

"Oh. Of course." Guire unsheathed his dagger and handed it to the old man.

"Forgive me, child." The priest drew a circle of blessing in the air with his left hand. With his right, he dragged the knife blade across his throat.

As the old man crumpled to the ground, Guire understood what had happened. Understanding brought only terror, and, free of the priest's spell of compulsion, he stood like someone ensorcelled.

"Guire? Why has old man killed self? Is this customary in civilization? Thraas will return to village while he is young, if so."

"He . . ."

"Yes, Guire?"

"He has . . ."

Thraas gripped Guire's shoulder to comfort him. "Speak, Guire. Thraas would help."

The pain made it easier for Guire to act. He laughed. "Help? You'd help?"

"Yes, Guire."

"The priest has escaped his doom, Thraas. And I'll suffer in his place. The Empress is . . . not known for kindness."

"Thraas doesn't understand."

"I wish I didn't, either," Guire whispered.

A column of smoke, or something like smoke, materialized near the ashes of the supply tent. A number of soldiers gasped and stared, but Guire only nodded in resignation. The smoke settled into the shape of a robed and cowled human, and a thin and reedy voice spoke. "I am Thelog Ar, not precisely in the flesh. I come on the Empress's business. Deliver the magician to me."

"See?" Guire said. "So soon. . . ."

"That is doom?"

"Yes."

"The priest has escaped his doom, Thraas. And I'll suffer

Guire smiled thinly. "It's futile, Thraas. He's a servant of the night lords, or so it's said, bound to the Empress. . . ."

The soldiers had formed a wide ring about Thelog Ar. None dared to move away or step closer.

"What magician?" Quentian asked. For the first time, Guire heard fear affect his captain's voice.

"A major magic has been done," the wizard said. "I sensed it, and have come."

A guard broke through the ring of men, then gasped at the sight of Thelog Ar. Seeing Quentian, he cried, "Sir! The woman remains, but the priest and the halfbreed are gone!"

"Oh?" said the wizard's smoky form. "What priest? What halfbreed?"

"Prisoners of ours," Quentian said. "They can't have done any significant sorcery."

"Who, then, has, if not they?"

"You see?" Guire whispered to Thraas. "The priest has done what he wanted, and I've allowed him to escape."

"Say nothing, Guire. No one knows."

"I know. I must—"

Quentian turned to Guire. His eyebrows drew closer together as he noticed the huddled figure in black cloth at Thraas's feet. "Is that your magician?" he asked, pointing a gloved finger at the Elder's body.

"Perhaps," the wizard replied, looking toward Guire.

"There's no need for concern!" Thraas announced, stepping forward.

"Yes?" Quentian circled Thelog Ar to approach them.

"Yes. Magician is dead!"

"Thraas..." Guire warned.

"Obviously," Quentian replied. He kicked the blind man's body to turn it onto its back. "Your knife, Lieutenant?"

"Yes," Guire admitted.

"Yes!" said Thraas. "Guire slew magician. Guire has saved us all!"

Thelog Ar's cowl dipped as though he nodded. "It's true that the magic is gone," he said. A tendril of smoke crept out of his white sleeve to approach the dead priest. At its touch, the body collapsed upon itself. Only dust remained.

"You will find those who escaped," Thelog Ar suggested. "It would be wise." The smoke of his form rose upward in misty streamers, and he disappeared as he had come, suddenly, silently, and without warning.

"Guire . . ." said Quentian.

"Sir, the priest magicked—"

Quentian stopped his protest with a shake of his head. "You'll have to answer to the Empress. You needn't answer to me. Until City Gordia, you're my lieutenant, as always."

Guire nodded gratefully. "Thank you, sir. I—"

"Don't thank me. You and your burly attendant now have a quest. Find the escapees and bring them to Castle Cloud."

"Yes, sir." He began to turn away to pack, then said, "If, ah, it's not possible to capture them alive?"

"Thelog Ar will learn the location of what we seek when he interrogates the girl in person. The others mustn't be allowed to obtain it before he does. Do whatever is necessary, Lieutenant."

"I understand."

chapter eight

Early Morning Conversation

LIZELLE WOKE TO the clamor of chaos in the Gordian camp. Though her guard had, for the moment, abandoned her, she found no advantage in his absence. Four silk cords bound her wrists and ankles to stakes at each corner of the tent, leaving her sufficient slack to turn to one side or the other on her bed of rough blankets, but not enough to bring her hands or feet together to try to untie herself. A fifth cord around her neck kept her from lowering her head to gnaw at the knots.

A flare of light, visible as a sudden glow through one khaki canvas wall, surely meant that a tent had caught fire. Fearing hers would follow, she pulled frantically at the silk cords, but the light soon died. A helmeted, jacketless guard ran in, stared at her, and ran out before she could question him.

She calmed herself. *Darkwind? Darkwind?*

The reply was surprisingly strong. *This one has failed. Again.*

Don't fret, four-legs. I'm no worse off than before.

One would help—

One's tried. Something's happened here. An attack?

If so, one senses no attackers.

The tent flap was jerked open, admitting cooler air and bright light as Quentian stepped in with a lamp in one hand.

Until later, she told Darkwind. "Good sir—"

"I'm not highcaste, girl. No more than you."

"Captain—"

"What, no harsh words, no protests of innocence?"

"I'm resigned to proving myself in Gordia."

Quentian squatted beside her and reached toward her wrist. "You're comfortable?"

She resisted the impulse to twist away from his hand. "Not very."

"Our facilities are somewhat limited."

"No more than your faculties."

He smiled. Lizelle looked away, at the wall. Quentian hooked a finger in the silk about her wrist and examined the knot, then stood and walked around her. "Come, girl. What do you expect? Should I slap your face, sneer, and say, 'Ah, my pretty, it's good you have spirit—the more will I enjoy breaking you'? I'm sorry to disappoint you."

She lay still while he checked her bonds. The jewel was so cool on her chest that she believed the stick to which it was linked had snagged in an ice flow. When Quentian stood to leave, she said, "If I knew where Lord Noring's gift lay..."

"Yes?"

"Not that I know anything of where my kidnappers hid it, but..."

"You wonder if giving it up would win you your freedom."

"Captain—"

"It wouldn't. So no one needs to worry whether you lie, Thelog Ar will glean its location from your mind. The process, I've heard, isn't pleasant."

"If you're trying to scare me, you succeeded long ago."

"Not enough. You're a tough one, girl. I begin to respect you, even if your strengths are seeming and deceit."

"Captain—"

"Tell me where the stone is and I promise you won't be tortured. And if you're to be killed, it'll be quick. I'll try to get you a short imprisonment in one of the better cells. Perhaps in five or ten years, you'll be free."

"Captain! I'm not—"

"If you think I offer little, you don't know the Empress. She is... inventive."

"I'm innocent."

"You'd do well to heed me. Well?"

She shook her head.

Quentian nodded. "Sleep as best you can. We depart early."

What had she gained from her act? Better quarters than the others, just in case she proved to be highborn. And none of the soldiers were permitted to visit her for their amusement. That was all. The priest and his friends would never aid her now, if they ever had the opportunity to do so. She had gained one thing: time. If only an opportunity would arise. . . .

She heard Guire speak to Quentian as he left. The young Gordian entered a moment later with Quentian's lamp.

"Lieutenant Guire!" she cried. "What's happened?"

His eyes turned toward the ground. "I'm not permitted to say, La . . . Lizelle. Would that I could."

"Withholding knowledge is a tiny torture."

"It's not Quentian's way," Guire said quickly as he kneeled near her. "He does this out of kindness."

"Then I hope he never decides to be cruel."

"He doesn't hold with magicians and their torments, reducing people to quivering things simply to learn their secrets. . . ."

Lizelle let herself laugh harshly. "I don't, either."

"Give up the miststone, Lizelle. Please. My family has some influence with the throne. We might lesson your punishment."

"Quentian made a similar offer."

"Accept it! Together—"

"I've heard that the Empress cares little what her subjects want."

"She accepts some political considerations. She can't rule alone."

"Besides, I've nothing to fear. I'm—"

"Innocent," he said sadly. "So you say. You should quit that role."

"It's no role."

"Everything's a role with you. If only you realized how serious . . ." Guire set his hand on her wrist. "I haven't time for this. I leave immediately on a mission."

Did that mean someone had escaped? That would mean she would be guarded more closely, if true. "For long?"

"No. I hope not. I'll try to be in City Gordia when the Empress sees you."

"You're kind, Guire."

"No. I'm a fool."

His voice was so sad that she said, "Not—"

He smiled gently. "Oh, I don't mind. At least I've learned that I'm a fool. That's wisdom of a sort."

"Guire . . ." She thought, *I'm to die or worse, and I feel sorry for him because he feels sorry for himself. The things the mind is capable of.*

The lieutenant laughed. "How Thraas would love to hear me now!"

"Who?"

"The barbarian I baby-sit. He thrives on philosophizing, simplistic or otherwise."

"Oh."

"I bore you."

"Never." *Only sometimes. I like you enough to endure it.*

"And I must go."

"Who's escaped?"

"I can't say. Oops."

She did like him. She smiled and said, "I won't tell."

"I am a fool."

"I tricked you. I hope the priest got away, at least."

"Nice try."

"See? You're not that much a fool."

"Thanks. Why do you hope one of your 'kidnappers' escaped?"

Who was the fool? "They didn't treat me badly. Perhaps they had no opportunity to, but imprisonment's given me some sympathy for the criminal classes." Guire winced, and Lizelle changed the subject. "The soldiers haven't abused the one-eyed man?"

"No. His guards gamble with him. They'd have done better to have gamed with the Wolf Lord. I think the man now owns eighteen royals, three quarter-royals, a good fistful of coppers, one flawed diamond, a spell to end diarrhea, and a particularly unlucky guard's entire family."

Lizelle laughed. "That's good. And the priest?"

"He receives a certain amount of respect. The Questers have few enemies."

"And you won't tell me who's escaped?"

He shook his head. "No."

"Nor who remains?"

"Neither— Damn! I've got to leave before you trick the plans for the winter campaign from me."

"Fare well, Guire."

"And you." When the tent flap closed behind him, she called, *Darkwind? You hear?*

Captivity is bad for that one. Of course one isn't there.

Catseye and Merry escaped?

Yes. One has already scented their trail.

They must've lain with the gods of luck.

One wouldn't know. Can that one get free?

I keep trying. Can you reach Catseye or Merry?

They wouldn't help, even if they could.

The priest might. He seems to need me for something.

No matter. One's approach would only frighten them. After a moment, Lizelle heard, *Perhaps if one followed, one could write in the dirt for them when the sun rises.*

Try, she suggested.

One shall.

And she was alone again. She pulled on the silk cords because it was something she ought to do. The knots did not slip free, the stakes did not come loose, the weave of her bonds did not part. She closed her eyes to wait for sleep.

Merry was frightened, weary, and lost. The trees near him swayed under the tread of demon racers. The moon, flirting with the storm, showed his face infrequently. Minions of the night lords peeked from every shadow, from every place where something was darker than night. The godlings slept, for Mother Sun had set, or if they were awake, they crept out to do mischief. Of the Ten, the Cruel One reigned while the Nine rested. Only the Bat Friend of the Night People did kind deeds in the evening, and she rarely aided strangers.

Perhaps, Merry thought, one should never learn much of his world's lore.

He called, "Catseye! Catseye! One minute, I beg of you!"
When no one replied, he was certain the one-eyed man had
abandoned him. Then he heard, "Quiet, priest. If you're in
such a hurry to die, you need only ask." Catseye was leaning
casually against an oak with his arms crossed on his chest.

"We must return!" Merry whispered.

Catseye nodded. "I see why you joined your Order. You
wouldn't survive long in the world with such impulses."

"We must save the woman."

"Ah. I've nothing against altruism in the abstract, but
the Gordians will send out searchers before sunup. They
may hunt us already. I intend to be far from here by morning.
You may do as you please." He turned to go.

In desperation, Merry cried, "You no longer desire
Yrvann's Egg?"

Catseye stopped perfectly still.

"There's no other way to win it," Merry added.

Catseye turned and studied him. Uneasy, Merry looked
at the ground, repeating weakly, "No other way."

"Oh? I could torture you for its location. Did I ever tell
you of my stay among the Hrota? They have one particularly
clever trick—"

Merry swallowed and said, "Only the members of the
Inner Circle know where the Egg's kept."

Catseye nodded. "Sit," he ordered. "We rest for five
minutes. No more."

Beginning to wish he had remained in Quentian's care,
Merry sat. Catseye dropped to a cross-legged position across
from him and said, "Tell me what we're supposed to do.
And tell me no tales of seeking truths in legends."

Merry asked hopefully, "Then you'll help free Lizelle?"

"Then I may help free Lizelle."

"You won't believe me," he warned.

"I haven't believed you yet," Catseye said. "Still, I'll
listen."

"My Order has read the World Pattern recently."

Catseye shrugged. "That I can accept."

"The Pattern grows dark and convoluted."

Catseye laughed. "And that's obvious."

"The Pattern suggests that four alone might set things

right. You, I, the woman, and the barbarian you've seen with the twin-bladed axe."

"Everything made right?"

"Yes!"

Catseye tugged at his mustache. "With that, I have a bit of difficulty."

"We've read the Pattern many times."

"How do you wish to change it?"

"The Empress of Gordia—"

Catseye stood and adjusted the sword strap on his shoulder. "I appreciated your story, priest. If ever you hope to find me, look in Port Rakar. I'll be sure to be elsewhere."

"This can be done!"

"I suspect I needn't care what 'this' might be. Oppose all Gordia? I? You flatter me."

"With assistance—"

"A woman who betrayed us in hopes of saving herself."

"Which you might've done, if you'd thought it would help you!"

"And a hillman who fights for the enemy. And you. Perhaps you'd add in a beggar boy or a blind man, just to even the odds?"

"Patterns can be changed."

"Not easily, priest. That much I know."

"But you don't know what you'll lose!"

"I'll lose my life if I follow you."

"There's hope of success. Would I be along otherwise?"

"There's always hope where there are fools. But, since we've two here..." Catseye sat again. "Continue."

"The Empress of Gordia wants to control the world."

"Hardly the most original of goals."

"To do it, she'll destroy much."

"This should bother me?"

Merry, wanting to scream his frustration, breathed deeply. "We speak of the fate of millions, Brother Yellow."

"No, priest. We speak of my fate."

"You don't care about your fellows?"

"They show little concern for me."

"Life under the Empress—" Merry began.

"Would be much the same as life under any ruler,"

Catseye finished. "Those in power may change, but for those of us who have nothing, life will continue as usual. This argument doesn't help you. I'd change it, if I were you."

"To what?"

"To the truth."

"I haven't lied."

"No. But you've chosen your truths carefully."

"The truth wouldn't interest you."

"It might, priest. Tell the whole story, this time. From the beginning."

Merry hesitated, then, knowing it was his only hope, no matter how slim that hope might be, he said, "Very well. What do you know of creation?"

Catseye sighed. "You needn't take me literally."

"I'm serious."

"I've heard the Elf legends about a God who shaped everything, then divided Herself among Her creations so they might have souls. I know the priests of the Nine say—"

"The first story is the truth."

"Of course it is." Catseye's tone carried considerable skepticism. "How good to know."

"This is relevant. The God gave Herself so we might all exist."

"And I certainly appreciate it. So?"

"She didn't intend to die forever."

"Who does?"

"She planned to reform Herself at some future date, to evaluate Her success, and to decide the fate of Her creation and all those in it."

"The entire universe?"

"Exactly."

"I appreciate those who think big."

"She planned for all the lesser gods and all the lords of existence, from the Empress of Ants to the Wisest One herself, to meet one day. When all were present, She would be reborn from them."

Catseye nodded. "And if they didn't choose to meet in this phoenixlike consumption, as well they might?"

"The God left no choice. They're all compelled to come."

"Good for Her. What's this got to do with us?"

"The Lord of Cats is missing. If he or she can't be found, can't join—"

Catseye's voice was suddenly harsh. "Yes?"

"Then the God will never again be."

"So?" he said carefully. "Perhaps it's best to miss Her final judgment. I agree that the world might be improved, but I find enough in it to content me." Though his words were glib, his tone was sharp.

"Anyone who'd prevent Her rebirth would judge us more harshly than She ever would."

"I take it . . ."

"Yes?"

"I take it you'll help this God you never knew, no matter what the consequences."

"We," Merry corrected, "will help Her, no matter what the consequences."

"Don't speak for me, priest. I'd . . ." Catseye grimaced, then said softly, "I would ask what you intend to do about the absence of the Cat Lord."

"Find him, if possible. Free him, if necessary."

"I see," Catseye said. "I'll help you." He stood.

"What's that?" Merry stared up at him.

"I said I'll help you. Let's go."

"You needn't hear more?"

"Later." Catseye ducked into the woods. "I'll help you. That's enough, eh?"

Puzzled and relieved, Merry followed. As he scrambled through the woods, he wished he had the one-eyed man's night vision. They were far enough from the Elf King's Road to be in the old forest, where little undergrowth hindered them and deer or elk trails were plentiful in the few areas of dense brush. But the ground was uneven, and the boughs overhead blocked the little starlight that slipped past the roiling storm clouds. The second time Merry's robe snagged on a branch, Catseye said, "Perhaps you'd prefer to make carvings in the rock: 'Those you seek passed here'?"

"I can't help it, Brother Yellow. I'm not a woodsman."

"Perhaps you'd rather carry your clothes in your arms?"

"It's cold!"

"Then be more careful."

A few minutes later, Merry almost bumped into Catseye, who waited where the path went between two very close birches. "What is it?"

"Something comes," Catseye whispered.

"Gordians?"

"No. Not human."

He tried to speak calmly. "I know a few defenses against the supernatural."

"Truly, priest? You did nothing against the Thief in Shadow."

"That was dif—"

"No matter. This is nothing occult."

"What, then? And how can you be sure?"

Catseye said, "It smells like a horse, or a unicorn."

"Surely we've nothing to fear from—"

"How do we know what we should fear? I thought you were the cautious one."

"Well, yes, but—"

"It approaches. Move off the trail. Quietly."

They slipped behind a large thorny bush. Soon Merry heard the hoofbeats that had warned Catseye. He thought it strange that this beast picked its way with such care. Did it sense wolves nearby? Merry shuddered. If it did, a horse would run madly away, wouldn't it?

The animal stopped where they had left the path, and Merry saw that it was riderless. More, it looked familiar. Its brow was splashed with white. He thought it larger, and possibly more graceful, than most horses he had seen. Something about it reminded him of circuses. When the Inner Circle had shown him those who might set things right, all had been alone, except for . . . "It's Lizelle's!" he whispered.

Catseye clapped his hand over Merry's mouth. The horse looked in their direction, whinnied, and began nodding its head while striking at the earth with one foreleg.

Catseye released the little priest, saying, "You may plan what we do, but I say how we do it. And you obey."

Merry coughed. "Cer . . . certainly."

"Horse," Catseye said, stepping out into the path, "I know that you're alone."

The horse nodded.

Merry, following Catseye, said, "I'll dine with the mad god! She's trained it well."

"He's as intelligent as you are," said Catseye. "And he may be as intelligent as I. Aren't there any legends left in the east about the offspring of horse and unicorn?"

"What? None that I know of. An interesting—"

Catseye spoke again to the horse. "Do you come to aid us?"

The horse nodded.

"Do you have a plan?"

It shook its head.

"Do you expect us to free Lizelle?"

It nodded twice.

"And if we don't?"

It reared without warning and lashed at the air with its hooves.

"The question was hypothetical, of course," said Catseye. "But you understand that this may take a while."

The horse did nothing, then nodded slowly.

"Good." Catseye turned to Merry. "Tell our ally our plan."

"Our plan? I thought you were heading—"

"Away," said Catseye. "That, and nothing more."

"Oh. You refer to our immediate plans?"

"Certainly. I assume he's more interested in freeing Lizelle than in saving the world, the God, or the universe, or whatever it is you say we must do."

The horse looked at Catseye, then Merry.

Catseye said, "Don't blab that to everyone you meet."

It nodded.

"Nor should you," said Merry.

"As if anyone would take me more seriously than I take you."

"The Empress has ears everywhere."

"And might not this beast be one?"

Merry covered his mouth in horror. "But you acted as if . . ."

Catseye's teeth flashed in a grin in the starlight. "Relax. No beast like this one would let itself be coerced by any other's will."

The horse turned its head to one side in an attitude of some doubt.

"True?" said Catseye.

It nodded vigorously.

"So!" said Catseye to Merry. "Your plan, if you please."

Merry rubbed the stubble of his unshaven head. "I think it's time to learn a little more about all of this."

"What?" said Catseye. "I thought you knew—"

Merry smiled, pleased to surprise the halfbreed. "So did I. But I didn't know of 'the offspring of horse and unicorn,' or anything of the Empress's fondness for miststones. We assumed that each individual was shown to us for his abilities, but the Pattern's rarely so simple. Perhaps you're each important for something you carry."

"Like the miststone?"

"Yes. There's your unusual sword, and I doubt the barbarian's axe is the product of mountain folk."

"You may make too much of a Faerie tale notion," Catseye said. "None of the things you've mentioned are objects of power."

"Oh?" Merry glanced at him.

"You know that, too."

"The things needn't be magical to be important."

"True," Catseye said. "So how do we acquire some answers?"

"There's one who was born in Sargoniom times," Merry said. "She might know."

"We continue the quest for the Wisest One?"

"Eventually. The Pattern suggests that success hinges on finding her. But I speak of another, one who's more accessible. At some risk, you could ask her about Lizelle's stone and these other things as well."

Catseye nodded. "There are times when I wish I were born a farmer. Very well. Who is 'she'?"

"Her name is Smyorin."

The horse whinnied softly.

Catseye looked at the beast, and then at Merry. "I suspect

there's more to tell, if this one knows her."

"True," said Merry. "She's a dragon." He waited, knowing that if Catseye left him now, the quest to find the Wisest One and arrange for the God's salvation was doomed; knowing that if Catseye stayed, there was hope for their mission, however small and fragile that hope might be.

When Catseye finally spoke, he said, "Yes, there are times when I wish I'd been born a farmer. Is your dragon far away?"

"No," Merry said. "Quite close, actually. That's why I thought of her."

"Good. It's embarrassing enough to put myself in situations that promise danger. It's worse to travel far to do so."

chapter nine

Tangles in
the Pattern

SMYORIN SLEPT ON her hoard in a cavern above Korz Pass and dreamt of the things under her: idols of ruby and ivory and gold from Bakh, carved Liavanese caskets of teak and pearl, Northland cuirasses of tooled leather, scarves of moonthread woven by the forest folk, chests of leviathan bone holding spices from the Dawn Isles, heavy tomes from Sargoniom's libraries that were bound in the dyed skins of extinct animals, sleighs from Torion that flew on command, casks of Lyrandol's red wine (many now empty), Thessalabakhan lyres of merfolk hair and narwhal tusk, mechanical Tyrwilkan soldiers who smoked cigars and blew rings of yellow smoke (a particular favorite), tiny clocks of Staryan's Metal whose hours were marked in diamonds cut like mythical beasts, opaque glass jars of mirthweed from Port Rakar (many also empty), paintings and statues from the Elfland cities, and, most important of all, somewhere in the midst of several thousand years of gathering, a small brown egg.

Waking suddenly, Smyorin cried, "Who's there? Who's there, I say?" She peered about, seeing no one. Morning light fell through a small hole in the mossy roof to splash against a curtain of pink flowstone. The rest of the cavern was rich in shadow, but Smyorin knew the shape of every boulder and every abandoned bone.

"I'm thought a particularly large dragon," she said, catching a new scent near the mouth of the cave. "You had best answer. Else I'll expel a bit of flame into, say, that dark corner near the entrance to my home. After that—"

A human stepped out from the nook she had mentioned.

It wore a green cloak, far darker than her scales and not nearly as attractive, and a sharp thing in a teak case on its back. Its hair was the hue of fire, which displayed uncommonly good taste. She wondered why it bound an eye in a band of leather, but humans, she knew, did many unfathomable things.

"No need, good Smyorin," it said, bowing low to her. "I feared I had annoyed you by waking you, and that I would never intentionally do."

Pleased, Smyorin smiled, knowing the human would only see her long white teeth and be unable to read her mood. "Perhaps you've annoyed me, little human," she answered. "And perhaps not. Who are you, and why have you come here?"

"I am called Catseye Yellow," the human announced with evident pride.

"Ah, Kephias!" said Smyorin. "I've heard so much of you. And how is your master?"

"I am called Catseye Yellow," the human repeated coldly, "and I acknowledge no master."

"Well, of course not," Smyorin said. "Who would? I merely wondered about your . . ." She had never met anyone quite so irritable, but then, humans tended to be uneasy in her presence. "Your patron?"

"I wish I knew how you'd learned these things. I had thought them secret."

"That's hardly an answer, little Kephias. Still, your master—"

The human glared.

"Excuse me," Smyorin said. "Your patron and I are friends, in our way. He managed to send a message to me."

"You are . . . ?" the human asked.

"The First Among Dragons," Smyorin said. "Of course. Who else might I be?"

"I came—" Catseye began.

"To ask some question or other," Smyorin said. "That's why your kind always come. Well, some come to steal or to win fame by slaying me, but I tend to think them aberrations of your species, hardly intelligent creatures at all, and therefore perfectly suitable for eating. Don't you?"

"If I were you—"

"You would, of course. It goes without saying."

Catseye said, "It certainly went without saying."

Smyorin smiled again. "Do I interrupt?"

The human said cautiously, "Some might—"

"For I certainly wouldn't wish to do so. I care little for those who are rude."

"Ah. You're—"

"But then, I care less for those who point out that anyone is rude."

"—the soul of courtesy."

She rather liked this agent the Cat Lord had found. "You really think so?"

Catseye shrugged, raising both hands. "Of course."

"Of course! I should think you more than the average human."

He smiled. "I am."

"Of course," said Smyorin. "Didn't I say I should think it? If I should think it, it should certainly be so."

"I . . . yes," Catseye said.

"You seem confused. I've noticed that those who come to me often have difficulty thinking clearly. But if they didn't have that difficulty, why would they come? But then, if they thought clearly about not thinking clearly, they'd go elsewhere for their answers. I'm noted for a savage sense of whimsy considered most becoming in great beasts of my age. Are you confused?"

"Quite."

"And frightened?"

"Rarely—"

Smyorin snorted, expelling smoke and sparks. "Truly?"

"—do I admit it."

Smyorin laughed and gestured with a talon for the man to approach. "I haven't eaten a human in many years."

"You wouldn't appreciate my flavor," said Catseye, backing away. "I'm lean, older than I look, and half Elf."

Smyorin laughed. "Move your hand from your sword, little Kephias. That clever blade's useless against me. You should find or purchase a magical one."

He took another step backward. "My thanks for your advice."

"It's nothing. Now, relax. I've had my little joke. I rarely eat my guests. So long as you mind your manners, you're quite safe, if not for your own sake, then for the sake of my friend, your mas . . . er, patron."

"Your humor would be much to his liking."

Smyorin purred with gentle laughter. "In truth, it is! Cats and dragons may have been kindred once."

"Can we bring this to a point? I have little time."

Smyorin closed her eyes. "The haste of the short-lived."

"Some of us hurry because we would live longer."

She examined him for a long moment and thought again that her friend had chosen well. "You're right. I apologize. I forget that others have concerns of their own, perhaps as great as mine. What are yours?"

"I'm a pawn in another's game. I'd prefer to be a player, or to escape the game entirely."

"Will you consider dying?"

"No."

"A shame. It's the easiest solution."

Catseye glanced suspiciously at her. "Hardly. Then I'd only be a pawn lost through careless play."

"True. Tell me of the game."

"I don't understand it fully."

"Of course not. If you did, you'd be a player. Tell what you know."

"The Questers are on one side. The Empress of Gordia plays for the other."

"For?"

"Yes. I thought Gordia and the Questers were the gamers, until my patron asked me to involve myself. Now it seems that this is his game, or rather, that he's decided to make it his. So the other players must be his enemies. I'd like to know who they are."

"I have suspicions, little Kephias. You're better off not knowing."

"I didn't choose to involve myself in a game of gods."

"None who play are gods, I suspect. No more than I am, myself. But some of us would like to be."

"Hmm?"

"Of course, you don't understand."

He shrugged. "I've come to you for answers."

"I give those I choose."

"I thought—"

"That I must answer because you're here?" Smyorin laughed in loud bursts of amusement, quickly filling the cave with smoke. When she heard Catseye begin to cough, she tried to stop and soon succeeded. "How naive, Kephias! There are always prices to be paid. You should know that."

"Only too well."

"What can you offer me?"

"Would a fat male human, not young but not old, interest you?"

"Only if he offered himself, or were truly yours to give."

"Oh." The human seemed disappointed. "What, then, is important to you?"

In her many years as First Among Dragons, Smyorin had chosen from thousands of offers; most of the pieces of her bed were gifts for her knowledge. Never had she been asked what she wanted. "Many centuries ago," she finally said, "when I was young and far more powerful and far less wise, an Elf came and tricked my egg from me."

"You refer to Yrvann?"

"You know of this?" Her eyes opened wider than they had in several centuries.

"A little. I'm versed in odd bits of lore." His voice mingled modesty with pride. "Speak on."

"Dragons rarely have more than one offspring. I have conceived and brought forth another egg."

"You should be content, then."

"You," said Smyorin, "have never been a mother."

"One of my many failings," admitted Catseye.

"I treasure the first as much as the second, perhaps more. It was an egg to engender pride, large and blue with a stripe—"

"I've heard it described."

"Save your sarcasm, small one. Remember my appetite."

The human pulled its cloak about itself as though it were cold. "I only try to speed this."

"It moves quickly enough." Smyorin tapped the dry stone floor with her talon to remind him who directed the conversation. "I would like my egg returned."

"Even though it's probably—"

"My child lives in its shell, little Kephias. Dragonkind are hardy."

"And how will you aid me if I return your egg?"

She considered this, then said, "I'll answer all questions that I can, and give what help I dare."

"Only 'dare,' great Smyorin?"

"Only 'dare,' little Kephias. It's not due to our constitutions alone that we dragons live so long."

"Very well," said Catseye. "If I live, I'll deliver your egg to you."

"And if you don't live?"

"Ask the Questers. One of them keeps it in a place unknown to me."

She said, "Agreed. What do you wish to know?"

"My sword—"

"Step closer."

Cautiously, the human obeyed.

Smyorin's sight may have been failing, but her memory for jewels and treasure was not. The elongated hilt and the pommel like a basilisk's skull were clues enough for her. "It was carried by the last mistress of Sargoniom, before the city's collapse," said Smyorin. "It was forged centuries before by Triskaliom Myrdana, who seized a comet from the sky to fashion it. It has no magical properties, but it's almost indestructible and rarely needs sharpening. What more would you know?"

"Is it important in the present affair?"

"Probably not. Of course, it may play a minor part, but I couldn't imagine the Questers, your patron, or Gordia's Empress going to much trouble for any sword, no matter how durable or sharp."

"I see," said Catseye, twisting an end of his mustache. "There is a huge hillman who carries an axe, twin-bladed, with a steel shaft that bears snake designs."

"About the man I cannot say. The motif on the axe was used long ago by the folk of Torion. It does not seem magical?"

Catseye shook his head.

"Then it was probably obtained in trade or war, and kept

as an heirloom. I'm sure it has an interesting history, but I doubt it's important."

"I thought as much."

"Then why do you ask?"

"My patron has . . . suggested that I ally myself with the Questers. One of them waits outside. He has fantasies of fate being moved by objects of power."

Smyorin bared her teeth in a smile. "Fate is directed by individuals and luck. Each of the people you mention may be important for themselves, but surely not for their possessions."

"There is one other," Catseye said. "A woman who carries a miststone in a necklace of Elvish work."

"Then again, your Quester may be right."

The human stared at her. "What?"

"Is the stone shaped like a drop of rain, perhaps half the size of your pommel?"

He glanced at his sword and said softly, "Yes. It is."

"Then it may be the Necklace of the Wisest One. The Empress of Gordia would seek such a thing, if she was ambitious. And I hear that Glynaldis is *very* ambitious."

"So. Fate weaves his web about the necklace," said Catseye.

"No. Luck has dropped it into your hands. Fate will only say who has it last. You should do your best to influence him."

Catseye nodded. "I always try."

"What else would you like to know?"

"Why is the necklace important?"

"Whoever controls the Wisest One has access to the knowledge of all living things. It's a key to power, if used for those ends."

"What do the Questers want?"

"They usually act to serve the God when She returns. What do they say?"

"They say"— Catseye's lip curled in scorn —"that my patron's absence will prevent the God from reforming Herself, or some such nonsense."

"Truly? Interesting." Smyorin stretched her legs and raised herself on her hoard.

"This doesn't seem to disturb you."

"Of course not, little Kephias. Who would look forward to dissolution that another might live, that another might decide whether one would ever live again? Not I." Smyorin spoke slowly as she toyed with dangerous thoughts. "And you say that the Cat Lord's absence will ensure the God never returns?"

"So the Questers say." Catseye cocked his head to one side and said, "You believe in this God and Her return?"

Smyorin nodded. "Your master is in a most precarious position, Kephias. He doesn't want the God's return any more than I do, yet he needs his freedom."

"He's your friend," said Catseye, edging away.

"Don't try to leave!" said Smyorin, and Catseye stopped where he stood. "My friend, yes. But he would think as I do, if our positions were reversed."

"I thought you wanted your egg."

"I do." She extended her wings to stretch them and almost filled the cavern. Retracting them, she said, "But it'll be offered to me again, in a hundred years or a thousand, if your master isn't found."

Catseye's sword was in his left hand, and he shouted over one shoulder, "Merry! Aid me, damn you!"

Smyorin let her laughter rumble through the cavern. "How kind of you to call the other morsel, my little sinister swordsman."

"Merry!"

"And you," said Smyorin, "are the cat's only hope, and thus, the God's only hope. How very convenient." She spat a lash of flame at him as he dodged behind a thick limestone column. "Your reflexes are excellent," she said. "but your strategy's rather simplistic. If you haven't noticed, you're trapped there. Though you may cry 'Happiness, ecstasy, and delight!' it won't help you escape now."

"Think, Smyorin! When the God returns and learns of this, She'll judge you harshly."

"Ah, but if She doesn't return, She will not judge me at all." Smyorin spat another burst of fire. "Does it grow warmer back there?" She began to crawl forward off the heap of her treasure, intending to edge about the rock that hid her prey.

"Quite warm," Catseye admitted. "You needn't do this."

"Quite the contrary, Kephias. It's fun. I should do this more often."

"I fear I can't say the same."

"In a moment, that'll be literally true."

"Merry, damn you! Help me!"

Smyorin felt her ribs expand as she prepared to end this conversation. She coughed fire . . .

. . . which caught in her throat and burned its way back into her lungs, hurting her more than anything she had experienced since she'd first learned to use her flame. She gasped for cooler air and found she could not breathe. A trick of Catseye's? She looked for the human, hoping to impale him with her talons before she died.

Behind her, someone said hesitantly, "If you—"

She whirled. A small, round, bald man in a grey robe peeked into the mouth of her cave. She leaped toward him, but the obstruction in her throat doubled in size as he gestured frantically, much like swatting at insects. Smyorin sat down. If the fat annoyance did not free her throat in twenty seconds, she would learn whether the thing that blocked her air would keep her from eating.

"If you promise to be reasonable, I'll free you," the priest said.

Smyorin nodded.

"That's reasonable." The priest did something with one hand, and she inhaled deeply.

"Thank you," she said.

"You're welcome," he answered. "You do understand why I did that? Catseye's important to the Pattern."

"You do what you must." Smyorin eased closer to him.

"Don't try anything rash," said the priest. "Please. I can do what I did in an instant, if I have to. And I don't like hurting you."

"I won't harm you," said Smyorin. "Not if you're no threat to me."

Catseye stepped out from the rocks where he had crouched and sat cross-legged before them. He nodded to the priest and said, "You took your time in coming."

"I had to think of a very simple spell. I've said that great magics will only reveal us to the Empress's wizards."

Catseye dismissed that with a wave of one hand. "You risked nothing more than my life. I'll return the favor sometime. What do we do now?"

"I don't know. What did you learn?"

"That the necklace belonged to the Wisest One."

The little priest slapped his forehead. "I'm a fool."

"I could have told you that in Tyrwilka."

"But a miststone! If it'd been something unique, I might've suspected—"

Catseye said, "It's not your first mistake, priest. And I'm sure it won't be your last."

"Thanks," said Merry. "We must go to City Gordia."

"What of World's Peak? Do you forget it in your concern for Lizelle?"

"I've no concern for her!" Merry snapped. "Not now, at least. The miststone's the key, and if it falls into the Empress's hands..."

Smyorin nodded, piecing the puzzle together as the humans argued. "Perhaps I could aid you," she said.

Both stared at her. "Why?" said Merry.

"Don't trust her," said Catseye. "She doesn't want the God returned."

"That's true," said Smyorin. "But it's a preference, not a passion. I hadn't considered that there might be an option to Her rebirth, and perhaps I acted a tad impetuously. But if sides are forming now, I'll choose yours."

"Why?" asked Merry.

She lifted her wings in a shrug. "Because you'll kill me if I don't."

"We will?" said Merry.

"Yes," Catseye said quickly. "We will."

"So I'll help you, then," Smyorin said.

"Hardly for the most altruistic of motives," said Merry.

"They're motives I understand," said Catseye.

Merry looked at Smyorin. "We can't trust you."

"But you can always kill me," she reminded him. "In an instant, you've said."

"I wouldn't dare to sleep," said Merry.

"I've another reason," said Smyorin. "Kephias has offered to return my egg, if I help you."

"Oh?" Merry studied Catseye.

Catseye said, "I use what's available. We'll discuss this some other time."

"And I wish to amend my attempt to hinder you," Smyorin said, "so the God will look more favorably on me."

"If the God doesn't return," said Catseye, "you needn't worry what She thinks."

Smyorin said, "Do you ever confine yourself to one side of an argument, little Kephias?"

Catseye grinned without humor. "Not unless I must."

Merry cleared his throat. "Um, you understand our hesitation to accept your turnabout, good Smyorin? Would the God really think better of you for helping us when we had forced you?"

Smyorin stood, snapping her wings to either side. "You could kill me, human, but death is not defeat to a dragon. I could easily kill you both before I died." Noticing the priest's hand turn while a tiny obstruction formed in her throat, she cried, "Wait! Follow my reasoning!"

The priest opened his hand and the blockage disappeared. "Very well."

"By killing you, I win the contest between us, for your plans die with you. But my first purpose is not to oppose the God. It's merely to survive. So I'd win against you and lose against myself."

"You think the God will look kindly on you for this?" asked Catseye.

"Kindly? No. But She must understand. She is, after all, the God." Smyorin hesitated, then said, "Well? What do you say?"

Merry looked at Catseye, who nodded. "I say," said the priest, "welcome to our company."

Catseye shifted the sword strap on his shoulder. "For now."

Ralka spat into the fountain that burbled in the garden beside the tower of time, then said, "I'd like to know what happened in the dragon's cave!"

"As would I," Asphoriel said, lifting a goblet of yellow wine from a tray that his girl servant held.

"I thought you knew everything," Ralka sneered.

Asphoriel smiled pleasantly. "Thank you."

"Let's act, eh? I despise this endless watching and hoping."

"Patience, Wolf Lord. You're very young."

"I'm as old as this world!"

"And I am much older. Still, one would think you might have learned something during your years of existence."

"I have. To take when I can and to run when I must. What else is there?"

Asphoriel laughed, and the girl smiled. He said, "If you believed that, you'd never have called on me."

"I want to succeed. You don't have my constraints."

"I have constraints of my own, young one."

"But they aren't mine! And that's where the God has slipped. Together..."

"You think much of your brilliance."

"And of yours."

"Thank you. In my case, you may be right."

"Ha," Ralka said bitterly. "Ha. Ha."

Asphoriel said, "Tell me, are you also Lord of Hyenas?"

"Yes," Ralka said, with his brow wrinkled in curiosity.

The girl giggled, and Asphoriel laughed. He stroked her bare flank and told the Wolf Lord, "You have no sense of humor, youth."

"I don't need one." After moments that might have been hours, Ralka said, "I'll tell you what I wish."

Asphoriel nodded. "How very thoughtful of you."

"I wish we could tell them the truth. I wish we could simply go up to the woman and the fat Quester and the Elfling and tell them that the Questers' Inner Circle has lied to the world, that the story of the God's return, judgment, and then paradise for everyone is their lie to make sure that no one prevents Her rebirth and our universe's end."

"They would never believe us," Asphoriel said.

"No. So we must stop them."

"And we shall, young one. One way or another, we shall."

chapter ten

Of Dragons, Dire Wolves,
Duty, and Death

THE NOON SUN was bright and warm, though Thraas smelled something in the air that said the first snows of winter would fall soon. He removed his beaver hat to wipe his brow with the back of his hand, then settled back to enjoy his pony's steady pace as he and Guire rode a narrow trail that gradually climbed up the side of Korz Valley.

It was good to be away from the Gordians, even if it was only for a day or two. Thraas liked them all, and he liked asking them about their customs and their land, but none of them, except for Guire, seemed to have a sense of humor. Nor had he liked plodding along in the dust raised by so many marchers. Perhaps a soldier's life was not his destiny, Thraas thought hopefully. But then he remembered that leaving Quentian's troop would mean leaving Guire, his new friend, and Thraas was loathe to do that.

This part of the valley reminded him of his own hills to the north. Perhaps there were more pine and spruce trees here, and fewer oaks, but the vista was similar, complete to the snow-capped barrier of The Wall to the west.

He noticed a scuffing in a place where the path widened and gently drew Silky's reins to halt him. "What is it?" Guire asked, riding up beside him. "Time to rest?"

"Might as well." Thraas swung one leg over Silky's withers to dismount, more a matter of stepping off his shaggy white pony than of leaping down.

He studied the clearing. "Strange," he said after a moment. When Guire said nothing, Thraas repeated, "Strange!"

Guire, checking his chestnut gelding's hooves for stones, looked up in surprise. "What's that? Are they near?"

"Yes," Thraas said. "But something odd here."

Guire left his mount to graze by Thraas's pony. "What now?"

"Look. Here." Thraas pointed at a clump of brown grass that had been bitten close to the ground and, beside it, the print of an unshod horse.

Guire squinted. "Very, um, interesting. What's it mean?"

"Means horse joins priest and one-eyed man."

Guire glanced about. "They have help? If they're leading us into an ambush..."

"Thraas would know. This is not help. Not help like that, anyway. Horse is riderless. Has no shoes. And neither priest nor One-eye mount it." Thraas pointed at a few scuff marks where the others had left. "They walk with horse up hill."

"That is odd."

They peered in silence at the ground. Thraas wondered why Guire stared to one side of the tracks. "What do you see, Guire?"

The Gordian laughed. "Nothing, Thraas. I wish I had your eyes."

"But then Thraas would be blind," he pointed out.

"That's, um, a figure of speech."

"Oh. Would unicorn come to them?"

"What?" Guire looked back at the ground, staring slightly to the other side of the tracks. "A unicorn? Well, maybe."

Thraas looked closer. "But prints are too large for unicorn, large even for horse."

"True," said someone behind them. "Perhaps it's neither."

Both hillman and Gordian spun about. Thraas snatched his axe from its loop on the pack on Silky's back, ready to chop, parry, or throw, as Guire flourished his saber.

A man seemed to have stepped from behind a small cluster of pine bushes on the far side of the clearing. His hands were held before him to show he was weaponless, and he smiled in greeting with very white teeth. His skin was darker than most mountain folk's. Though his hair was as grey as his eyes, his face was handsome and smooth, unseamed by weather or age. His simple clothing, grey like his hair and his trimmed goatee, consisted of a Gordian kilt, low boots of dyed leather, a sleeveless tunic, and a short cape of wolf hide. In all, his appearance suggested great wealth, and Thraas thought it odd that he walked alone in the hills without provisions or company.

"Y-you are . . . ?" Guire asked.

"A friend," said the stranger, nodding.

"I . . . appreciate that," said Guire. He glanced beyond the grey man.

"Have no fear," the stranger said. "I come alone."

Thraas said, "You are bold to come with no weapon."

"There's little I need fear."

"You're very fortunate, then," said Guire, suspicion still in his voice.

"And you are fortunate that I'm your friend," the grey man said. "I come to tell you that those you seek are in a cavern near here."

Thraas wondered how the man knew this and why he told them, but Guire only said, "Good."

"With a dragon," the grey man added.

"Oh."

"Thraas has not slain a dragon," Thraas said. "Nor does Thraas wish to. Thraas might slay basilisks, but—"

"You've little choice," said the grey man, "if you wish to advance the Empress's goals. I fear the dragon may help our foes."

Talk of the Empress reminded Thraas of her sorcerer. "Are you Thelog Ar?" he asked.

"No." The other laughed. "Fortunately! I'm merely one who wishes your Empress well."

"Forgive me for asking," said Guire, "but how do we know that you speak the truth?"

"You don't."

"Thraas is not reassured," Thraas said.

The grey man looked at him. "But you have some small ability to know the truth, don't you?" He held out his hand. "Touch my palm and ask me your questions."

Guire looked to Thraas. "Your gift? Of sometimes knowing things?"

"Grey man knows more than Thraas."

"True," said the stranger. "But you can learn from me. Take my hand!"

Watching the man for the slightest suspicious movement, Thraas reached out with his empty left hand. The stranger's middle and index fingers were of equal length, and grey hair grew on his palm. When Thraas recognized the wolfish cast to the man's features, the telltale merger of the eyebrows above the nose, he wanted to leap away, cry, "Shapeshifter!" and behead him.

More quickly than Thraas could move, the stranger snatched his hand. The image of a wolf's head superimposed itself on the grey man's features. Remembering stories told by his village's wise woman, Thraas gasped, "Ralka!" and tried to twist free of the Wolf Lord's grip.

Beside him, Guire dropped one knee to the ground. "Lord!"

Thraas ordered himself to be calm. Though he did not like Ralka's smile, the Wolf Lord had done nothing more than grip his wrist. If Guire thought Ralka was not a danger to them, perhaps he was not. And, if he was, perhaps Thraas would yet learn whether the Wolf Lord was faster than his grandmother's axe.

Ralka kept his hold on Thraas's hand as he told Guire, "Up. Had I wanted obeisance, I'd have identified myself earlier. You believe me now when I say that my goodwill lies with Gordia?"

"Of course!" Guire said. "Our patron—"

"Your companion still mistrusts me."

Thraas said cautiously, "Thraas thinks question is not of trust, Wolf Lord. Thraas has heard that Ralka's interests are always his own."

"Of course!" Ralka laughed. "As is true of everyone."

Thraas shook his head. "It is not true of Thraas. It is not true of Guire."

"You're both young, in different ways. I am as old as this world."

Guire said, "W-what can we do for you?"

"No. What can *I* do for you?"

"I . . . I don't know."

Ralka laughed again. "Then I'll tell you! I'll help you in your quest."

"Thank you, Lord," said Guire, bowing slightly.

"Don't thank me yet. My aid means danger, son of my favored country. It requires total trust—trust that can only be achieved, I suspect, if your companion also believes me!" Ralka yanked Thraas to him, embracing him as though they were lovers, and peered into his eyes. "You have power, hidden deep, power to know truth when it's spoken. The power wakes within you as I speak. Feel it!"

Thraas felt like someone struggling to reach the surface of a lake into which he had dived too deeply. "Something . . ."

"Yes?"

"Something . . . changes." Thraas stepped back, gesturing broadly with his hands. "Living things . . . all around here, throughout woods."

"Of course," Ralka said. "There's prey everywhere."

"But Thraas senses it now, Wolf Lord. And you . . . are not what you seem."

The Wolf Lord raised his shoulders in the imitation of a human shrug. "None of us are. You knew before that this wasn't my form."

"No. Thraas *thought* it before. Now Thraas knows."

"I don't particularly care how your power manifests itself, human. It is nothing, compared to mine. But do you trust it?"

Thraas could not conceive of doubting the ability within him. "Yes."

"Then keep hold of my hand. In contact, you can sense trust most accurately."

"True," Thraas said, and then he grinned, knowing it was.

"I come to help you defeat the Questers and their allies."

"True."

"I would further the Empress's plans, for they coincide with mine."

"True, too." Delighted with this gift of recognizing certainty, Thraas snickered and ignored the glance that Guire gave him.

Ralka continued to speak slowly, so Thraas could weigh each word. "Though it may seem dangerous, my plan will result in the dragon's death, and the thing that Guire must eat will not harm him."

"True," Thraas said.

"What . . . what thing, Lord?" Guire asked.

"This." Ralka tossed a small dark biscuit to Guire. Thraas could not tell if it had been plucked from a pocket or created as Ralka spoke.

Guire caught the biscuit in one hand. "What is it?"

"I've said that your deed will seem dangerous. This will make failure impossible."

"True," Thraas said.

"Oh! In that case . . ." Guire nibbled at it. "Tastes vile."

As Guire swallowed another bite, Ralka extended his hand. "Pass your blade to me."

"Certainly, Lord."

The Wolf Lord smeared Guire's steel with black paste that may have also come from the pocket on his grey tunic. "This is a very potent poison. Don't touch it."

Guire returned his saber gingerly to his sheath. "So I'm to stab the dragon? I admit that doesn't sound easy, but—"

"You must stab it in the roof of its mouth."

Guire stared for a long instant. "Godlings! What of its flame?"

Ralka smiled kindly. "The biscuit will ensure success, even if Smyorin tries to burn you."

"True," said Thraas.

"Oh." Guire crammed the last bit of Ralka's gift into his mouth and chewed. "Doesn't taste so bad after all."

Ralka laughed, a sound like barking. "Good."

"Thraas?" said Guire.

"Yes?"

"I have two nieces."

"No, Guire."

"That's right. I don't." Guire turned to the Wolf Lord. "Forgive me. I . . . I had to be sure."

"You must be sure," said Ralka. "You won't get close enough to succeed otherwise."

"True," said Thraas, still amused with his new ability.

"What now?" Guire asked.

"You must go. Immediately," said the Wolf Lord. He stepped away from Thraas, releasing his wrist. "Hillman, your duty is almost as important as the lieutenant's. While he slays the dragon, you must distract the priest, and the one-eyed man as well."

Thraas felt the truth in this, even though he no longer touched the grey man. He nodded in agreement.

"You won't help us more?" said Guire.

"I've helped you all that I may. Go!"

Guire bowed. "Yes, Lord."

The grey man strode into the brush without glancing back at them. At the point where the foliage closed behind him, he seemed to fade into mist.

"Thraas does not like these visitors who come so strangely."

Guire smiled as if to reassure him. "Thessis Ar and the Wolf Lord both came to help."

"Thraas would rather not need such help."

"Ah. You're just afraid of magic."

"Yes. Thraas is wise. Thank you."

Guire grinned. "You're welcome." He ran toward their horses, which had wandered back down the trail in search of better grazing. "Come on!" he called. "I have a dragon to slay and a future to forge!"

"Odd," Thraas said as he took his pony's reins. "When you said that, it was true. But was it true because it was true, or true because you believed it?"

Guire glanced at him and frowned. They mounted and rode on in silence.

After half an hour, the trail turned to climb sharply through an ancient landslide. They had to lead their horses, and at one point, Thraas would have left the mounts picketed by a bit of scrub if he hadn't seen Darkwind's tracks continuing upward, telling him that horses could make it. Beyond the landslide, the slope was less steep, so they rode on.

"Soon," Thraas said, noting horse dung no more than a few hours old.

"Good." Guire had turned up the collar of his blue cape and tucked his blond-bearded chin into it. Few trees stood this high above the valley to protect them from the wind. "Think they've gone up as far as the snow?"

"Thraas hopes not."

"Me, too. Thraas?"

"Yes, Guire?"

"Do you trust Ralka?"

"No. But Thraas believes him."

"He wouldn't lie to us," Guire said, and Thraas heard a trace of question in his voice. "For whatever reason, Ralka wants what we want."

"Wolf Lord cannot lie to us. This much Thraas knows."

"Good."

They almost rode into the cave before they realized they had come upon it. Thraas spotted it first. The mouth, a tall gash in the side of a sheer cliff, was partially shielded on either side by walls of fallen rock. Enough of the ground was clear before it, Thraas realized, for a large dragon to land. "There!" he whispered.

"Ah," Guire said. After a moment, he added, "Dare we enter?"

Thraas scratched at the braids of his beard. "Thraas thinks not," he decided. "Thraas may not recognize signs of dragon magic."

"We have to get close, if we're to surprise them."

"True. Crouch above and leap on those who exit?" To climb above the entrance would not be easy, and there was nowhere to stand. He did not like to think of clinging to the side of the wall, waiting for the dragon to leave.

"Perhaps. If—" Guire halted. A large night-black horse stepped out from behind the far rockfall. "That's Lizelle's mount!"

"Interesting," said Thraas, seeing its lineage in the star on its brow and the bits of shaggier fur below its underlip and at its fetlocks. "Woman must be wondrous horseman."

"Why do you say—"

The horse lifted its head to sniff at the air, then faced Thraas and Guire. "If horse spooks..." Thraas said. The horse stared, then reared and drummed at the rocks with its hooves.

"Damn!" Guire swept his sword free. "So much for surprise."

"Unusual horse," said Thraas.

"Come on, philosopher!"

They hurried their mounts up the remaining fifty yards of dirt and scree. Lizelle's horse darted around the rockslide to flee along the path. "If they noticed . . ." Guire said.

"They noticed," said Thraas. Something huge moved in the shadows of the cave.

"Thanks for telling me."

"You're welcome, Guire."

"If it weren't for Ralka, I'd be frightened," Guire whispered.

Thraas felt his friend's lie and clapped Guire's shoulder to comfort him. "Wolf Lord did not lie."

The Gordian's gelding shied as the dragon's head, larger than a poor man's hut, poked out of the dark cavern. Guire tossed his reins to Thraas, leaped nimbly to the ground, and ran on, holding his sword high. "For Gordia and my Empress!"

"For dinner," murmured Smyorin as she extended her claws. Her wings were folded tightly against her back.

Thraas struggled to control his pony. He patted its neck, saying, "Easy, Silky. Guire will kill dragon, as Wolf Lord promised. Then Thraas will ride to Gordia, and Silky will eat many oats."

The dragon had padded into the sunlight, and its scales sparkled. "At least this will be quick," she said. "Some fools take hours to gain courage enough to act."

Guire slipped on the loose rocks, and his sword clattered from his hand. He stood again with one knee bleeding, picked up the saber, and walked on. "I need no courage," he said in tones of prayer. "I have faith."

The one-eyed man came out behind the dragon, dusted off a boulder with a corner of his green cloak, and sat to watch. The little Quester followed in his bedraggled robe, crying to Guire, "Young sir! Don't throw your life away like this! Surely you realize—"

"I will win," Guire said through clenched teeth, with only a hint of doubt.

"Guire will win," said Thraas to his pony. He still felt, ever so slightly, the delight he had known with the birth of his power and knew that without it, he would be very frightened for his friend.

Catseye shielded his eye from the sun and called, "I'll only offer advice once, Gordian. It's far better to be a live coward then a dead hero."

"You can't dissuade me." Guire advanced with deliberation. "You know that without the dragon, you're our captives."

Catseye sighed. "Obviously."

"Surrender," said Guire, pausing perhaps thirty paces from the dragon, "and I promise to help you all when you face Gordian justice."

"A kind offer," said Catseye. "But how can we face something that doesn't exist?"

The priest called, "Don't be a fool, lad! How many have slain a dragon alone?"

"None yet," said Guire. He dashed forward with his sword held close to his chest, its point before him like a lance.

Smyorin waited until Guire was within reach, then swatted his saber from him. The blow knocked the Gordian to the ground, and his arm gushed blood from a claw's caress. If they had not been given the Wolf Lord's promise, Thraas would have believed the battle was already over.

"No!" Guire cried in agony or terror. He scrambled across the rocks for his poisoned weapon.

"Yes," Smyorin said, catching him in one taloned hand and lifting him to her mouth.

The priest screamed, "Smyorin! Please! Don't—"

Thraas kicked his heels into Silky's sides, charging with his axe ready, his mind filled with the thought that the Wolf Lord had said, and had spoken truly, yet—

Guire's shriek was muffled as Smyorin's jaws closed over him. His cries ended with the sounds of bones breaking and grinding. "I do like humans," Smyorin said then, turning to meet Thraas.

Guire! Thraas wheeled his pony before her claws could reach him. He had no time to escape if she decided to torch him, so he charged again. The Wolf Lord had said that the inner mouth was vulnerable. If he could reach Guire's sword and finish what his friend had begun . . .

Smyorin inhaled loudly, announcing her intention. Thraas

knew he moved too slowly. The pink flesh of the dragon's maw filled his sight, and a ripple of flame danced from the dragon's throat. Then she coughed. Her eyes snapped wide in surprise as she fell forward onto the dirt and rocks.

Thraas stared about the hillside for an explanation. The priest was vomiting helplessly, obviously not responsible. The one-eyed man lifted an eyebrow and asked, "What magic—"

"Not . . . magic," the dragon answered, trying to lift her head. "Dragonsbane. Yet I smelled none. The human . . ."

Thraas understood then. "Wolf Lord!" he screamed, and felt his throat hurting from the force of his cry. "You killed Thraas's friend, Wolf Lord!"

"The dragon?" Catseye wondered. The priest glared at him from where he stood by his puddle of vomit, and the one-eyed man said, "Sorry. Not the best time for a joke."

"To be sure," said Merry.

"Ralka?" gasped Smyorin. "He would do . . . something like this. Yes. How?"

Thraas said bitterly, "Wolf Lord gave Guire something to eat. Something that meant success, he said."

"He didn't lie," Catseye noted.

"No," Thraas agreed. "Wolf Lord did not lie."

"Your friend was a bit of a fool," Catseye said.

"He was Thraas's friend."

Merry stumbled to the dragon and touched her snout. "What can we do? Anything?"

"Not . . . to help. But . . ."

"Yes?"

"My egg . . ."

The priest glanced at Catseye, then again at Smyorin. "Yes?"

"I can help you," she coughed, "though I die. If I help, will you . . . will you see that my children are hatched? Both of them?"

Catseye looked away, out over the valley below them, but when he looked back at the priest, he nodded. Merry whispered, "Yes. We can do that."

"You need to reach City Gordia. Soon, you said."

Merry nodded again. "Yes."

"In my hoard, there are two sleighs from Torion. I would watch them fly, sometimes. . . ." Her concentration seemed to be crumbling, but her great, leatherlike lids flicked, and she said, "You control them—" She murmured several words of power.

"Thank you," Merry said softly.

"You'll find my egg in . . . in a jewel chest lined with yellow satin. The egg is . . . very small. Small and brown. Take it and the other. Build a fire about them. Keep it . . . keep it going for a month and a day, and they'll hatch. You'll do it?"

"I'll do it," said Merry.

"Th . . . thank you. Leave soon. The one who will be First after me may already be coming." Smyorin's eyes closed, and her clawed hand slackened.

"Is dragon dead?" Thraas asked.

"Yes," Merry said.

"Good."

The priest's eyes were wet with tears. "It was not her fault."

"She did not have to kill!" Thraas said.

"It was her nature," said Catseye gently. "Your friend did not have to attack."

"It was not Guire's nature! Wolf Lord tricked him."

Catseye grimaced suddenly, bringing his hand toward his covered eye. "If you would have revenge on this Wolf Lord . . ."

Thraas thought about the word, knowing that revenge was exactly what he wanted, but he said, "People of village at Fork In Stream do not believe in revenge."

"Ah." The one-eyed man began to turn away.

"But Wolf Lord's plans should be stopped," Thraas said.

Catseye smiled. "Come to Gordia, then."

The hillman stared at the dragon, but that hurt too much, so he glanced away. "Thraas has seen Tyrwilka," he said. "Thraas intended to see Gordia. Yes. Thraas will come to Gordia."

Merry said, "I'm glad Catseye convinced you to join us. The Pattern suggested you should, but—"

Thraas whirled and shouted, "Thraas will come if you

tell no more of *Pattern* and *shoulds*! Guire died because of *shoulds,* because of *duty*!" He stopped, hearing himself and suddenly sure that leaving his village had made him less than he was before. He said softly, "Thraas thinks Thraas will be philosopher no more."

Merry frowned. "What?"

Catseye pointed at his own head, then made a gesture as if throwing something away. Thraas did not understand it, so he ignored it, as did the priest, who said to him, "I apologize, friend. I'll try to avoid any subject that pains you."

Thraas nodded slowly. "Thank you."

"We should go," said Catseye. "I'll call the one who let Lizelle ride him." He strode away from the mouth of the cave.

"And I'll find the sleighs." Merry nodded to Thraas, then entered Smyorin's home.

Thraas sat upon a rock near Smyorin's corpse and studied her. Before he finally stood and followed the priest, he said, very softly, "Poor dragon. You were tricked. And poor Guire. You were Thraas's friend, Guire, but maybe . . ." Thraas looked away, at the woods below them, then back at the dragon's body. "Maybe you were not wise, Guire. You should not have trusted Thraas. Thraas is very, very sorry. Very, very sorry. Good-bye, Guire. Thraas hopes we will be friends again, somewhere, someday."

chapter eleven

The Streets
of City Gordia

THE WORST PARTS of the ride through the city were the startled recognitions by people Lizelle had known: a former landlord, a lover whose name she barely remembered, a woman who may have been at every party that she and Noring had attended, a merchant from whom she had bought apples for Darkwind. Each saw her and turned away quickly, before they could be linked in any way with a prisoner of the Empress. The taunts from strangers were expected and therefore easier to bear. She heard such envy in one old woman's cry of "Noring's slut!" that she could not contain a smile.

She wished the troop had not arrived at noon when all of City Gordia came out from the low red-tiled buildings to shop and gossip. The tiny streets were crowded with dark-haired people in bleached cotton kilts, robes, and ponchos. Many of the more religious Gordians wore headbands appropriate to their caste, brown for the lowborn, white for the high, and gold for the caste of merchants that had been decreed during the Empress's father's reign.

The troop's progress had almost ceased in the press of people. Lizelle sat quietly on a pack mule with her hands tied before her and watched for any sign of inattention from the soldiers or aid from the crowd. She saw none. The smell of roasting chestnuts drifted above all the scents of too many people in a small city. She saw the vendor, a legless girl in rags who sat before a brazier, and realized that she would trade places with that girl without a second thought, if some god offered her the opportunity then.

"Some think public humiliation is punishment enough for any crime," said Quentian, riding near her on his grey gelding.

"And you agree?"

The captain nodded. "When the humiliation is that of losing one's head."

Quentian had played a constant game of testing her fears as they rode from Korz Valley and across a corner of the northern plains. Guire had called Quentian's comments a kindness, said they were made so Lizelle would surrender and face simpler, more immediate punishment. She had begun to think she would rather face every torment the Empress's servants could give her than hear once more of them from the captain.

"Sir!" cried a soldier, running back through the troop. "A noble party comes our way! Shall we take another street to let them pass?"

"The Empress is impatient," Quentian replied. "Ask them to go back."

The column of soldiers turned onto Victory Street, which climbed to the sprawling marble structure that was Castle Cloud. For all that the avenue was wider than any other in City Gordia, it was also more crowded with wagons and carriages and people on foot, all of whom had to make their way about beggars and street merchants and wandering musicians. Lizelle could see, winding through the traffic toward them, the silk sunshade of a carried litter. Its colors were scarlet and jet, which suggested no castes or families to her. The porters were blond, bare-legged northlanders in very short blue woolen tunics.

"Thessis Ar wishes to speak with the prisoner!" someone shouted.

Lizelle remembered Daerko and the sailor's wooden finger bone. Witch-kin to Gordia's sorcerer was surely no friend to her.

A soldier at the head of Quentian's column was shoved aside by a small brown Islander in an indigo loincloth and jacket. The wiry little man wore on his back a long two-handed sword sheathed in red leather. "Make way!" he cried in a high, foreign voice. "Make way for Thessis Ar!"

Behind him came the litter. Its curtains were a heavy translucent gauze that bore the shadowy outlines of the woman inside it. "Captain Quentian?" she asked. Her voice said she had seen forty or fifty years. Her accent was patrician, almost a parody of the speech of the First Caste.

Quentian brought his chin down to his chest and up again. "Lady."

"This woman is the one called Lizelle?"

"Yes."

"I should like to speak with her, if I may."

"This is hardly—"

"What place could be better?" The woman sounded very pleased with herself. "The Empress knows that Thessis Ar would never betray her, and certainly not in the middle of the noonday market."

"The Empress wishes to see the prisoner soon," Quentian said.

"And she will," said Thessis Ar. "Our conversation won't take long. And I act now for Glynaldis, as I always do."

"Very well." Quentian turned to Lizelle and gave a tiny, guarded nod that told her nothing about what was expected of her. She dismounted from the pack mule and waited.

The Islander, shorter than Lizelle by several inches, drew back the curtain. Lizelle, peering within, said, "Thessis Ar?"

"Yes." The woman smiled. Her face was thin and faintly lined, with the beauty of one who aged slowly. Her hair was a color somewhere between iron and silver, but her eyes were a cold, pale green. She wore a jacket of albino sealskin over a dress of scarlet moonthread. She said modestly, "You've heard of me?"

Lizelle nodded politely. "Rumors only, Lady. No one knows much about you."

"That's as it should be." Thessis Ar waggled a finger to beckon her into the litter. "Don't stand on ceremony, girl. Get in before the sun steals what looks still remain to me."

"Yes, Lady." Lizelle climbed slowly in on her knees. The litter's floor was a padded black mattress on which several grey, white, and pale yellow pillows were scattered. The Islander, with the hint of a sneer, closed the curtain behind her. Lizelle remained kneeling before Thessis Ar. She wondered what this meeting might portend.

"Saji?" said the woman to her guard.

"Yes!" he cried, stiffening into a salute.

"Bid the porters to sing."

He nodded and moved away to speak to the northlanders in a guttural tongue.

Thessis Ar said, "He's an officious little fellow. But he's very, very good at what he does."

The litter bearers began a northern song pitched surprisingly high, yet pleasant to hear. While Quentian's soldiers looked on, mostly amused, the crowd of native Gordians who had clustered around them began to clap time and yell encouragement to the rich woman's servants.

"You won't tire me with your pretensions to nobility, I trust," said Thessis Ar. "You can't play that part much longer. And you need a friend. True?"

Lizelle bit her lower lip for an instant, weighing possibilities. Finding none, she whispered, "True."

Thessis Ar smiled in approval. "Good."

"Your servants are singing to foil any listeners?"

The woman nodded and handed her a pillow to sit on. "I've heard that there are those who watch mystically and deduce speech from the shape of one's lips, though I doubt their efficiency. Particularly if you don't enunciate."

Lizelle caught the hint and said, "Yes?"

Thessis Ar laughed. "How wonderfully you do that!"

"I began my circus career as an aide to the puppeteer. She claimed my mouth flapped so much that I'd blow the audience away."

"Ah." Thessis Ar twined a lock of her iron-grey hair about one finger. "I know something of puppeteers."

"I'd perform for you," LIzelle said, "if I could."

Thessis Ar's lips curled upward in a smile that disturbed Lizelle. "Never fear," the woman said. "One way or another, you shall."

What I dislike about people who make games out of life, Lizelle thought, *is that they make such long games out of life.* "Is there anything I might do for you?" she asked.

"You are blunt."

"Forgive me. I think of your Empress, who is eager to see me, I hear."

Thessis Ar laughed, covering her mouth with one hand and beating against the pillows at her side with the other. "Oh, I do like you. I thought I would. Noring speaks well of you, if somewhat bitterly."

"He's . . . ?" Lizelle tried to keep her concern from her voice.

"As he always is, but more so. Your leaving caused him to settle even deeper within himself."

"I'd hoped it'd do otherwise," Lizelle said.

"You'd hoped to escape with a small fortune."

"I . . . Yes. I did. But he wouldn't have let me leave him unless—"

Thessis Ar stopped her with a shake of her hand. "You're not on trial yet."

"I'm sorry. I . . . get excited, and—"

"No. You scheme, like me. That's part of what I like about you."

"But—"

"You took a miststone with the other jewelry."

Lizelle expected this. She said innocently, "Yes?"

"The Empress wants it."

"And wants to slay me when I give it up."

"What else can she do? Her justice must mean something. If every thief could avoid punishment by restoring what was stolen . . ."

Lizelle nodded. "I understand. Yet it's small incentive, you must admit."

The woman frowned, and her eyes became narrow slits. "You dicker like a gypsy."

Shrugging, Lizelle said, "Or a lord."

Thessis Ar laughed. "True." She looked out through the gauze at her bearers. "They sing well, don't you think?"

Lizelle wished the woman would keep to the most important subject, which was whether Lizelle had any reason to hope to live. Thessis Ar's perfume was an oppressive scent of roses, and though the gauze did little to retain heat within the litter, Lizelle had begun to sweat. She loosened a button of her dusty black jacket and answered casually,

"Yes. But their song seems rather long."

"It's an epic for northern winters. It takes hours to finish."

"You expect to be here so long?"

Thessis Ar shook her head. "Not nearly. I would like to have the miststone."

"Yes?"

"I could arrange for your freedom, if you gave it up."

Lizelle met the woman's gaze and said, "I would give it up, if I were free."

"Hah!" Thessis Ar's amusement seemed sincere, as did her frustration. "Impass?"

"Not insurmountable, I hope," said Lizelle, praying it was not. "You have the advantage on me, as you only lose a stone. But I don't dare give up anything until I'm sure of keeping my life."

Thessis Ar dismissed that with a flip of one red-gloved hand. "You'll surrender the stone when my brother questions you, you know."

"Perhaps," Lizelle said carefully. "But that hasn't happened yet. And I know how the mad god's followers will their own death. I'll do that, if I think there's no hope for my freedom."

"You are a contrary bitch," said Thessis Ar. "No wonder Noring loved you."

Whether he ever did was not a question to ask now. She said, "Free me, and you'll have the stone."

"No. I rather like you and greatly respect you, but I trust you not at all. Nor you, me."

"True."

"Could we negotiate an exchange on neutral ground?"

"I hope so," said Lizelle.

"Good," said Thessis Ar, nodding thoughtfully. "Leave me, then. We'll talk again, I promise you."

Lizelle bowed from the waist and climbed out of the litter. As the gauze fell shut, the Islander directed her toward Quentian with a sharp jerk of his narrow chin. For a moment, she thought herself out of reach of Saji's blade and considered darting into the crowd. She knew these streets well enough to lose most pursuers, she thought. But she also remembered the reputation of Dawn Isle fencers, so she remounted the patient army pack beast.

Thessis Ar's train turned and preceded them up Victory Street, squeezing soldiers and citizens against Gordia's cool, white-washed brick walls. "Onward!" cried Quentian then, and Lizelle and her company moved toward the distant, heavy castle that watched over City Gordia and the world.

In a room of low couches in the temple of time, Asphoriel said quietly, "You've botched things." The girl who sat by an open hearth, watching scenes in its flame that made no sense to her, became as still as a statue when she heard her master speak, then relaxed when she realized he did not speak to her. His words were like the events in the flames: if they did not affect her, they meant nothing.

"I've saved us!" the Wolf Lord cried, clenching a furry grey fist at Asphoriel. "You'd watch until—"

"Until we've won. Yes."

"Won? Perhaps," said Ralka. "But the dragon—"

"You did not need to intervene."

"You did nothing! With Smyorin's help, they might've—"

"The Pattern did not say that the dragon was important."

"Perhaps because I was destined to eliminate her, as I did. I assume the Gordian lieutenant wasn't important, either."

"True."

"Hah! I listen to you too much."

"Too little."

"Too much! I have an idea."

"I cannot tell you how eager I am to hear it."

"Let the Empress know where the miststone lies. In return, she kills the woman for us. I'll arrange for the deaths of the priest and the one-eyed man."

"How?"

"A pack of wolves."

"Very subtle."

"Or a thunderbolt to knock their flying sleighs from the air!"

"Which the weather lords will be sure to notice. Why not bid all the God's regents come to your home for a ball to celebrate your rebellion against their creator?"

"Very funny."

Asphoriel sighed. "Listen to me, Wolf Lord. I cannot *give* the miststone to anyone. We demons must be paid for all we do; it is our first constraint. Glynaldis has called on me once to know its price. When I told her, she refused it."

Ralka's face wrinkled in puzzlement. "You'd have our plans fail because of your pride?"

"It is not pride, Wolf Lord. It is discretion. I dare not do anything that falls outside my role of Demon Lord."

Ralka stared at the slim, naked man. "Then we can only watch and hope?"

"No. I've acted to aid our cause."

"How?"

"Watch the flames. Or the fountain, if you would be alone. You will see the results." After a moment Asphoriel said, almost kindly, "At least your interference was as circumspect as your nature would permit."

"Thank you."

"You are welcome."

"If only we knew who might help us!"

"Your God gave Her offspring a strong sense of duty. Wouldn't you have done the same in Her place?"

"Of course!" In a quieter voice, Ralka said, "Do you think less of me for rebelling against Her?"

"Self-preservation is in your nature, Wolf Lord. Your God should be proud, if She could know how well She had wrought."

"You speak sarcastically?"

"Not now. Cheer yourself, Ralka. You betray one who created you from a whim and asks your death to show your gratitude. What cause have you for shame?"

"None!"

"Quite so. Now I, however, betray an equal, one who was once closer than friend to me. Should I feel shame?"

Ralka squinted his suspicion. "Do you?"

"Of course not. She chose to create this universe, when She might have stayed in mine."

"You were lovers?"

"That word does not do justice to what we were, Wolf Lord. You may think of us that way, if you wish."

"But why—"

"This is not the whole of the truth, but this you may be able to understand. She loved power and glory . . . and maybe, beauty . . . more than She loved me. Hence, this universe, Her creation. I only follow Her principles in trying to acquire it for myself."

"Why not take it, then? If your power is equal to Hers—"

"It's not, here, even though She has spread Herself so thinly among all of you. That I can manifest myself in any form in Her realm is tribute to my strength and cunning, which you should appreciate." Asphoriel smiled the same smile he always employed, possibly the only one he knew. "And, since I'm being honest, my presence may only be possible because of Her absence. But Her weaving is elaborate, and I must know every thread before I dare to pluck at any. In this form, I could be easily destroyed." He looked at Ralka. "Easily as I think of things, not as you do."

"You're my ally, Asphoriel. I wouldn't turn on you."

"Thank you. Now do you understand why I demand that we do little, if we would win?"

"Yes. You are . . . cautious."

"A kinder word than 'cowardly,' Wolf Lord. I thank you again."

"Eh."

"I think it'll cheer you that we'll have something to do soon."

"Oh?"

"Yes. The end of the game draws near. I can feel it. Someone will reach World's Peak in another day, or maybe two. If my tweakings at the Pattern are successful, it will be the Empress, but whether it is she or Lizelle or some unknown other, you and I will then act, and win."

chapter twelve

A Game of Blades,
A Test of Truth

CASTLE CLOUD WAS a sprawling mass of pink-veined marble blocks that had been cut in the hills and hauled hundreds of miles, dragged across the northland plains and then floated on rafts down River Gordia. It may have been intended to appear to float on air, but its architect's knowledge was less than his vision. Its many soaring spires and gables and parapets were buttressed with heavy columns and wings until the whole resembled a leviathan frozen in its death throes. It sat atop Gordia's highest hill in a tangle of outlying buildings—barracks, temples, stables, kitchens, smithies, manors, and more—all forming a walled city of government that rose above and within City Gordia.

Two of Quentian's soldiers pulled Lizelle from the pack mule she rode and untied her silk bonds. "You free me?" she said hopefully. "At last you realize that I'm—"

"The Empress doesn't care to see anyone bound in her throne room," Quentian answered, dismounting from his grey and handing its reins to a corporal. While Lizelle rubbed her sore wrists, the captain selected four of his tallest pikemen to accompany them and sent the rest of the troop on to their barracks. The four stolid guards flanked their prisoner, then Quentian led them up the wide steps. Ornate palace doors of walnut inlaid with glistening brass wolf heads opened silently to a fat doorman's tug. He bowed to Quentian and said, "The Empress awaits."

"And we hasten," Quentian replied, marching into a wide, cool entryroom and removing his hat.

Lizelle felt some relief to be out of the crowded streets.

Here, at least, no one was likely to throw stones, epithets, or filth at her. She told herself she was glad that the confrontation with Glynaldis was near, glad that her fate would soon be known. If the goblins had stopped tying knots in her intestines, she might have believed herself.

As they strode through long halls lit by skylights or stained-glass windows, they passed servants in blue tunics and sandals who discreetly eyed the prisoner and nobles in white linen robes who stared openly. Lizelle expected every slender dark man to be Noring, which made her realize that she did not expect to die. If she did, how could she dread something so small as meeting a hurt lover? Lizelle's only comfort of the last few days was that the stick Merry had magicked must have found warmer waters, for the miststone no longer chilled her.

They soon passed through open portals to the Empress's throne room. Noring had taken Lizelle to a few parties, but he had never brought her to court. She expected a gaudy display of wealth in the decoration of the chamber and its occupants. Instead, both were so austere as to make the first seem almost unfinished and the second almost undressed.

The room was of moderate size, capable of holding no more than fifty people or so. The walls and the floor and the empty throne were carved of polished white marble; the ceiling was a vaulted mosaic in which a number of birds flew through a sunny, afternoon sky. Two long, simple benches, also of marble, flanked the Empress's seat. The room was crowded with chatting men and women in plain white gowns, robes, or tunics worn with unadorned jackets or shawls. Lizelle wondered whether wealth was still in fashion in Gordia, then saw that their clothing was mostly of silk and moonthread.

"Not what you expected?" The voice rose from the silence that followed their entrance.

Lizelle turned to see a young woman in a gown so little tailored as to seem a sheet belted at her narrow waist with a cord of golden links. Her auburn hair curled about her face as though no brush could ever tame it, and her eyes were as green as jade. Her skin seemed soft, yet very brown from the sun; her figure was lush, yet athletic. Lizelle's first thought was that this woman was more beautiful than anyone she had seen. Her second was the certainty that she stood before Gordia's Empress. Though she wondered how she knew, Lizelle curtsied immediately and said, "No, Majesty."

The woman smiled. Her lips were full and pliant. Her teeth were small, sharp, even, and whiter than the marble throne. She said, "My father's style was more showy. I follow it in parades and at most public functions, but I thought this room should symbolize my ideal of the world as ruled by Gordia, a world in which essence had surpassed appearance."

"A glorious ambition, Majesty," Lizelle said, noticing that everyone deferred to the Empress in such subtle ways of expression and posture that they might as well have pointed and shouted, "This woman rules us all!"

Glynaldis told Quentian, "Your men may leave us."

"Yes, Majesty." At his nod, the guards backed out, closing the oak doors behind them.

The Empress took Lizelle's elbow to lead her through the crowd. "How was your trip?"

Lizelle smiled slightly, growing hopeful though she knew she had no good reasons for hope, and said, "Hurried, Majesty."

Glynaldis laughed in pleasant, husky tenor notes. "I can imagine!"

Could she? What would royalty know of imprisonment and deprivation? Lizelle wanted to hate her, or resent her at least. She found she liked the woman's cordial manner. Still, she feared what might lie behind it. "The waterfall at Korz Pass is magnificent, Majesty."

"Truly. I saw it, long ago. I wish my duties allowed me to travel."

"Surely you could take a vacation."

Glynaldis smiled. "Ah, don't let me babble of the difficulties of ruling. I enjoy myself enough to pay any price for my privilege, and would therefore be the greatest of hypocrites."

"I would never—" Lizelle stopped as the last group of nobles stepped back. There, waiting patiently, stood Lord Noring in a chiton of moonthread and high basilisk-skin boots. He glanced at her, then flicked his gaze away. Lizelle bit her lower lip and thought, *As always, your face is a mask, Uyor. Have you ever cared for anyone?*

"Ah," said the Empress. "It warms my heart to see old friends meet again."

Bitch, Lizelle thought.

"So, Noring," Glynaldis began, "was this woman born to the First Caste?"

He lifted his chin and said, "No, Majesty."

Lizelle's trial had begun. The nobles around her understood as soon as she did. They moved quietly away, arraying themselves to face Glynaldis and the throne. Most of the elder men and women, wearing black embroidery on one sleeve that undoubtedly meant they were senators, sat along the two marble benches.

"Is she of the merchant caste, then?" Glynaldis asked.

"No, Majesty."

"To the best of your knowledge, she has no right to present herself as highborn."

Perhaps this troubled him, for his voice grew fainter. "Yes, Majesty."

"Speak louder, Noring, that all might hear."

"Yes, Majesty!"

"You know her well?"

Noring stared at Lizelle. She locked her gaze with his and prayed, *If ever you loved me—*

"Yes, Majesty," he said, looking away from Lizelle.

"What's her ancestry?"

"She was born to peasants who fished the lake district, or so I've been told."

"And her upbringing?"

"She was sold to a circus as a small child. She became its star attraction, a performer on horseback. A year ago, I . . . met her."

"I see. That seems to clarify the first charge. Did she steal a necklace from you?"

"Majesty!" Lizelle interrupted, knowing she must say something, no matter how feeble. "I wouldn't!"

"Did she?" Glynaldis repeated.

"Yes," Noring said.

"No!" Lizelle cried.

"Captain Quentian, please." The Empress spoke as though she asked for butter at dinner.

Quentian stepped forward with one hand on his saber hilt and bowed. "Yes, Majesty?"

"Did you see this woman with a miststone necklace of Elvish work?"

"Yes, Majesty."

"Did she explain how she happened to have it?"

"She said that she bought it, Majesty. From a jeweler."

"I see. Did she, Noring?"

Lizelle saw tension about his eyes, and she wondered if that was for her sake, or only because Noring had never liked being the focus of attention. He said coolly, "No."

"You speak the truth?"

Noring nodded. "Yes. Majesty. On my honor as one of the First Caste."

"And you, Captain Quentian?"

Quentian's nod was a tiny bob of his black beard. "I am of the farmer's caste, Majesty, but I still claim honor. Yes. I speak truly."

Glynaldis smiled. "That seems to settle the second charge. What say you, the accused?"

"It's . . . a mistake. Some horrible mistake, Majesty!" *Godlings, let Thessis Ar help me, somehow. I'll trust her with the necklace. I must.*

Glynaldis continued to smile. "That's hardly the most original of defenses, I daresay. Can you add anything to substantiate your claim?"

Frantically, Lizelle weighed possibilities. A magician had hypnotized both Noring and Quentian? No. She had a twin who had done these things? No. Someone formed a simulacrum of her that acted . . . No. Lizelle would have begged for mercy, if Glynaldis had ever been known to show any. "No, Majesty," she said.

The Empress looked at Quentian. "Where's the necklace now?"

"I don't know, Majesty."

"No?"

"No. The Tyrwilkans insisted on taking both girl and necklace—"

Her lids narrowed. "You let them?"

"They . . . they said this was a matter for our diplomats to settle, Majesty."

"It may be a matter for our armies to settle."

"I doubt they have it, Majesty."

"No?"

"No, Majesty. I believe that one of the woman's confederates has hidden it somewhere."

"Ah." Glynaldis's good humor returned. "And you know who these confederates are?"

"Yes, Majesty. A Quester and a one-eyed halfbreed."

"A Quester?"

"Possibly a renegade."

"We must ask the head of their local Order about this. Where are these confederates now?"

"They escaped us, Majesty. My lieutenant hunts them now."

"He has not found them?"

"Not that I know, Majesty."

"I see." Glynaldis touched her lip with a long fingernail as she thought.

Noring cleared his throat and said, "Thelog Ar will learn where—"

"If the girl doesn't know its present location, he can hardly learn it from her. I am . . . most displeased." Glynaldis glanced at Lizelle. "Will you surrender the necklace?"

It had never felt so heavy about her neck. "Majesty, I didn't—"

"If you give it up, I'll have Noring grant you a quick death here. That'd be doubly kind, wouldn't you think? Otherwise, you will beg me for a month before I let you die."

"But I don't know—"

Glynaldis silenced her with a wave of her hand. "Captain?"

"Yes, Majesty?"

"You have failed me."

Quentian put one knee to the floor and bowed his head. "Yes, Majesty. I shame myself, my parents, my country, and my caste."

"True. But I'll offer you a chance for redemption."

"Thank you, Majesty."

"Defeat my champion, and you'll live."

Lizelle thought of Noring's skill. Glynaldis would have been kinder to offer Quentian the opportunity to tread water for an hour in a pool of sharks.

Quentian nodded. "Here, Majesty?"

"Yes."

An older man, whose embroidered sleeve proclaimed him a senator, stood and said cautiously, "Majesty, is this appropriate?"

Glynaldis said, "How could it be more so? Let the game of life and death be enacted where it's decided."

The senator looked down both benches of robed elders for support. His fellows appeared reluctant and embarrassed, yet eager to watch what came of the Empress's whim. The man said, "Yes, uh, I suppose it, uh . . ."

"You may sit," said Glynaldis.

"I, uh, yes. Thank you." He sat, smiling gratefully.

Glynaldis said, "Well, Noring?"

"I don't have a sword with me."

"You have your dagger. That should serve."

"I . . . Yes, Majesty." He fingered the tiny hilt guard of the ornamental knife that hung from his belt. The knife's blade was no longer than his hand.

Quentian removed his cloak and money pouch and placed them with his hat on the floor near the wall. "Lord?" he asked Noring.

"Yes?"

"Would you see that my wife gets these? She lives above a potter's on The Lane of Yellow Flowers."

"Of course," Noring said softly.

"Thank you." Quentian drew his saber and saluted the Empress, then Noring, then all in the room. Noring, with a trace of embarrassment, did the same with his knife.

Noring, in soft boots and moonthread tunic and armed with a tiny dagger, seemed a sacrificial offering to the gods of war, and Quentian, with his heavy saber and martial clothing, seemed the god who would take Noring, yet Quentian circled, unwilling to attack. After several long moments, Glynaldis called, "Noring! You must engage him!"

Noring said, "As you wish," and skipped forward. Quentian feinted at his shoulder before committing his blade to a stomach slash. Noring ducked, caught the saber with his dagger, and lifted it aside. Quentian tried to back away, but Noring grabbed Quentian's boot in his free hand, and the captain fell. The pressure of Noring's blade sent Quentian's sword spinning into the midst of a group of onlookers. For an instant, Lizelle considered snatching it up, then decided that suicide, however brave, did not suit her.

"You shouldn't have been so quick," the Empress told Noring. Then, to Quentian, she asked, "Well, Captain. Are you ready to die?"

Quentian bowed low. "Yes, Majesty. As ever."

Lizelle saw that his fists were clenched at his side, but she heard neither rage nor fear in his voice. She supposed he thought this an ignoble end and his life a failure. By her definitions, he was right, but only because he would not die in bed of old age.

"Good," said Glynaldis. "You'll live."

Quentian stared at her, his knuckles turning whiter, then said coldly, "Thank you, Majesty."

"Leave us, Captain."

Quentian bowed, retrieved his bundle of possessions, and backed away. Lizelle thought Glynaldis had made a mistake if she expected Quentian to be grateful for his life. She saw that he hated her for not allowing him to die well. Then, noting Glynaldis's pleased smile, Lizelle understood that though Quentian might hate his Empress, he would spend the rest of his life trying to prove his worth to her.

Glynaldis said, "Well, girl? Will you give up the necklace now?"

Lizelle nodded.

Glynaldis laughed. "Excellent! Where is it?"

"It's hidden in Tyrwilka," Lizelle said. "A magician, for good payment, fashioned a pocket in the fabric of time, keyed to a specific location, a recurring hour, my presence, and my voice. The necklace lies in that pocket. I will fetch it for you."

Glynaldis laughed. "And we have only your word that this is so?"

"I'm afraid so, Majesty."

"There's a way to test this, you know."

"You'd have Thelog Ar peel my mind?"

Glynaldis laughed again.

"The key demands my sanity," Lizelle added, striving to make this sound as though it were no afterthought. "Or the pocket will never give up its contents."

"That wasn't the test I thought of." Glynaldis nodded to a young noblewoman. "Fetch my mage. He rests in the next room."

Lizelle told herself to be calm while she waited. Her shirt was damp with perspiration, and she wondered if she had sweated so much that everyone smelled her fear.

The noble returned, and a moment later Thelog Ar shuffled into the throne room. He was covered from head to foot in a coarse white robe. Its cowl hid his head; its folds, his form, which seemed to be that of a wizened and slightly hunchbacked man. Only the tips of his fingers showed beneath the robe's baggy sleeves. They were sheathed in ill-fitting gloves that only told her how very thin his hands must be. "You have a task for me, my Empress?" he whispered, and his words filled the room.

Lizelle stepped back, very afraid and unsure why. The sorcerer's voice was gentle, but somehow inhuman. All in the court, excepting Glynaldis, appeared similarly cowed by the muffled little man, for they moved discreetly away from him.

"Yes," Glynaldis said. "Do you carry the trifle you found?"

"The token I forged for . . . my sister? Yes." He reached into a pocket and brought out the wooden finger bone to which Merry had linked the miststone necklace.

Glynaldis watched Lizelle's reaction. "You recognize it?"

"A finger bone?" Lizelle asked. "Is it a charm for luck, Majesty?"

"No, not a charm. And it's only carved to resemble a finger."

"Oh."

"A spell of transference has been done, you see. Anyone seeking Noring's missing necklace by magic would only find this bone. Which, in fact, has happened."

"That seems clever of the thieves, Majesty."

Glynaldis's eyes showed annoyance, yet she smiled. "Yes, but there's an aspect of this that they've overlooked."

"Yes?" Lizelle asked, afraid to hear the answer.

"Yes," Glynaldis said. "They didn't consider what we might do with the finger bone if we found it."

"Ah." Lizelle nodded. "You'll destroy it?"

"In order to search for the necklace directly? No. Even if the finger bone was burned and its ashes scattered, the spell would still link the necklace to the ashes. But we have another option." She turned to Thelog Ar. "Begin."

The sorcerer spoke a word or two of the First Language. The miststone began to grow warmer between Lizelle's breasts.

The Empress said, "What the bone undergoes, the stone experiences. Thelog Ar heats it, not enough to burn it but enough that soon, if the stone is hidden in cloth, that cloth will begin to smolder. If it lies against flesh, well . . ."

Thelog Ar's glove glowed with red light, and the court gasped its awe. Lizelle kept her face impassive. "This won't damage the necklace?"

Glynaldis laughed. "No. Though I appreciate your concern. Of course, this little show of my magician's power is quite unnecessary, since the miststone lies in a mystic pocket somewhere."

"Quite," Lizelle agreed. She had watched people play endurance games with fire. She had never expected to participate.

In Thelog Ar's hand, the finger bone began to smoke.

chapter thirteen

A Second
Game of Blades

A SMALL GIRL in a blue tunic ran into the throne room, crying, "Majesty! Majesty! An envoy arrives from the Elflands!"

The Empress glanced at her. "Now?"

Taking advantage of that instant while all eyes shifted to the messenger, Lizelle leaned slightly forward so the miststone would dangle between her skin and her baggy shirt. The stone's heat still hurt, but she could bear it. Then she saw that Noring watched her with an expression that no one else might have interpreted. It was a look of sudden understanding, and Lizelle knew that if he spoke, she would lose whatever advantage she might have won from the messenger's interruption.

The girl bowed awkwardly to Glynaldis. "Yes, Majesty! His sleighs sit before the palace."

"Sleighs?" Her tone shifted from annoyance to amused interest.

"Yes, Majesty!" the girl cried. "They fly, faster than birds! Two of them, one carrying the Elf and a merchant who accompanies him, the other bearing a bodyguard and a horse."

"A horse."

"Yes, Majesty. It's magnificent!"

"I'm sure it must be, to ride in a sleigh, rather than before." Glynaldis turned to Thelog Ar. "Enough of that. It's obvious the girl doesn't have it."

"Yes, my Empress." The token in his hand lost its glow.

The necklace about Lizelle's neck began to cool. The

steady pain of the burned flesh between her breasts remained. She wished she could stamp around the room, cursing and throwing things, or simply cry a little, but even a wince might give her secret away. Noring had said nothing of what he saw. Did that mean that her fear had made her think he recognized what she had done, or was he merely waiting for reasons of his own?

"Perhaps the necklace is where you say," the Empress said to her, "and perhaps not. No matter. We'll learn more, later." She looked to the messenger. "Tell the Elf that though he arrives unannounced, we shall assume his cause is urgent and see him now."

The girl bowed, calling, "Yes, Majesty," as she ran from the room.

Glynaldis asked Thelog Ar, "What do you know of this Elf?"

"Nothing, my Empress."

"Truly?"

"Yes."

"Tsk, tsk. Your skills fail you."

"The sleighs were undoubtedly imbued with magics of concealment. Knowing of them now, I might be able to learn something."

"Much good that would do me."

"One never knows, my Empress."

"True, mage. You do serve me well."

"Of course."

"Return to your tower, but come quickly, if I call. And learn what you can, while you can."

"As you wish." Thelog Ar's cowled head dipped low in respect, and then, in the traditional puff of white smoke, he disappeared. Lizelle, after a moment of awe, noted that the smoke smelled of lilacs.

The burn on her chest was a dull but constant pain. She knew she should treat it soon, but when she realized how many things might kill her before any infection could, she suppressed a shudder.

"Majesty!" cried the messenger as she returned. "I announce Lord Kephias of Castle Thramering, Master of the Iron Woods and personal envoy of Ih..." Her brow furrowed. "Of Islvann, High Lord of Faerie!"

"Well done," said Glynaldis.

The girl blushed and backed away. Behind her, resplend-
ent in a blouse of sea-green moonthread, black tights, and
boots of ermine, with a cloak of burgundy wool and a richly
jeweled scabbard holding his odd sword on his back, Catseye entered. Flourishing his cape with one hand, he bowed
low to Glynaldis. His hair was dyed Elf black and hung
loose about his shoulders, his mustache had been shaved,
and his skin was so much paler that, for an instant, Lizelle
thought Catseye must have an Elvish twin, a thought rein-
forced by the new, extended points to his ears. But she
doubted a twin would have cause to cover an eye with a
patch of fine gold mesh. The ears must be the result of a
subtle spell. If so, she prayed none of the Empress's magicians would discover it.

Somewhere in the middle of wondering what trove Catseye had looted for his attire, Lizelle thought, *Nice legs, in
addition to his other charms. I think I'd sell Darkwind for
a night with that man.*

Immediately, she heard, *One's comforted to know that
one has been missed.*

Darkwind!

*Of course. Could any other react so calmly to so vile an
act as that one proposes? Never. Any other would close
away all consideration of ever aiding one so ungrateful—*

I was joking.

—unkind—

And I'm sorry.

—incompetent—

Watch it, fumble-foot.

—impetuous—

Oops. Sorry, O quick and wise and ever-capable one.

—and yet, one grants, ever so slightly endearing.

Thanks. Where are you?

*In the Empress's stables. Here, one is treated with the
respect that is one's rightful—*

*I'll buy you a godlings-be-damned stall of gold and dia-
monds, if you'll be quiet and help me out of here!*

Certainly. Does one prefer the quiet or the help?

Lizelle imagined a sigh. *The help.*

One does what one can. For now, all hope rides with the Elfling.

Oh, joy.

Catseye rose from his bow, and Glynaldis nodded to him. "Lord Kephias."

He smiled. "Lady Glynaldis."

The Empress frowned.

"I may address you in Elvish fashion?" Catseye asked, lilting each word with a flawless Faerie accent. " 'Majesty' is a tribute to power only, and cannot acknowledge such beauty, grace, or wisdom as are also yours."

Glynaldis pursed her lips in a failed attempt to conceal flattered amusement. "We permit this, out of respect for Faerie. And for the glib tongue of its ambassador."

"Thank you, Lady."

They would appreciate each other, Lizelle thought. *I wonder if Noring thinks Catseye a rival?*

"You come in unusual company," Glynaldis said.

"Alas, my entourage was attacked by Hrotish savages soon after we left the Iron Woods. I, alone, survived."

"You were most fortunate."

"Yes. A merchant and his attendants passed overhead in flying sleighs and chose to aid me. Many died in the battle, but when we had won, I asked him and the most valiant of his company to escort me here." Catseye turned toward the doors and snapped his fingers.

Merry, wearing a yellow silk cloak and a robe of blue and grey, was almost unrecognizable with sorcerously grown red hair and beard. He stepped in, followed by a tall, clean-shaven hillman wearing a red tunic, purple breeks, and silver-furred boots. Each of them bore a pile of costly cloths, gilt boxes, and sealed bottles of obvious age.

Catseye said, "My saviors, Merriar of Tyrwilka and his aide."

Lizelle stared. *The aide is . . . the barbarian who helped capture us? Yes! Then, where's Guire?*

Darkwind answered, *The barbarian is whom you think. He calls himself Thraas Thunder's son, or Lightning's lad, or some such. Guire died in the mountains.*

No!

Does this one lie?

No. I . . . I wish it hadn't happened. He was kind.

Glynaldis nodded to Merry and Thraas, whose bows were made awkward by the burden of their gifts. "You've done a great service for all of humankind," she said.

Merry replied, "We would certainly hope to do so, Majesty, in whatever small way we might."

Lizelle winced. *This isn't a place to indulge in innuendo.*

Darkwind said, *Some prefer to lie as little as possible.*

Yes. Some also prefer to survive.

Catseye quickly said, "We bring a few small and unworthy gifts, that are as nothing when next to your glory, Lady."

Glynaldis nodded and motioned for two pages to take the presents. "The gifts of Faerie are ever treasured by the peoples of Gordia."

Too true, thought Lizelle. *As witnessed by, what, four invasions of the Elflands?*

Glynaldis told a third page, "Have Colonel Ianin show the merchant and his man to suitable quarters."

Merry bowed low. "Thank you, Majesty." Thraas imitated Merry's bow, and both followed the page.

"So!" said Glynaldis. "I must assume that you did not come to make clever compliments and part with your riches."

"True, Lady," Catseye said. "Shall we speak of important things?"

"Yes."

"As you wish." Catseye turned slightly, to address all who listened in the throne room. "Word has come to Faerie that an ancient heirloom has been found and lost, and possibly found again."

"Yes?" asked Glynaldis.

"Yes. I speak of the Necklace of the Wisest One."

The Necklace of . . . Lizelle contemplated the burn on her chest. *Now I have a name for this thing, but I still don't know what it is.*

"I understand that you've captured its thief, and I assume that she is this woman"—Catseye nodded at Lizelle—"who is dressed too inappropriately to belong to your court."

"You've much knowledge of what happens in the lands of men."

"As we must," Catseye noted.

"That's understandable. And if your guesses are true?"

"Then we would have our necklace returned."

"Your necklace?"

"The Wisest One has always been Elvish."

In Tyrwilka, Catseye doubted that the Wisest One existed, Lizelle realized. *Is this a game he plays, or . . . ?*

Who knows? Darkwind answered. *If so, one prays he plays well. He and the priest spoke of many things in their sleigh. Perhaps this is the truth.*

Glynaldis said, "I think there should be a new Wisest One, one who is not of Faerie. Her purpose, after all, is to serve all of humanity."

Catseye's smile was like the one he gave the Thief in Shadow when they dueled in Tyrwilka's alleys. "Hasn't the Wisest One always served all of humanity?"

"True, Lord Kephias, but she serves Faerie first. Humanity's fate no longer lies with the Elves."

"You think so?"

Glynaldis laughed. "I don't care to be rude, Lord, but we have invaded your lands four times in the last century."

"And never held them. How quickly would you expel Elves from your domain?"

"Surely you don't threaten us?"

"I hope never to do so, Lady."

"Ah. Is this token so important?"

"You know it is, Lady. Otherwise, you'd give it up."

"I don't have it, yet."

"We'd be content to have its thief. We might learn something from her."

"As might we."

"Elvish methods are gentler."

"Does this thief deserve kindness?"

Catseye glanced at Lizelle, and she remembered calling him her kidnapper. He looked back at Glynaldis and shrugged. "Don't we all?"

"Perhaps," Glynaldis said. "But there are times when expediency must come before all else."

"In affairs of state, perhaps."

"And this is one. So, where do we stand, Lord Kephias?"

"If expediency is your sole concern, I could take the thief from you now, and let Gordia return to its affairs."

Glynaldis laughed. "All affairs are the concern of Gordia, Lord Kephias; this woman, no less. She is a citizen of our state, she stole from one of our lords, she is held in our lands."

"I ask this for Faerie, and for all of humanity."

"And I must refuse."

Catseye and Glynaldis gazed at each other like warriors or lovers. "In Gordia," Catseye said, "is expediency more important than honor?"

Among the watching nobles, several hands moved to dagger hilts. Someone muttered, "Elf scum!" and most of the senators stood. From the general whispering, one Gordian shouted, "Majesty, must we endure—"

Glynaldis quieted them with a tiny turn of her hand. "No, Lord Kephias," she said sweetly, "it is not."

Catseye nodded. "Then I demand the right of champions."

Lizelle bit her lip. *Catseye, you fool....*

"Faerie will accept what is decided here?" Glynaldis asked.

"Yes."

"Then I grant it. Who fights for you? The merchant's man?"

Catseye drew his strange sword with his left hand. "I fight for Faerie."

"Honor demands that this be to the death."

Lizelle tried to catch Catseye's glance, to hint he should try something, anything else. He never looked at her.

"Of course," he said.

"And the terms?" Glynaldis asked.

"If I win, the thief is mine, to take where I will."

"And if you lose?"

"Faerie surrenders all claim to the necklace."

"Very well. These grounds have been inaugurated for fencing. Will you fight here, and now?"

"Certainly." Catseye snatched off the buckler that held

his sword's sheath, then slipped a golden brooch from his cape to whisk it to one side of the room. He grinned. "I am ready, Lady."

Glynaldis looked calmly at Noring. "Well, Lord? Will you serve me again?"

Noring nodded with hints of weary resignation. "With swords?"

"Of course," Glynaldis said. "We would not wish to insult Faerie." She turned to the dark-haired girl page. "Deo, fetch Noring's blade."

"Yes, Majesty!" The girl ran from the room.

Glynaldis said, "Lord Kephias, I give you my champion, Uyor, Lord Noring, Master of the Barren Lands and High General of Gordia's Army."

"High General?" Noring asked her.

"You needed a better title."

"Thank you."

Ah, Lizelle thought. *Your plots advance you, Noring. I do hope you're happy.*

Glynaldis spoke as if Noring's new rank were no great matter. "Fight well, Lord Noring, and keep it."

"As ever, Majesty."

Catseye told Noring, "Your skill as a swordsman is even known in Faerie."

"I'm sorry I can't say that yours is known here."

Catseye shrugged. "Nor will you, whatever the outcome."

Noring laughed with a twinge of nervousness. "You have a strange sense of humor."

"It serves me."

"Lord Noring," Glynaldis said, "has made a study of fencing. Do you favor a particular style?"

"Yes," Catseye said. "My own."

"Ah." Glynaldis turned away. "Here comes Deo." The girl bore a sheathed sword, plain and straight, but slightly heavier and shorter than Catseye's. Glynaldis told Noring, "Do make this more interesting than the last bout. I'd hate to send you bare-handed against your next opponent."

"I'll try." Noring glanced at the blade in Catseye's left hand, then took his in his left, also. Lizelle wondered if that gave Catseye a chance. She found herself wanting to warn them both and wished she did not have to watch this.

Catseye said, "And what are the rules?"

"Survival," answered Glynaldis.

"Excellent," said Catseye as he thrust at Noring's throat.

Lizelle thought Catseye's face bore a trace of disappointment or fear when Noring deflected his lunge, yet Noring also seemed surprised. Several members of the court cried "Foul!" and "Be wary of Faerie tricks, Noring!"

The duelists separated after the first clash of steel. Lizelle expected Glynaldis to order them to reengage, but the Empress only watched intently, as did the rest of her court. She realized that Noring's moment of surprise meant this was that rarest of duels, when masters met.

Catseye took a careful step forward. Noring stepped back a pace, almost mimicking him. Lizelle began to forget the stakes as she studied each fencer and wondered who was better, Catseye employing his stronger hand or Noring using his weaker.

Noring brought his sword overhead to invite an attack. Catseye stepped away, moving his blade low to the side, also opening his defense. When Noring did not take it, he raised his sword high to mirror Noring's pose.

Do they fight or dance? Lizelle wondered.

Darkwind said, *From what this one sees through that one's eyes, they do both. Noring has studied Dawn Isle fencing, and the one-eyed man knows something akin to it.*

Noring moved forward, lowered his blade, then stepped forward again. Catseye's rapier descended with deliberate slowness. The swords seemed to kiss shyly, then whisked apart as Catseye jumped back. The sleeve of his sea-green tunic was marred by a line of blood.

The court whispered its approval. Catseye, angry at them or himself, raced forward. His strange rapier eased by Noring's guard to slash the man's left arm and leg. The cut at Noring's thigh seemed of little importance, but his upper arm bled freely.

Glynaldis called, "Noring! Don't kill yourself for my amusement!"

"I wouldn't," he answered, then said to Catseye, "You're very good."

"Thank you," Catseye murmured. "You could be worse."

Noring laughed, though sweat beaded his brow. "I could be better, and am. My masters would think me a fool for underestimating so capable an opponent."

"You do them no shame."

"Ah, but I do. You see..." Noring passed his sword from his left hand to his right. "Alas for you, I'm right-handed."

Lizelle saw her death and Catseye's written then. She bit her lip and watched with fatalistic calm as Catseye managed to parry Noring's next two thrusts. The third opened his shirt above the ribs and drew blood. Catseye retreated, but Noring pressed him, backing him into the crowd of watching nobles, who hurried out of the way. Every time Catseye began an attack, Noring forced him to defend against a flurry of feints and thrusts. The one-eyed man took a second wound in the arm, then managed to separate from Noring for a moment.

"You were right," Catseye gasped. "Your previous performance was truly poor tribute to your teachers. This one would fill them with pride."

"Thank you."

"Unfortunately for you," Catseye said, "I'm also right-handed."

Catseye tossed his sword from his left hand to his right. As Noring's eyes widened for an instant in fear, surprise, and disbelief, Catseye kicked him in the groin.

No, Lizelle thought, smiling, *no one should ever trust that man.* She heard the Empress whisper, "Uyor!" in one second, and noticed her hiding her concern in the next. *She cares for him! From what I've heard, I'd not thought it possible.*

Noring staggered, curling forward but still standing. Catseye returned his sword to his left hand, batted the weapon from Noring's grip, and placed the tip of his blade against Noring's throat. "To the death?" he asked Glynaldis.

The throne room rang with shouts of rage. Several of the younger nobles had drawn their daggers and seemed ready to use them against Catseye. Glynaldis only looked at them all until they quieted, then said to Catseye, "That's not necessary."

"I've won?"

"You've won."

"Good." Catseye wiped his sword on his torn sleeve and sheathed it. "I'll take my prize and leave then, if I may."

Glynaldis glanced at Noring, who leaned against a wall and tried to stand erect. "No," she said softly.

"Lady," Catseye whispered, "this is a matter of honor."

"No," Glynaldis repeated. "For Asphoriel himself has told me that you, Lord Kephias, are a Tyrwilkan rogue called Catseye Yellow, your 'merchant' is a renegade Quester, and his aide is a deserter from my own armies. This charade no longer amuses me." She clapped her hands twice, and pikemen rushed in to surround Catseye. "Your friends have already been escorted to 'suitable quarters.' You may join them there, in my dungeons." She smiled. "You may be amused by the dungeon keeper, who is a more-than-mortal being sworn to my service. If not, take what comfort you can in knowing you will not stay with her long."

In the room of low couches in the tower of time, Ralka asked in surprise, "What's this mean?"

Asphoriel said, "What it seems."

"You chastise me for making my plottings known and let the Empress toss your name about as though she recommended a hairdresser?"

"How amazing."

"Something happens?"

"Yes. You display the rudiments of wit."

"Hah. I doubt it'll happen again."

"I, too. A shame."

After an hour passed, Ralka asked, "Why did you intervene?"

"It was the tiniest of interventions, youth."

"Yet, you said—"

"I state principles, Wolf Lord, not absolutes. I want to win."

"So you say. I only wish to know—"

"You have need of much knowing."

"Perhaps," Ralka admitted.

Asphoriel looked at him in surprise, then said, "Ah.

Well, then, know this. The Elf might have succeeded, if I had not warned Glynaldis."

"I thought it didn't matter who gained the necklace."

"She who has it now does not know how to use it."

"But you know."

"Of course. How else could I have captured your old enemy, our guest?"

"I thought you used your own powers to capture the Cat Lord."

"You'll never learn anything about discretion, Ralka. I had another do it for me, using the miststone."

"Oh. Well, now that you've revealed to the Empress and the world that you play a part in this—"

"I have not."

"I heard—"

"You heard that a demon named Asphoriel told the Empress that she entertained an imposter. That's no astonishing thing; a wise ruler would verify the identities of all 'visiting dignitaries.' That's within a demon's ability, and certainly within the power of Asphoriel, who is thought the mightiest of demons."

"You aren't—"

Asphoriel laughed. "How slow your kind are! Demons are of this universe. Didn't I say I was not? 'Asphoriel,' much like this tower, is a part of my means of acting in your God's realm, and nothing more."

"Ah. I see."

"You can't, but no matter."

"You don't tell Glynaldis where the miststone is because that isn't something a demon would do."

Asphoriel nodded. "And because I watch her to know her capability. If she learns too much, we may have a new opponent."

"Why?"

"Her pride might not permit her to rule her world as another's regent."

"So slay—"

Asphoriel smiled. "No, you'll never be subtle."

"Probably not. How long until the God should return?"

"For those we watch, but two more days."

"Aii!"

"Calm yourself, Wolf Lord. All continues well."

"I hope I'm never around to hear you say things go badly."

"As do I, youngling." Asphoriel stroked the shaven scalp of the girl who slept with her head in his lap. "As do I."

chapter fourteen

The Fate
of the Necklace

WHEN CATSEYE HAD been disarmed and escorted away, Glynaldis told two of the departing northland guards, "Wait a moment." She tapped her finger against her lip, then turned to Lizelle and said, "My servants will take you to a place where you may bathe, and then we shall speak again privately about fetching my necklace."

The Empress dismissed her with a tiny wave of her hand. Lizelle bowed, and the guards stepped to either side of her to accompany her into the hall. One said, "This way, miss," and they began their trip through the maze that was Castle Cloud. The soldiers were handsome, muscled men with long, straight swords at their hips to complement their heavy pikes, and Lizelle suspected she could outdistance them, if only she had a place to run, if only they did not pass other guards at almost every door.

A flight of stairs took them down to a narrow, humid hall lit with oil lamps in copper bowls. For an instant, Lizelle thought the guards were actually leading her to the dungeons to join Merry and the others. Then she noticed that the floor was a mosaic in black-and-silver patterns and had been swept recently, luxuries that would be wasted on prisoners. When one guard opened a plain cedar door, she stepped into a low, warm room devoted entirely to a tiled pool, perhaps four yards wide and seven yards long. Standing on a flooring of wooden slats that encircled the pool, a barefoot Island woman in loose green cotton pants and jacket watched them enter.

"You may leave us," the small brown woman told the northlanders.

"The Empress did not say—"

The Islander nodded. "That is correct. She did not. Now, go. Or do you think this woman will escape me?"

"No, madam," one said meekly, and the two men backed out.

"Good." The Islander ordered Lizelle, "Undress. Bathe. You know how, girl?"

"I'm no Hrota," Lizelle answered. Though she wished the woman would look elsewhere, she was grateful to shed her dusty riding gear.

The pool seemed too hot to bear, at first. Once she was in, she decided she would stay there forever, if her guard allowed it. Scrubbing herself with a heavy sponge, Lizelle called, *Four-legs?*

One hears.

The pampering continues.

Good.

No. Why haven't I been given to Thelog Ar? Just because I told them I had to be sane to retrieve the necklace? I'd expect the Empress to test that a little more before she accepted it. And what really scares me is that Asphoriel takes a part in this—poor Catseye's act might've succeeded otherwise. I want out, Darkwind. I want—

One will help.

I know. Thank you.

That one would do the same.

Maybe. I hope so. Darkwind?

Yes?

Nothing. I ... only wanted to offer some melodramatic expression of gratitude.

Do not hesitate on this one's account.

Forget it, vain one. My attendant's jerking her head for me to leave the bath. I don't want her coming in after me.

"Time to go?" Lizelle asked.

The Islander only repeated the snap of her head, then narrowed her dark eyes.

"I get the idea." Lizelle dried herself with several plush towels, and left one draped over her shoulders to hide the red and blistered skin between her breasts. When she reached for her clothes, the Islander kicked them away, indicating a pale blue robe. Lizelle checked her impulse to push the woman in the pool. "Never a word when an action'll serve, hmm? I met a relative of yours." The woman glanced disdainfully away. "Thessis Ar let him carry a sword, at least."

The Islander turned and smiled something that was not quite a sneer. "My husband still needs weapons, but he's very good with them."

Lizelle let respect show on her face. "You're a Dancer?"

"I am what I am."

"I hadn't thought Dancers served anyone."

"We each choose a path, Dancers like others. Come."

"As you wish." Lizelle slipped on the short robe, knotted its cotton belt about her waist, and looked for sandals.

"Now."

"Very well." They dressed her as a slave, she realized, so she would feel like one. Understanding the intent helped to lessen the effect, but she still wished for warmer, more functional clothing.

The Empress's men had left the hall. Lizelle asked her guard, "You have a name?"

After a moment, the Islander said, "I am Taisho Eanara."

"I'm Lizelle Davinschild."

The woman grunted softly.

If the Dancer would serve one master, she might serve another. Lizelle said, "I've access to much wealth."

"Not while I watch you."

"Oh."

They passed a few servants and an occasional First Caste on their way to the Empress's quarters. All recognized Taisho and seemed to decide that they had no interest in these two women, so little, in fact, that they would quickly walk elsewhere.

Taisho stopped before a gilded door. "You proceed alone."

"You trust me?"

Taisho smiled. "The Empress has guards of her own."

Lizelle twisted the latch, glanced again at Taisho, and stepped into the next room. Its nearer walls held shelves of scrolls and books and piled parchments. At the far wall, two large windows of thick, leaded glass opened on a small garden, letting in light and the subtle smell of autumn flow-

ers. A brown upholstered chair sat before one window with
its high back to Lizelle, and a second door was directly
opposite the one at which she stood. The tan-and-gold Liavanese carpet was soft beneath Lizelle's bare feet, and the
distant playing of a lute filled her ears. For a moment, she
felt as though she could, at last, rest.

The door closed quietly behind her. Lizelle spun to try
its handle, then realized that Taisho probably waited on the
other side. When Lizelle turned back, thinking to see if
anyone waited in the garden, Noring stood before her.

"Uyor!" she gasped.

He rested an arm on the high-backed chair in which he
had sat. "So. You remember me."

"Of course. Uyor...." She tried to make her tone con-
soling, apologetic. Opening her arms for an embrace, she
hurried toward him.

He stepped back from her. She halted, then said, "Please,
Uyor. I wouldn't use you."

"No?"

"Well..." She smiled sadly. "I might. But I'm still fond
of you."

"I loved you."

"Not very much, if you already use the past tense."

"Damn it, I—"

"See? You really want a stupider companion, Uyor."

He nodded. "Or a smarter one."

"Perhaps." She remembered his look in the throne room
when he'd seemed to realize that she wore the necklace.
"You wanted to see me?"

"No. The Empress asked me to wait here."

Surprised, Lizelle said, "She tests you?"

"Perhaps. She may only wish to talk with us both, since
we're the last to have had the necklace."

"Oh." Lizelle took a random book from the shelf and
riffled its pages loudly, whispering, "Will you help me?"

"Not to escape," he said in conversational tones.

"You haven't changed."

"I have my position to think of."

"As I said...."

Noring looked away, as if he thought someone might be

in the garden, or as if he searched for the player of the lute. "I'm better rid of you."

"I told you that."

"Why'd you leave?"

"I had to."

He turned back to face her, and his expression seemed bitter. "Some answer, that."

Can I say that my life as your toy was destroying me in ways I couldn't understand, Uyor? Could you understand, if I did? Lizelle shrugged. "I was bored."

"Thanks."

"You asked."

He nodded, closing his eyes for a moment in resignation. "You should surrender the necklace, you know."

"That's what everyone says. And what am I offered in return?"

"You could beg for Gordia's mercy."

"Or for the intervention of a god. I don't expect either."

"I'm trying to help."

"You've often tried to help me. You've rarely . . . I'm sorry. You've helped me. But . . ."

He reached out and touched her cheek. "Don't apologize. You can't hurt me, anymore."

Hah. We can still tear each other to shreds. "I'm glad of that, at least."

He smiled, then hugged her. She relaxed and hugged him back. A kiss seemed to follow without planning, though as it did, Lizelle wondered if she should offer to become his companion again, in return for his aid. *Oh, there are things you do well, Uyor. I wonder how Catseye compares?*

The far door opened without warning. "My Empress!" Noring gasped, pushing Lizelle away. "We . . ."

Glynaldis smiled her small, secret smile. "You are friends, Noring. I understand."

Lizelle smoothed the front of her robe. *So. Noring avoided one trap and fell into another. But I have another question to add to my list: If Noring wants to stay in the Empress's grace, as he so obviously does, why hasn't he told her that I wear the miststone? Is he waiting for the most dramatic moment to reveal it?*

Glynaldis said to Noring, "I hoped you'd persuade your friend to help me."

"Majesty," he replied, "perhaps the necklace isn't important."

She shook her head impatiently. "You shouldn't speak like a fool, Noring. It doesn't become you."

"Forgive me, Majesty. I've just now heard that it belongs to the Wisest One, and I've always thought the Wisest One a myth."

"A legend," Glynaldis said. "There's a difference."

"As you say, Majesty."

"It's a thing of power, Noring. More than that, you needn't know."

"I see," he said quietly.

The Empress placed her hand on Noring's shoulder. "Don't be insulted. I trust no one. But I'll share this world with you, when I rule it, if you remain faithful to me."

Lizelle squeezed her fist until her knuckles ached.

"As ever, Majesty," Noring replied.

"I'll give it up," Lizelle said.

"What?" Noring's eyes widened.

"The necklace. I'll return it." Noring might have her interest at heart, but Lizelle suspected he had his own. If she couldn't depend on him, she would play the game her way. And with luck...

"I expect you have terms," the Empress said.

"Of course. Announce that I'm innocent of all charges to save your reputation for justice. Have a few trusted aides, such as Noring here"—that might keep him from speaking out before he knew her plans—"accompany me. Only a few, so the Tyrwilkans won't wonder what Gordia does in their state, yet enough to be sure I can't escape. I'll give the jewel to them, and they'll leave me free in Tyrwilka."

"Perhaps," said the Empress. "I thought to offer a similar proposal, though not so soon. These are all of your conditions?"

She knew she should not request too much, yet she also remembered Merry's face when she called them her kidnappers. "No. My companions go free, too."

"It'll require a considerable troop to escort four of you."

"Take the others to the border post at Winterberry. When I have the jewel, your aides can accompany me from Tyrwilka to Winterberry, and we can make the exchange there."

The Empress tapped her finger lightly against her lip. "This calls for much trust on my part."

"More on mine," Lizelle noted. "That's why I'd like two of King Milas's representatives present, as observers."

Glynaldis was quiet while Lizelle wondered if she had demanded too much. At last, the Empress said, "You're clever."

"I wish I were cleverer." There were too many ways left for the Empress to trick her, but at least Lizelle would be in Tyrwilka, where Gordia had to act circumspectly.

Glynaldis turned to Noring and smiled. "No wonder you loved her."

"I have a greater love now."

Glynaldis glanced back to Lizelle. "It'll be done. You may leave us, Noring."

Noring bowed and took the door into the hall.

Glynaldis took two goblets and a bottle of amber wine from a tray that sat by the plush chair. She filled each goblet and held one out to Lizelle. "You'll learn that I always treat well those who serve me well. Here." When Lizelle hesitated, Glynaldis laughed and sipped from both goblets. "The wine's a trifle tart, but good."

"Thank you." Lizelle smelled it, noted the hint of resin that was characteristic of Lyrandol wines, touched her tongue to it, and then swallowed a tiny bit. "A trifle tart," she agreed.

"As your friends so thoughtfully provided sleighs, you can leave for Tyrwilka in half an hour," Glynaldis said. "And you can hardly travel dressed like that. Follow me."

The next room was a dressing room, or perhaps the Empress's closet. Painted in shades of blue, it held her clothing as the first room had held her books. Its shelves and racks extended from the floor to the ceiling, and on them, Lizelle recognized items of dress from every time and nation she knew and saw some that were so strange she could not imagine where they were from or how they were worn.

"There must be something here that'll suit you," Glynaldis said absently. "Take off the robe."

"I—"

"You needn't be modest."

"The values of my people—"

"Are practically nonexistent, judging from your behavior. Or do you hide something?" Glynaldis smiled sweetly.

"Of course not."

"Then be quick."

Lizelle faced away from the woman and let her robe fall.

"Try this," said the Empress, handing her a purple woolen
tunic.

"Thank—" As Lizelle reached for the garment, Glynaldis
snatched her wrist and spun her.

"Ah!" The Empress's free hand darted to the burn on
Lizelle's chest. "I suspected—" Her fingers snatched for
the invisible miststone, and something exploded in the room
like silent fireworks, flinging Lizelle to one side, Glynaldis
to the other.

Lizelle rose unsteadily, feeling dazed and confused, but
unharmed. The Empress remained motionless on the floor.
Her eyes were closed like someone unconscious or dead,
and the miststone necklace was visible in her hand. *So,*
Lizelle thought, *Merry provided a second defense.* She
wished he had warned her about it.

She stepped across the room to kneel by the Empress.
As she reached out, Glynaldis's green eyes snapped opened,
and, with a weak gesture and a gasped word, the Empress
disappeared, the Necklace of the Wisest One with her.

"Godlings!" Lizelle cried. *Please, let her be invisible,
and not gone. Without the necklace, I've nothing to bargain
with, nothing.* . . . She searched the room futilely. *Glynaldis
moved herself with a spell. If I understand anything about
magic, she's probably nearby, unconscious from such ex-
ertion. But how can I find her?*

The farther door, almost certainly to the Empress's quarters, was locked. *If only I had tools, or time.* . . . The guise
of a palace slave would give her some anonymity, she knew,
so Lizelle dressed again in the robe she had dropped and
slipped through the library into the hall, thinking, *What
now? As ever, what now?*

* * *

His guards had taken Catseye through undecorated corridors meant for the quick, discreet passage of servants and soldiers through the castle. The flagstone floor was clean but not polished, and the walls bore scuff marks. A quiet, grey-bearded man who had been addressed as Colonel Ianin led him, two burly northlanders flanked him, and three more followed behind with lowered pikes. He supposed he should be flattered but wished the compliment took a subtler form.

Ianin stopped before an iron door and unlocked it with a large key taken from a kilt pocket. It swung open without a sound. Beyond it, stairs lit by a few oil lamps circled down into darkness. Catseye caught a faint whiff that reminded him of the worst of a field hospital and a coffiner's, a blend of unwashed humans, their feces, unknown illnesses, and death. A strong scent of lye only made the other smells seem stronger.

At the bottom, the stairs opened on a tiny room of unmortared granite blocks. A balding, crooked-backed woman looked up from a game of one-hand kabibble and said, "More guests for me hostel, is it?"

"Yes," Ianin answered.

As they all came into the room, the woman peered at Catseye as though she were nearsighted. "Ah, it's a handsome fellow you bring me, indeed. What do they call you, dearie?"

Catseye nodded and said, "Catseye Yellow, most recently of Tyrwilka, Lady."

"Oh, ho! And well spoken, too! I be Mother Makari. Do the wax tips on your ears have aught to do with this visit?"

Before Catseye could answer, Ianin said, "He's to be kept for the Empress. Watch him well. There's more to him than may appear."

"Ah." Makari bobbed her head in understanding. "That'll make two of us, now, won't it?" She reached for a staff that leaned against the wall and hobbled closer to them. Ianin, by the stairs, stiffened warily. "Oh, come now, you're not afraid of me?" asked Makari. Only then did Catseye see that the staff which seemed so light in her hands was a black, misshapen bar of steel.

She glared at the guards. "Well? What're you waiting

for? I've me business to attend to, and you should be doing
the same. What does the Empress pay you for, eh? To
dawdle about and get in an old woman's way?"

Ianin said, "We'll be going," and his men hurried up the
dungeon stairs. He gave Catseye a look that was either of
warning or pity, then followed them.

Makari clutched Catseye's upper arm with a wrinkled,
clawlike hand. "So, it's a cell for you, dearie. Can you pay
for a room of your very own?"

"I haven't—"

"Oh, you must've forgotten this." She plucked his profit
from gambling with Quentian's troop out of an inner pocket
of his tunic. "Thank you."

Behind her was a narrow corridor lined with iron doors.
Most had small grills at top and bottom for ventilation,
though a few did not. One prisoner moaned loudly, and
Makari said, "Pay no mind to that. The fellow has the
Rotting Death. He'll be quiet in another day or two."

Her grip and her ease with her steel staff told him that
he could not overpower her. Thinking to try to trick her,
he said, "Do you know who I am?"

"No," she answered. "Nor do I care."

"It would be wise for you to free me, for I—"

"Watch your tone, sonny."

"You are the one who should be careful, woman. I—"

Makari snapped her hand against his diaphragm, and
Catseye fell back, unable to speak or breathe. She smiled
and said, "You don't want to be threatening Mother Makari,
no matter how politely you do it. I fear we'll have to punish
you now, you naughty, naughty boy."

Thraas looked at Merry. "Suitable quarters? Empress did
say, 'Suitable quarters,' yes?"

Merry sighed. "Yes, Thraas. That's what she said."

"Thraas hates the Wolf Lord's gift." He smashed the flat
of his hand against the door of their cell.

"Quiet, laddie," called Makari from her stool by the
stairs. "Lest I be forced to thrash you a bit, as I did your
handsome friend. The old need their rest."

Thraas and Merry shared a stone cell two paces wide

and three paces long. Its floor was clean sand, recently spread. At the back wall, a short pipe trickled cold water into a sewage hole. A few slits in the iron door admitted the tiniest bit of light and air.

"Why did One-eye get room of his own?" Thraas asked.

"They trust him less," Merry answered, closing his eyes and wishing Thraas had bathed recently.

"What will you do now, Merry?"

"Pray," he said.

"Oh. Thraas will not bother you." The hillman began drawing pictures of horses in the sand. After several minutes, he said quietly, "Thraas hopes Silky is safe in mountains."

"I'm sure your pony's fine. I cast a little spell to lead it to one of our temples."

"Many dangers in mountains, Merry."

"True."

"Poor Silky. Poor, poor Silky."

chapter fifteen

Of Revolution
and Revelation

As LIZELLE CLOSED the Empress's door behind her, some-
one in white lunged from behind a tapestry for her wrist.
She dodged aside, driving a fist into the man's stomach.
"Wait!" Noring gasped. "It's me!"

They were alone in the short hall. Annoyed and wanting
to hurry away before any alarm could be given of her escape,
Lizelle said, "You should've warned me."

Noring rubbed his belly and nodded. "I wondered if your
reflexes were still good. We used to play—"

"Sorry. No time for reminiscences." She kissed him
quickly on the lips and walked on. He would follow if he
wanted to help her.

She heard his footsteps as he ran after her, calling, "Wait!
The Empress let you go?"

Lizelle turned to face him, spread her arms wide, and
turned again to continue down the hall. "So it seems."

"And the necklace?" he asked.

She glanced at him. "It's important to you?"

"I don't know. If it's important to the Empress."

"In the throne room . . ." she said carefully.

"Yes?"

"Did you notice . . . anything?"

"That you wore something around your neck?" Noring
nodded.

"Why didn't you say so?"

"I care for you."

"And?"

He smiled.

No, he had not changed. Lizelle said, "You have a use for it."

"Perhaps."

"Uyor!"

"Yes?"

"Choose sides, Uyor."

"I choose my own."

"You're predictable."

"Perhaps. Where're you going?"

"To find my friends." As she said it, she wondered when she had decided.

"Oh? They're in the dungeons."

"I figured as much." When he continued to follow her, she said, "I want to visit them alone."

He stopped her with a hand on her shoulder. She looked at it, and he moved it away to ask, "What happened in the Empress's rooms?"

Lizelle shook her head, then said, "If you intend to help Glynaldis, it's safe for you to leave me."

He frowned slightly. "Why?"

"Because she has what she wants, and all I seek is escape."

He stared. Lizelle nodded and said, "You shouldn't be seen with me, you know."

"And if I oppose the Empress?"

She shrugged. "Then do what you can, immediately. If the Wisest One exists and the Empress controls her..." Lizelle grinned bitterly. "Safer to stay her lover, Uyor. Now, go. Please!"

He continued to follow as she descended a flight of stairs. They had passed several people as they talked, and Lizelle realized that Noring's presence helped protect her, for the moment.

He said, "Do you really hope to free your friends?"

"No."

"Then why—"

"It's worth the try."

"Could they do anything to stop Glynaldis, if they escaped?"

"If you help us, maybe. If not, I doubt it."

He nodded. "I'll help." Lizelle squinted at him, suddenly suspicious. Noring said, "There are those who plan a revolt. They follow someone called the Hooded Man. I . . . am one of them."

"You never told me."

"I didn't dare."

She laughed and wondered if she sounded a little mad. "You're a rebel, and you're going to help me free prisoners from your lover's cells. How very convenient."

"It's true. The revolt could begin within the hour—*must* begin within the hour, if Glynaldis has the miststone." Noring tugged her arm, directing her away from the dungeon stairs. "Come."

She stood still. "This isn't necessary, Uyor. If you want to arrest me, just shout for a guard. I'll kill you with my hands before one arrives, of course."

"Lizelle . . ." He reached out to stroke her cheek.

She stepped back, raising her hands before her. "Or you could leave me, and then call a guard. Or several. For the sake of my pride, make it several."

"Please. Come."

Lizelle sighed. "You're more devious than I thought, Uyor. But I have one request."

"You have thousands."

"If I don't escape . . ."

"Yes?"

"Let my horse loose in the woods."

He raised an eyebrow, then nodded. "Of course." Taking a corridor Lizelle did not know, they passed several white-garbed members of the First Caste, a few blue-robed clerks, and a priest of the Nine before Noring found a soldier and ordered, "Carry a message to Colonel Ianin. Tell him Noring wants a new guard at his quarters, and immediately. You have that?"

"Yes, sir!"

"Be quick."

"Yes, sir!" The boy departed at a run.

"I wish I knew what you're doing," Lizelle said, not liking her decision to trust him.

"I told you—"

"Right. Is there anything else, or may we go on to the dungeons?"

"You're obsessed."

She wondered if she was. "There's only a little time left for me to act, I think. I could get drunk. I could seduce someone. Or I can try to make amends for something I wish I hadn't done."

"You have a plan?"

"Of sorts. You'll really help?"

Noring nodded, and she decided it was time to stop questioning him. He was either sincere or he wasn't, and questions would not help her know which. She said, "Is it true the jailer's some half-mortal creature?"

"Yes. Old Makari. She's either half god or half demon. Most people suspect she's Asphoriel's child, though no one knows the mother. I have my suspicions."

Lizelle asked with a raised eyebrow.

"Glynaldis," Noring said.

"But she's—"

"Makari ages much more quickly than humans do. That's part of the reason she hates us. You won't get around her easily, you know. And she only takes orders from Glynaldis."

"I hear," Lizelle said, "that demon children are very fond of luxuries."

Noring shrugged. "I've heard the same. So?"

Lizelle smiled. It felt good to be making decisions again, even if they were bad ones. "So where can we get a large goblet of red wine and three—no, twelve leaves of Sleep's Ease?"

Noring frowned as he studied her. "That's a very old trick."

"Yes," Lizelle said. "Which is why it usually works."

The wine was obtained at the kitchens; the Sleep's Ease at the infirmary. The clerk who gave them the powdered leaves said, "I don't know why you intend to drug several teams of oxen, but I hope you realize they won't walk for a week after you give them this."

Lizelle laughed. "Good." Noring stared at her and said nothing.

His key got them past the door to the dungeons, and she wondered what she would have done if she had not met him. As they walked down the dark stairs, Lizelle said, "Glynaldis won't be amused by this."

"No. Not at all."

She stopped on the steps and glanced at him.

"Something?" he asked.

"Yes." She reached over and squeezed his hand. "I . . . may have misjudged you."

"Probably not. I've done things I wish I hadn't."

"Hmm. Have I heard that somewhere?" Lizelle squeezed his hand again and moved on before he could say anything embarrassing.

At the bottom of the stairs, an old woman with thin white hair looked up from her game of one-hand kabibble. "Why, Lord Noring himself comes to visit, and here I haven't cleaned the place!"

Noring smiled thinly. "That's all right."

"And who accompanies you? Oh, ho! A pretty slave girl!" The old woman winked. "You do keep busy, don't you, me lordshipness? This is an odd place to bring her, but then, who'm I to wonder about the fancies of others? Why, when I was young, I'd sometimes . . ." Makari's wrinkled features stretched in a grin. Her teeth were white and strong. "Well, never you mind. Treat me little realm as though it were your home." She gestured freely with a thick staff that seemed light in her hands.

"Thank you," Noring said.

Lizelle stepped forward, thinking she would have halved the dose of Sleep's Ease, if she'd known how feeble the old woman was. "The Empress sends a gift," she said, offering the drugged wine.

"Oh, isn't that kind! What a dear, dear lass." Makari leaned her staff against the wall to take the goblet in both hands, as if its weight were all she could bear. "You must thank her." She drank it down in a single draught. "A bit sweet, but who'm I to complain, eh?" She upended the cup to drain a few more drops. "Right tasty, it is, right . . ." Her sentence ended in a snore.

Noring whispered, "Is she—"

Lizelle released a breath, nodded, and began to search the old woman's robes. Makari burped once. Noring started, and Lizelle smiled as Makari's snore resumed. "Here," she said, showing him a ring of keys.

"Good."

They ran down the dark hall. Prisoners began to yell, and not all the cries seemed to come from human throats. Lizelle heard someone shout her name, and with a sudden, strange confusion of emotions, she recognized the caller. "That's Catseye. The one you knew as Kephias."

"I'd prefer to leave him, but . . ."

Lizelle was already trying keys at Catseye's door. She opened it, and he limped out, blinking. The dye was washed from his skin and hair, a ragged green scarf covered his right eye, and his tunic hung on him in tatters. His skin was badly bruised. Clotting blood marked his nose and several scrapes on his chest and arms. His gaze focused on Lizelle's short robe. "I like that." Then he looked at Noring. "I do hope you haven't come for a rematch."

Noring shook his head. "We're allies for now, it seems."

"Oh?" Catseye looked at Lizelle.

She nodded and said, "Can you walk?"

"I can run, if it'll get me out of here."

"Good. Hurry. Things are getting worse."

"That'd fit the Pattern, so far."

"Down here!" Merry shouted from farther away.

When they opened the second cell, Merry and Thraas rushed out, barefoot and stripped of their jewels and rich clothing. Merry, in only his blue-and-grey robe, rubbed his eyes and said, "Where's the necklace?"

"With the Empress," Lizelle answered.

The little priest grimaced. "And how will we escape?"

Noring said, "The revolt begins in minutes."

Thraas glanced at him. "Revolt?"

Noring nodded. "The followers of the Hooded Man finally act. We're well organized. We hadn't planned to move so soon, but with the necklace in the Empress's hands . . ."

"If time's pressing," Catseye said, "let's go."

They ran down the dark passage. Lizelle tossed the key ring into another cell so the prisoners could free themselves, then bumped into Thraas, who suddenly halted. Some twenty feet ahead, Makari stood, blocking their way.

The old woman spun her staff in her hands like a baton, and, shocked, Lizelle recognized it as forged steel coated with black paint. "That wine," Makari said, "was a trifle more potent than most. But it was tasty." She caught the staff and slammed it against the floor. "So, how'd you lot get loose?"

Catseye stepped past the others and bowed low. "I tired of your hospitality."

Makari laughed. "You, laddie? No need to pretend to be the great magician. I'd know."

"My talents don't come from me, but from my patron. As I would have told you earlier, had you let me speak." He tugged the scarf from his head, and Lizelle wished she were standing closer to see what lay under it.

"Oh!" Makari cried. She slumped back into her crone's posture and said again, "Oh!"

"The game is up, Makari. My patron would have his vengeance."

"I didn't aid them against him! Honest, I didn't!"

"You did not treat me well, Makari."

"I didn't know, Lord! Honestly, I didn't. I'm so very sorry, I am, and that's truth, I swear it!"

"Calm yourself," said Catseye. "I like you, and will offer advice."

"Oh, thank you, sir! Thank you, thank you!"

"Your mistress is about to experience the gravest of setbacks. If you wouldn't suffer with her, depart this place, and soon. And you see that your friends' efforts were of no use against my patron. Prove your innocence by staying away from them. Then you shall not share their fate, either."

"Oh, I will, Lord. I will." She bowed again. "Thank you. Thank you!"

"You have our possessions?" Catseye said.

"They're in the wee room by the stairs, Lord. You should have no trouble getting them."

"No," Catseye agreed as they filed past Makari. "I shouldn't."

Upstairs, Merry exhaled in relief. "How did you dupe

her, friend Cat? I hardly followed any of that, but it was very well—"

Catseye turned. His right eye was golden, like a tiger's. "She recognized my patron's mark, but didn't know he had suffered . . . reversals."

Lizelle, staring, said, "Cat, what—" *Which is his, the human eye or the cat's?*

Catseye shook his head. "Ask your questions when we have more time. I might even answer them."

Noring pointed at a storage room. "Your things are probably in there."

"Thraas will open that," said Thraas. He hurled himself against the oak door, and it swung wide on shattered hinges. Thraas stood rubbing his shoulder as the others entered.

The "wee room" was larger than the homes of most poor folk, and held aisle after aisle of deep wooden shelves where the clothes and weapons of hundreds of Mother Makari's guests were neatly stacked. While Lizelle, Catseye, and Thraas ransacked it for former possessions and new ones, Merry asked Noring, "Can your rebellion succeed?"

"If you can stop Glynaldis."

Merry scratched his skull and seemed surprised when his hand encountered his long, sorcerously grown hair. "Are the flying sleighs still here?"

"I believe so," Noring said.

"If we can get to them, we might reach World's Peak and the Wisest One. And then . . ." He shook his head. "Then we'll think of something. You'll stay behind?"

Noring nodded. "There are things to be done here, if we're to succeed."

Lizelle heard Catseye exhale in satisfaction when he found his sword, but her own clothes were not in the room. She dressed in soft buckskin breeches, a cotton riverman's shirt, and a boy's riding boots, then found a black wool jacket that reminded her of her old one. Buckling on a fencer's sword, she asked Noring, "You'll proceed with the revolt? I thought we might all flee—"

"Where?" Catseye said, joining them. He wore green forester's clothing and a dark cloak, and thrust a pair of moccasins and a soldier's overcoat at Merry as he explained, "So long as Gordia's fair ruler keeps the necklace, there's no hope of escaping her. It's true we shall only need to avoid her if she's annoyed at us, but I rather suspect she might be."

Merry nodded grimly as he donned his shoes and coat. "I'm sorry I involved you all."

Lizelle glanced at Noring. His face was still a mask to her, as it had always been. Then he smiled sadly, perhaps a little wistfully, and, ever so tenderly, she kissed him. When they separated, she said, "I wish..." Wondering what she did wish, she shrugged.

After a moment, Noring said, "I, too."

Embarrassed, Lizelle turned and gestured at the others. "The stables are this way! Let's go!"

Noring called after them, "Good luck!"

Lizelle prayed they would not need it.

Noring walked briskly through the halls of Castle Cloud so no one would stop him for any casual matters. As he considered what remained to be done, he wished for a moment that he were anyone other than Noring, the Hooded Man, the one whose fear was so great that he always plotted to make himself safer and thus set himself farther along dangerous paths. And then he began the long climb to Thelog Ar's chambers.

Though dusk was just arriving, the magician's tower felt as if only the hour of midnight existed within it. Noring slowed, telling himself to save his strength. He remembered the girl he had used, the homeless Riawn. Had she taken these stairs eagerly or afraid?

Something in them seemed to sap his will, though perhaps that came from knowledge of his goal. The stones felt colder than they did in any other part of the castle, far colder than the dungeons he had left. The windows were narrow slits spaced well apart, and the gloom was more oppressive than any he had known. Perhaps, if his message had not already been sent to Ianin, he would have turned back. But he had begun the revolt he had planned for so long, and so, as always, self-preservation kept him moving forward.

When Noring neared the top, he heard a whispering voice in the wind. "You come unbidden, Lord Noring."

"I wish to talk with you," he said, hiding his fear.

"Obviously."

The large room was dark and drafty. In spite of the open windows, it smelled like an apothecary's storeroom in which several items had begun to rot or grow moldy. A torch burned near the head of the stairs where Noring stood, and some candlelight spilled down from the stairs across the room that led to the floor above. Noring peered at various shapes among the shadows. "Are you here, Thelog Ar?"

"Yes," the magician whispered. "In my usual seat. You may bring the torch closer, if the magic of night does not comfort you."

A heavy chair sat in the far corner, and someone occupied it. When Noring had crossed halfway to the sorcerer, Thelog Ar said, "No closer, please. I see things too well, and need no more light."

"I'm . . . sorry." The room heightened Noring's discomfort. He did not like the musty smell of strange and ancient things, and the shadows sometimes moved in ways that had nothing to do with torchlight.

"Don't be sorry," Thelog Ar said. "The fault isn't yours. What would you speak of, Lord Noring?"

"Some say you don't serve the Empress willingly."

Thin laughter filled the chamber. "I do it. Isn't that therefore of my own accord?"

"Many people are bound to Glynaldis in different ways. In my own case, it is my fear of her that holds me."

Thelog Ar's quiet was unsettling, as if he had left the room, and only his muffled body remained. After a moment, he said, "Why do you come?"

Noring considered the distance to the magician. His thrown knife would be quicker than any spell. "I rebel against her," he said.

Thelog Ar laughed again. "And you come to me for help? How very, very foolish, Lord Noring."

"You won't help me?"

"I can't."

Hearing sadness in the magician's reply, Noring said,

"But would you, if you were able?"

"I would."

"Then do so!"

"How simple is your world."

"It is! Make your freedom!"

"I've no escape from our ruler." Thelog Ar's voice was rich with longing. "None."

"You've power...."

"So does a river. Still, humans harness it, not it humans."

"Don't play with my words, mage!"

"I don't mean to offend you, Lord Noring. Believe that."

"Will you tell her of our conversation?"

"If she asks."

"You'll help her against me?"

The magician's answer came more slowly. "If she asks."

"Why?"

"I tried to betray her once," said Thelog Ar. "She did not care to lose my aid. Draw nearer, if you will, and you shall see, and know."

Without thinking, Noring stepped forward. As the torch-light fell on Thelog Ar's face, the magician asked, "Do you understand now?" His lips did not move, and his eyes were closed. Something moved from one lid like a tear.

"I, I . . ." Noring's throat filled with conflicting needs to vomit and to scream.

Thelog Ar sat in his high-backed chair with his head resting on his shoulder. Under his white cowl, his face was that of a mummified corpse. Several ants, like black tears, walked across his shriveled cheeks.

"I taught her magic," said Thelog Ar, opening dry eye-lids. The sockets beneath them were murky, writhing ruins. "She learned to use it against me. She slew me, yet she did not. She kept my soul as a pet, as a mentor, as an instrument, as—"

"No!" Noring whispered.

"Yes," said Thelog Ar, almost with glee. His head lifted as though to regard Noring with absent eyes. "And she will use me against you."

"No!" Noring whispered louder.

Thelog Ar's hands moved to place themselves on the

arms of his chair. "Yes." He began to stand. "She will send me against you like a demon's hound, and I—"

"No!" Noring shouted, flinging his torch at the magician's shrouded figure. It ignited with a roar, as though made of tar. "No!" Noring cried again as he reeled away from the sudden heat of the flames.

The wind within the room seemed to speak as someone far, far away said, "She you seek lies in the chambers above." The blaze grew even brighter, then flared. At the fire's brightest, the wind whispered, "Thank you. . . ."

Noring's face was wet with tears. He had drawn his sword for some reason that he could not understand. He would have fled had it not been for Thelog Ar's last gift of information. "She I seek," he mumbled. "She I seek." He staggered to the far stairs.

The room above was much like the one below, though it was better lit. The walls and the ceiling were a lattice work of windows. Candles, mimicking the stars, burned in chandeliers and wall niches. Someone slept in scarlet robes on a white satin couch.

Noring stepped forward, then recognized her. "Thessis Ar!" The woman's features seemed more deeply etched than he remembered, and her hair was almost white.

Her eyes opened. "Who?" she said, blinking. "Noring?"

"Yes."

She looked at the sword in his hand and said warily, "What do you want?"

"Need," he corrected. "Your help."

She shook her head to clear it. "Are you well?"

"Very. I freed your brother." As Noring spoke, he felt certain he had both helped and defeated Thelog Ar. Coping with the magician's sister should be far easier.

"He's no longer the Empress's pawn. Do you want to remain that?"

She studied him. "No."

"Then join me."

"I thought you loved her."

Noring laughed harshly.

"Or, at least, cared for her."

"How could I? For someone who's done what she has?"

"Which is?"

"Whatever she had to, to keep power."

"And what do you do now?"

"I rebel against her."

"How very noble. Why?"

"To begin a better government in Gordia."

Thessis Ar shook her head. "No. You'd become the new ruler."

"Yes, but—"

"You'd give to some that Glynaldis has taken from, and take from some that she has given to. How would you be better?"

"I would never degrade myself—"

"Go to your apartments," said Thessis Ar, lowering herself back on the couch. "Think this over for a few weeks, or months—"

"It's begun."

"What!" She scrambled to her feet. "You damned foolish—"

Noring raised his sword. "Speak nicely."

"You're serious."

Noring nodded.

"Or mad."

"A little of each, I suspect."

"What started this?"

"She's obtained the Necklace of the Wisest One."

"Oh. I can help you, then." Thessis Ar opened her hand. The miststone necklace lay in her palm.

"You've stopped her!" Noring cried.

"No." She spoke softly. "I am her." Thessis Ar's body shimmered like mist in the sunlight. Her features filled out while every trace of age left her face. As her thin grey hair became lush and auburn, she said, "What will you do now, my Uyor?"

The tip of Noring's blade leaped for the woman's chest, but she rolled backward out of reach, snatching from under the couch a sword much like Noring's. He stared in disbelief, then laughed. "You hope to save yourself?"

She parried his lunge with ease. "Your master had another pupil, Uyor. One who began her studies years before you."

"You're some demon—"

Her sword beat against his, deflecting his thrust, and passed through his heart.

As he fell, she whispered, "It would be easier, if I were."

chapter sixteen

Climbing
World's Peak

STEALING THE FLYING sleighs was a simple matter. The courtyard was almost empty while most Gordians sought their evening dinner, and the sleighs, each aglow with bright hunting scenes that seemed fresh-painted, still sat to one side near the outbuildings. Crouching in a recessed palace door close to the stables, Lizelle called to Darkwind, *Can you create a small diversion, fleet one?*

With pleasure, he answered. She heard a crash of splintering wood as Darkwind kicked open the door of his stall, then two young stablehands ran screaming into the courtyard with Darkwind close behind them. Several grey-bearded soldiers were lounging near the sleighs, playing a last game of cards while the sun set, and a few servants walked through the yard toward the castle. All stopped to watch a stallion loose on the palace grounds, and to laugh as the stablehands desperately tried to dodge Darkwind's nips at their buttocks.

"That's a minor diversion?" Catseye whispered.

Lizelle shrugged. "Be glad I didn't ask for a major one."

One stablehand, a girl, managed to scramble onto a high stack of hay bales, but the boy's kilt tore in Darkwind's teeth. While the Gordian audience guffawed at the stableboy's plight, Lizelle slipped aboard the nearest sleigh, a low, sleek thing with an exposed driver's seat and an enclosed bed in back for passengers and cargo. Catseye, Merry, and Thraas walked over to the second sleigh, pointing all the while at the wild horse like the other gawkers.

When Darkwind had chased the stableboy past Lizelle, he leaped behind her and settled on his knees in the sleigh bed. Merry and the others rushed aboard the second, smaller sleigh. One soldier saw them and shouted, "Hey! What're you—"

As the soldiers dropped their cards to snatch up pikes and bows, Lizelle whispered the words that Merry had told her, and prayed she remembered them right, prayed that flying would be less frightening than it appeared. In a shower of Gordian curses and arrows, her red-and-yellow sleigh rose into the sky.

One should open one's eyes.

Why?

Because World's Peak is not on the moon.

We're high enough?

Quite.

Lizelle peeked out one eye and quickly closed it. Castle Cloud hurried away beneath her.

One hears that air is weakened when it is far from the earth, and grows thin and cold. One would rather not learn if this is true.

Lizelle shouted, "Rise no more!" Their sleigh halted as if it had hit a bump, and Lizelle clutched at its railing to keep from being thrown out.

The priest said all commands should be carefully phrased.

I forgot. The view's not all that bad.

It's the world as seen from above.

You're such a romantic. Lizelle commanded the sleigh, "Go west and south, to World's Peak." Below, to the left, their companions kept pace with them. Catseye waved, and Lizelle thought she could see him grin. Timidly, she raised one hand to wave back.

Watching farmlands and woods slide away beneath the sleigh's bright runners, Lizelle soon forgot her mistrust of flight. To the north were the plains, and a line of white that said winter was already creeping toward Gordia. Ahead of her, the sun set behind the dark ribbon of The Wall. As Lizelle looked, she wondered, *How does the sleigh understand my commands?*

Darkwind thought something that felt like a shrug and said, *Magic.*

Thanks a lot. Horse.

She snacked on sausage and cheese and Lyrandol wine, all from the dragon's cave, while Darkwind told her of his travels and what he had learned. When he finished, she said, *Ralka, Asphoriel, the Wisest One, and the Lord of Cats. And, if She exists, the God. I think we're a little out of place in this.*

One knows. It would be simple to flee during the night.

That doesn't sound like you.

One suggests what one expects that one to suggest.

No. We go through with it.

Why?

They need me.

Oh?

And if the Questers tell the truth about the God, this is a chance to make amends. We help Her, She'll help us, hmm?

Perhaps.

And it feels like the right thing to do.

Ah. A few minutes later, Darkwind said, *Does one wish the one-eyed man flew in this sleigh, rather than this one?*

Are you kidding? It's been a long day. I need some rest.

Oh.

And you're good company, Darkwind.

Ah. Thank you.

Lizelle slept beside Darkwind under a heavy pile of soft blankets of Faerie moonthread. At dawn, when she woke, she first saw the cloud of her breath, then, below her and before her, the snow-covered peaks of the mountains of The Wall. One rose far ahead of them that was so tall and so grand that it could only be the Wisest One's home. *It's beautiful!* Lizelle thought.

It's cold.

That, too. Thank the godlings the Gordians hadn't unloaded these sleighs yet. She threw a yellow blanket over Darkwind and tied it on him with bits of cord, then cut a red one to make a poncho for herself. When she pulled up the hood of her jacket and slipped on the mittens taken from the storeroom in Castle Cloud, she decided she might survive the trip to World's Peak, if not the trip up it.

Soon after she was dressed, the second sleigh swerved toward them. Merry waved at Lizelle to land on an ice-covered plateau. "Descend, sleigh," she said. "Slowly!"

A small fire burned in a hastily made clearing beside the second vehicle. Merry and Thraas sat next to it with purple-and-orange blankets draped over them, and Catseye stood nearby in his dark cloak. Darkwind and Lizelle both jumped out as their sleigh touched ground. While Darkwind nosed at a bale of hay that lay near the fire, then began to munch at it, Lizelle squatted close to the flames and said, "Oh, that feels good! Who built it so quickly?"

Merry looked down with an expression of embarrassed modesty.

"And the hay as well?"

The priest shook his head. "That was Catseye. He snatched it from the stables before we left. At no small risk to himself." Admonishment or annoyance crept into his voice as he added, "Or us."

Lizelle glanced at Catseye in surprise and said, "Thank you."

He shrugged, then smiled. "Best to keep your mount fat, in case we have to eat him." Darkwind turned quickly, and Catseye raised both hands in peace. "A jest, fleet one. And a very poor one. Forgive me." He looked at Lizelle. "Will he forgive me?"

One would have preferred oats, Darkwind said.

"He thanks you for the hay," Lizelle said, then turned to Merry and, indicating the fire, said, "I thought you hoarded your magic."

"No more. We give up stealth for speed," Merry said.

"Oh? Then why do we stop?"

"To rest. Who knows what obstacles we'll face in the final assault?" The little priest turned his face into the wind to look up at the daunting crags of World's Peak.

Lizelle glanced at Catseye, who shrugged, then at Thraas, who stared glumly at the fire. "What obstacles?"

Merry said, "No one knows for certain. The first and greatest is the mountain itself. To climb that . . ."

"We have the sleighs," she said.

"If the winds aren't too strong for them. And there's the prophecy: World's Peak is gained by one who is less than Man, and more."

Catseye drew his cloak tightly around himself. "There

are always prophecies. Can we do anything more to pre-
pare?"

"No."

"Then let's go. The Empress surely follows as quickly
as she can."

"The revolt—" Lizelle began.

"It may slow her," said Catseye. "It won't stop her, I
suspect."

"I, too," said Merry.

"Thraas knows power," said the hillman suddenly, and
they all turned toward him. He pointed at World's Peak
with his axe. "Power is there. Empress knows power. Empress will come."

They flew until the winds tossed them like woodchips
in a waterfall, then settled onto the mountain slope and
continued to race the sleighs upward, faster than horses or
gravity could ever pull them. When the terrain grew too
rough, when sheer cliffs jutted from the snow like walls,
they left the vehicles behind and hiked up paths that were
sometimes as wide as Elvish roads, sometimes barely wide
enough for goats.

At noon, when all were weary from climbing and dinner
seemed the best excuse to stop, Catseye called over the roar
of the wind, "Is that the first of your obstacles, priest?"

Lizelle could see little more than the swirling snow that
had battered at them since morning. Then she noticed a
radiance like firefly light, dancing as a barrier before them.

"I don't know," Merry said.

Catseye nodded. "I'm so glad you came with us, priest."

"Look beyond!" said Lizelle.

The snow ended at the field of light. Past it, green grass
and trimmed hedges abruptly abutted with rock and ice as
if summer and winter had come to this place to kiss.

They tested the glow by passing the tip of Catseye's
sword through it. "Well?" he asked.

Merry pursed his lips and poked a finger in. "Nothing."
Smiling, he waved his entire arm through. "It must exist"—
he stepped forward—"for the sole purpose—" He slumped
forward on his face and lay still, halfway into the field of
light.

Lizelle threw herself down, pulling the sword from her belt and glancing about. *Are we attacked?*

One sees no one, senses no one.

Oh. Feeling foolish, she stood, then felt better when she saw that Catseye and Thraas were also rising cautiously and brushing snow from their clothes.

Merry's boots were still in the world of winter. Lizelle grabbed them to drag him back. As his head came out of the dancing lights, his eyes opened and he said, "Of maintaining the tempera— What happened?"

Thraas laughed, and Catseye and Lizelle joined him. Thraas said, "Remember legend, Merry? You are Man, yes?"

"Oh!" The priest glanced at Catseye. "Might you..." His voice trailed away as Catseye studied the light barrier with extreme skepticism.

Lizelle laughed then, understanding Thraas's meaning. "No! Less than Man, and more. Right, friend Thraas?"

Catseye and Merry turned to her as though she were the answer. Thraas said, laughing louder, "Are all city folk so simple?"

"Careful," said Catseye.

Lizelle pointed behind them. As the others turned to follow the line of her finger, she heard Darkwind say, *This one always has to help. Were this one less understanding ...*

Darkwind carried each of them through the wall of light, and each regained consciousness in the land of summer. A slight breeze blew, and butterflies flitted across a field of white, purple, and yellow crocuses. A flagstone path led on to a series of terraces that rose beyond them in three tiers. A small marble pavilion sat atop the third and highest terrace.

Lizelle pointed at it. "The Wisest One's home?"

Merry shrugged. "If we're lucky."

After a short discussion, they left their coats, blankets, cloaks, and bundles of supplies by the border of snow, then followed the stone-paved path. It took them through the crocuses to a curved wall of polished marble, perhaps twenty feet high. At its top, rowan trees and bushes could be seen where the second terraced garden began. A ladder of golden rungs set into the stone offered their only hope of access.

This one could not climb that, Darkwind said.

"Is there another way?" Lizelle asked.

"I doubt it," Merry said. "But we'll see."

Circling the wall in either direction brought them to a sheer cliff where land and summer ended in the glowing field of light. White fog or clouds billowed far below them, and they heard furious winds whip past them, just beyond the barrier of light. Merry shrugged. "I'm sorry, but . . ."

"You're right," Lizelle said, and they hiked back to the golden rungs, where she hugged Darkwind's neck. *Be careful, clumsy.*

As ever. That one ought not to do anything clever, unless that one must.

She touched his nose and felt his breath on her hand. *Don't worry. The prophecy got us this far. We'll be fine.*

Catseye saluted Darkwind with his sword. "Farewell, fleet one, until we meet again."

Merry looked at the others, then touched Darkwind's mane and said embarrassedly, "You've been, ah, a fine companion."

Thraas reached out and stroked Darkwind's nose. "Good horse."

As Lizelle climbed the golden ladder, she heard Darkwind mutter, *Good horse? This is praise? Good horse?*

The grounds of the second terrace were like those of the garden below, though the flowers here were tulips and daffodils. Hedges of boxwood lined another flagstone path which led to another golden ladder which led to another terrace. They walked quickly for several minutes toward it. Though the second ladder continued to gleam before them, no matter how they hurried or how far they seemed to walk, they came no nearer to it.

"Magic," Thraas said in disgust. He snatched a white stone from the ground and hurled it forward. It disappeared, then something hit him in the back of the head, and he yelped in surprise. When they all turned, the white stone lay on the path behind them.

Merry sighed and sat. "I'll stay here."

"What? You surely won't quit when we're so close," said Lizelle.

"That's our second obstacle," Merry said. "Someone's created a, well, a loop in space, and perhaps in time as well. If any of us will ever reach the top, someone has to anchor the path, to make this spot"—he pointed down—"be 'here,' and that one"—he pointed at the ladder—"'there.' I can't do it unless I stay. . . ." He shrugged.

"Here," said Catseye.

"Exactly," said Merry.

"It sounds like nonsense," said Lizelle.

"Do you know any other way?" asked the priest.

Catseye said, "It's hardly the first nonsense in this affair."

Lizelle said, "But what do we tell the Wisest One, if we find her?"

"What you know," Merry answered. "That's all I could do. If we're lucky, that's all she'll need."

"What I dislike," Catseye said, stroking his lip where his mustache had been, "is how easily we're succeeding."

Lizelle frowned at him. When she was younger, she had believed that confidence attracted the attention of the capricious masters of luck, and the ghost of that belief still lingered. "Who says we're succeeding?"

"We've come this far easily enough. The rest can't be much more difficult."

Merry added, "The Pattern suggested that we four—no, Darkwind, too—we five could succeed in climbing World's Peak. It's obvious we won't all make the top, but a few of you should. The only thing I worry about is what you'll find there."

Catseye nodded. "Very well," he said, and walked on. Thraas slapped Merry on the back, and Lizelle, surprised to feel so fond of the little priest, waved to him. Merry smiled after them as he began to chant.

Perhaps his spell was more successful than he intended. A few steps brought them to the second ladder. Catseye scrambled up before Lizelle, and Thraas followed her.

Lizelle heard the clash of swords before she glanced up. Catseye, half on the ladder and half on the next terrace, battled something above him that was cloaked in light, reminding her of the magical wall that surrounded this place. The thing's sword might have been forged of bound sunbeams, for Lizelle could not look at its blade without squinting. Catseye somehow managed to see. He fought, gained a foothold on the terrace, and stood. "Hurry!"

Lizelle scrambled up to stand among a sea of blue irises. "How can I help?"

"Find the Wisest One," Catseye grunted. "As Merry wishes. Then ask her to call off her watchdog."

In the cloak of shimmering light, a feminine face smiled. "I'm a guardian," it said. "Not a watchdog. And I'm not here to slay. Only to halt."

"I haven't so many restrictions," Catseye stated, lunging. His sword passed through the Lady in Light, and she laughed gently. Catseye parried a thrust that almost took his heart. He said, "I thought you wouldn't kill."

His opponent said sadly, "I only answer your intent."

"Ah."

"You could go back," it suggested.

"Never." He parried another thrust.

Lizelle watched, searching for some way to help. Catseye shouted, "Hurry, damn it! I'll hold this thing off for a while, I think, by fencing defensively. But hardly forever!"

Lizelle nodded and ran, and Thraas lumbered behind her. The third and last terrace was very near. Lizelle darted for the ladder. Then, with a gasp, she stopped short of it. A heap of dirt lay in the path before her, and it wriggled, and grew, and took the form of a small, stocky man, who grinned at them. "Hah! How long has it been since anyone passed my sister?"

"I . . . couldn't say," Lizelle said, wondering what might divert it, or if their quest was over.

"A long time," replied Thraas beside her.

"Indeed," said the other, chuckling. "Would you pass me?"

Lizelle nodded.

"Well, then!" Its arm lengthened suddenly, and its fingers closed about Lizelle's wrist. Before she was aware that she had been caught, she found herself hurtling through the air. Old habits took control, and she tucked to somersault among grass and irises.

Thraas's eyes widened in delight. "A game!" He buried his axe in an oak tree, then looked at this newest guardian.

"Would you kill?" he asked it.

"Only if you try to pass me."

"Then Thraas will not try to pass, dirt-man."

"No?" It almost sounded disappointed.

"No." Thraas grabbed it by one wrist and one ankle, raised it over his head, and threw it far to one side. "But Thraas will ensure Lizelle passes you!"

He had tossed the guardian so its head would strike the ground. While Lizelle watched, the sands of its form seemed to crawl as it reshaped itself. What had been its head became its feet, and the man-shape landed comfortably.

"Ah!" cried Thraas. "This will be a match to make sagas of!"

The fate of the world is at stake, and Thraas is having fun. Lucky bastard. Lizelle reached for a golden rung and climbed, expecting the thing of dirt to pluck her down. The sounds of its bout with Thraas accompanied her to the top of the final wall. Scrambling over, she rolled with her hand on her sword hilt and wondered what obstacles waited for her here.

Nothing attacked. No one was near. There were no paths, only a row of neatly trimmed hedges, a lawn of yellow-and-bronze chrysanthemums, and the small, marble pavilion. In the middle of the pavilion sat an ornate chair decorated with silver and gold. Beside it was an open door or gate, fashioned of strange metals and mounted so it stood alone near the throne. It wavered like a mirage, but instead of seeming an illusion, it made everything around it seem false.

A tall woman waited near the chair, covered from head to foot in a white robe and cowl. She stared away from Lizelle, away from the terraced gardens, watching the clouds surge far below them. Only the slight movement of her shoulders as she breathed proclaimed her woman and not statue.

Lizelle stood still for a long moment, hardly believing she was so close to her goal. An unaccustomed awe filled her, and she felt afraid to approach, afraid to disturb this tableau of perfect peace. Knowing she had no choice, she walked slowly to the pavilion and bowed low. "Wisest One?"

The woman turned and smiled. "You could call me that," said Glynaldis of Gordia.

"Now?" asked Ralka.

"Soon," said Asphoriel.

"Why do we wait?"

"The hour hasn't arrived."

"You want the necklace."

"Yes. We both do."

"Then take it."

"We will."

"Now."

"No."

"I'm impatient."

"As ever."

"*I* could take the necklace, now."

Asphoriel smiled. "You think so? You couldn't cross the barrier that the horse passed through so easily."

"No?"

"Nor could I." He pointed to the girl who watched them. "Ree might have a better chance than either of us, had she the wit."

Ralka stared at him. "You've doomed us!"

"No."

"You . . . you duped me. You serve Her! You're a third safeguard, aren't you? From the Elves, the Wisest One. From humans, the Questers. And from the gods—"

"Calm yourself."

"I should kill you."

"There's no third safeguard. Her mind doesn't work that way."

"Then why've you let them escape?"

"They haven't escaped."

"We might've stolen the necklace from the girl! Or from the Empress before she used it to reach World's Peak. True?"

"It would have been of no use to us, then."

"No?"

"No. It must be used in conjunction with the Wisest One's Portal of Passage."

"You didn't tell me this."

"I did not tell you many things."

"Why?"

"You might have been afraid to continue."

"And with good cause. But I'm no more a coward than you, Asphoriel."

"True."

"Why must we use it with the Portal?"

"Because the Portal is the passage to the underside of your universe."

"I'm sure that's clear to you."

"You're displeased."

"Of course. Will you tell me anything more?"

"Certainly."

"Can I trust you?"

"Possibly."

"When do you act?"

"It is still 'we,' Wolf Lord."

"When!"

"When the gem is in the Portal of Passage. Then we'll use the necklace like a needle to sew the fabric of your world as we wish. We'll change the Pattern so your God can never return, no matter what contingencies She has prepared."

"And how do you get the necklace into the Portal? Ask Glynaldis to carry it in for you?"

"Only one person will leave World's Peak, Ralka. That one will use the Portal, and then we'll have the necklace, and victory."

"Or?"

"Or you'll be happy. We'll take a last chance, and act within your God's world."

chapter seventeen

The Wisest One

THE TWO WOMEN stood atop World's Peak in silence. A slight wind toyed with Lizelle's hair and carried the scent of chrysanthemums to her. If Catseye and Thraas still fought the guardians on the terrace below, the sounds of their battle were muffled, perhaps by the hedge of honeysuckle that encircled the Wisest One's garden.

As Lizelle reached for the hilt of her sword, the Empress said gently, "I'm in no hurry to kill you."

Glynaldis appeared to be weaponless in her white, hooded dress. Still, her presence meant that they had all underestimated this foe. Lizelle thought she could attack with her hands or her sword almost as quickly as the Empress could speak, but Glynaldis would never be here without precautions. Knowing herself to be a prisoner again, Lizelle said, "I'm glad of that," and let her hands drop innocently to her side.

Glynaldis indicated the mountains about them with a sweep of her arm. The icy range of The Wall glistened blue and silver in the afternoon sun. "A beautiful view," Glynaldis said, and Lizelle believed the woman was sincere.

"Yes," she answered. "It is."

"There's no Wisest One," announced the Empress, turning to face her. "Yet. The last was slain centuries ago, some say by Asphoriel. This was about the time that the Lord of Cats disappeared."

Wondering what Glynaldis wanted now when she seemed to have won, Lizelle said, "There's a connection?"

"Perhaps. The necklace also disappeared then. I believe

the Wisest One's apprentice was seduced by the Demon Lord and stole the necklace for him. Perhaps it was used to further some plan of Asphoriel's. But the apprentice either returned to righteous paths or walked too far on a willful one. She betrayed Asphoriel and hid the miststone from him."

"Why do you tell me this?"

"To talk. If I talked to myself, I'd wonder if I was mad."

"Oh."

"And I rather like you, I think. Would you serve me?"

Lizelle nodded cautiously. "I might."

"Take this." Glynaldis tossed the miststone to her. Lizelle caught it in one hand and stared at it, then at Glynaldis, who said, "Don't act simple, girl. Put it on."

"As you wish." Trying to hide her confusion, Lizelle slipped the silver chain over her head. It felt *right* about her throat, and she hoped that Glynaldis would not take it again.

Glynaldis pointed at the jeweled throne. "That's the seat of the Wisest One. Whoever sits in it receives all the knowledge of all living mortal beings. In a single instant."

"But . . ." Lizelle frowned, wondering what this had all been about if Glynaldis would give up the necklace so easily. "Don't *you* want that?"

Glynaldis laughed. "I'd surrender much to experience that. But not my sanity, which it might take. Do you begin to understand?"

Lizelle bit her lip and nodded.

"You needn't be too frightened. Many have sat in that seat before you. Most have survived. Of course, they were all Elvish. . . ."

"What can I expect?" she demanded, thinking, *Catseye and Thraas risk their lives, and Merry as well, for all I know, and I stall for time. I haven't changed.*

The Empress lifted and turned a dismissing hand. "Who knows? Some say the experience is greater than any other, this losing of the self in the world's life. If you prove that someone other than Elf can endure it, I'll be grateful for a new thrill."

"And what's that?" Lizelle pointed at the jeweled door

by the throne, the gateway that pulsed with a power that seemed wrong in the world as she knew it.

"Ah. The Portal of Passage. If I were foolish enough to let you leap into it with the miststone, you could travel anywhere in the world by wishing to."

"Oh."

Glynaldis laughed again. "Do you wonder how I arrived before you did?"

"A little."

"The necklace brings anyone up here who wishes to come. And the Portal takes one away, wherever one wishes. Your trip would have been easier, if you'd known." Glynaldis nodded toward the chair. "Sit."

"If I don't?"

Glynaldis whispered a single syllable. A globe of fire appeared at her fingers. She juggled it casually in one hand, as if weighing it, and cocked an eyebrow at Lizelle.

"I'll sit," Lizelle decided. *Farewell, Darkwind, Noring, Catseye....* She braced herself with a palm on either arm of the Wisest One's chair, looked again at the Empress's blazing sphere, then, with a last plea directed to the godlings who, if they had never helped her, had never hurt her, either, Lizelle lowered herself until ...

... she was herself, and yet far more than herself, for beings lived within her body, simple beings who only understood consumption and reproduction, and those things, dimly; and ...

... similar things moved on her skin, and in the air near her, and on her neck was a creature whose thoughts and needs and physical size seemed so immense that she could not begin to comprehend it, and then she realized that it was a gnat; and ...

... things lived in the ground under her feet, and the grass itself lived, and reacted to warmth; and ...

... she was Glynaldis, and emotions and memories were too rich to absorb, though she felt the woman's great loneliness, which became her own loneliness; and with this sense of identity came the certain knowledge that she would kill someone called Lizelle when she had learned what she needed to know, for the girl was too dangerous to her plans for world rule; and ...

... *she was a woman and her brother who had given up their humanity to protect the Wisest One from those who would disturb the perfect solitude that the Wisest One required; and* ...

... *she was Catseye, whose mind was as guarded as his manner, who had lived by his wits and through his own ability, who had been a child in a world that despised humans and an adult in a world that hated Elves, who kept his loyalties and his passions to himself, so they could never be shattered, who served a great cat that was trapped in a place beyond the God's universe; and* ...

... *she was Thraas, who devoted himself with single-minded glee to battling a creature of dirt, and he was happy because his opponent fought without tricks, with fists and feet only, and, if Thraas lost, only Thraas would die and no one else, for Lizelle had already passed this thing; and* ...

... *she was Merry, sitting on the flagstone path and trying not to let his fears for the others disrupt his concentration, for the chore of linking the Wisest One's terraces so Catseye and Thraas and Lizelle might return was one that almost any of the Inner Circle might do with ease and one that he was neither skilled nor strong enough to do, though he noted with pride that he had held the way open so far; and* ...

... *she was Darkwind, who paced in the lowest garden and worried that this time his silly human rider would kill herself for sure as he munched angrily at purple crocuses; and* ...

... *she was Quentian, lying in his wife's arms in their small apartment on the Lane of Yellow Flowers and wondering if he should resign his commission in Gordia's Army; and she was Tikolos, who arranged a row of blue ceramic cups on the bar in The Wanderer's Roost and wished he had become a potter; and she was Hessabeth, who swept the stairs of The Roost and hoped Merry would return from his pilgrimage, leave the Questers, and marry her; and* ...

... *she was Serenity, who had been Felicity before the older man had fled from their Order, and when none could find his pattern among all the threads of the World Weave, she had succeeded to his position, though she had not wanted to; and* ...

... here Lizelle halted for an instant, if she can be said to have halted when time did not pass, yet while she was Serenity of the Questers, she felt a truth that transcended all other truths, that the story of the God's return and rebirth from the lords of all beings and judgment on all living things was a half-truth, that the God would be reborn from all the life in the universe and then do as She chose, thus ending all individual life, and no sentient being could honorably prevent this, for She had lent her own life to everyone, and all loans must someday be repaid; and ...

... Lizelle was simultaneously every human and every creature almost human and every creature that once was and every creature that never would be, all of whom formed the ten hundred billion parts of a being who was the God, who slept and knew the time to wake drew near, who wanted to wake and could not, for one tiny part of her was missing, and that part was the Lord of Cats; and then ...

*... Lizelle fell forward from the Wisest One's seat, un-*sure that she had sat in it, or who or what she was. She felt euphoria, fear, and confusion. Her memories were tangles of her own history and uncountable histories that were not hers. Clouded impressions quickly faded from her consciousness, leaving only a few facts gleaned from so many minds, and the most important fact of all, pieced together from fragments of legend and children's lore remembered by unknowable thousands of people and beings who thought them no more than amusing stories, was *the miststone could right all, or end all*.

Glynaldis gripped Lizelle by one shoulder and shook her. The sphere of flame remained in her other hand. "Well?"

"The necklace, the necklace..." Lizelle rolled her eyes like a madwoman and began to sing a tune to which she had skipped rope, long ago. "The necklace is the treasure, the treasure is the key, if I had the necklace, the treasure would belong to me!"

Glynaldis demanded, "Tell me!"

Lizelle winced under the woman's grip and said, "The necklace lets one travel..."

"Yes?"

"To this plateau."

"Yes. So? We're here already."

"Anywhere on this plateau," said Lizelle, wishing herself five feet away and beginning to smile.

Glynaldis whirled. Though her mouth was agape in uncustomary surprise, she threw her fire ball directly at Lizelle.

"Anywhere," said Lizelle, appearing farther away, grinning now, enjoying this power and her success. *It's like tumbling! I start here, end there, and trust the in-between to fate and skill and luck.* "Anywhere at all," Lizelle said, arriving behind Glynaldis. She hit the Empress hard on the back of the head with the pommel of her sword. With a gasp, Glynaldis slumped to the ground.

So. It's over. Lizelle sheathed the sword, then remembered her companions and ran past the hedges to the garden wall. Peering over, thinking, *I could have used the necklace to get here,* she saw no one. A pile of dirt shimmered at the base of the ladder. Someone tapped her shoulder from behind.

Suppressing a gasp, she turned, drawing her sword again. *I thought I hit Glynaldis hard enough—*

Catseye smiled at her. As Thraas, grinning, stepped from behind a farther hedge, Catseye said, "Well?"

If I answer, I'll have to tell you . . . what? That we can't free the Cat Lord without unleashing the God and destroying ourselves in the doing. You'll have to remain his servant, friend Cat. And what do I say to Merry? He thinks we only sought to stop the Empress and learn the fate of the Cat Lord, which we've done, but his superiors believe we all must repay our debt for the God's gift of life, and that means—"How'd you escape?" she asked.

Catseye shrugged and said, "I wondered why the guardians were so different and stationed so far apart. Thraas and I drove them together, and . . ." He indicated the radiant mound of dirt in the lower garden. "That's the result. They destroyed each other, I think." He looked at the marble pavilion. "Where's the Wisest One?"

"There isn't one," Lizelle said. "Unless you count me."

"Huh?"

She held up the necklace. "Yep." She willed herself behind him, and he spun to confront her. Amused by his surprise, she kissed him lightly on the nose, then skipped back. "Believe me now?"

"I—"

Thraas called from the pavilion, "Empress is here! Sleeping!"

Catseye glanced back at Lizelle. "Hmm?"

"Odd place to sleep," said Thraas, scratching the stubble on his chin.

"She'll rest for a while yet," Lizelle answered.

"Then the revolt failed?" Catseye asked.

"No. It's succeeding." She remembered a fragment from her instant as the Wisest One. "When her followers learn that we've captured her, Gordia will belong to Colonel Ianin's forces. I suppose they'll restore the senate's power."

"Probably," Catseye said.

They stood quietly, and Lizelle knew that she had noted something during the time she had been Catseye, but she could not remember what. She only knew that she liked him very much and felt sorry for him, too, though she was not sure of the reason—unless it was that he was the Cat Lord's servant, and not of his own choice. Unsure what to say to him, Lizelle turned and called to Thraas, "Watch Glynaldis! Bind her mouth and hands. If she begins to work free of the bonds . . ."

"Yes?"

It was easier to say than she'd thought it should be. "Be ready to kill her."

"Someone should fetch Merry," said Catseye. He moved toward the nearby rungs.

"I will." Lizelle smiled. "There's a toy I haven't tried yet." She wished herself before the Portal, then hesitated as she was about to enter. It felt wrong, somehow, in ways she did not understand. *But so did the trapeze, when I first tried one.* Focusing on Merry on the lower terrace, she stepped in, expecting something like the sense of tumbling that came when she had used the miststone.

Someone seized the necklace in the darkness, pulling it taut against her throat, strangling her. Lizelle flailed, hit something, and prayed to return to a safe place, any safe place. As she fell from the realm between time and space onto the ground in front of the Wisest One's Portal, she felt the necklace slip over her head. Three strangers had fallen with her.

All three had human form, but only an adolescent girl in a short, flimsy tunic seemed truly human. One was a male of eerie beauty who wore fire instead of clothing. The other, a bearded man garbed all in grey, was—

"Ralka!" Thraas cried, hefting his axe.

The wolfish man was closest to her, so Lizelle kicked him in the stomach and thrust with her foot, driving him back into the Portal. *Ralka?* She had no time for fear, only time to recognize an enemy and act. *Whoever wears the necklace controls the Portal.*

The Necklace of the Wisest One dangled from the young girl's hand, and she stared at it, bemused or insane. The fiery man, standing beside her, said, "Give it—"

Lizelle kicked again. Her instep caught the girl's wrist, and the necklace flew from her to land in a clump of rust-colored flowers. Lizelle dived for it as the other stranger, the burning man, reached out. His touch grazed her shoulder, and she shrieked in agony, but her fingers closed on the miststone. The burning man sighed his resignation as he released her. The pain left her shoulder as his hand did.

The shaven-headed girl stared at them all as though she were dreaming. Catseye watched with his long sword in his hand and confusion on his face, or, perhaps, helplessness. Thraas had crossed angrily to the Portal, where grey hands gripped the sides of the doorway as Ralka pulled himself back.

Remembering what she had learned while she'd sat in the Wisest One's seat, Lizelle pulled the necklace over her head and wished the Wolf Lord far away, trapped in a place hidden outside or folded within their universe. And, seeing then the only bearable solution to Catseye's servitude, she brought back from that impossible place a great striped jungle cat. It padded out of the Portal to calmly study them all.

The man in flames bowed to Lizelle. "Lady, we've no quarrel now."

"You are Asphoriel?" she asked.

"Some know me by that name."

"I never knew we had any quarrel at all."

The cat growled at the fiery man.

"Nor have we," said Asphoriel to the cat. "Your foe languishes where once you were trapped."

The cat, unsatisfied, growled again.

Asphoriel looked to Lizelle. "I've done you no disservice. In fact, I've served you well. You know your God would have returned if I had not removed a piece from Her gaming board. You obviously agree with the tactic, for you only brought back this pawn in casting off another."

Lizelle nodded slightly, afraid to speak.

"Then," said Asphoriel, "I ask a favor. Allow me to depart."

"Why?" she asked. *And why don't you simply leave on your own? Oh. I brought you all when I fled from your attack in the Portal. You have to use it to return to ... wherever you wish. And I control the Portal with the necklace, which makes you a prisoner, of sorts. I wish you weren't such a dangerous one.* She looked to Thraas and Catseye for advice. Catseye only appeared cautious, and Thraas seemed fascinated.

The young girl's lip began to quiver as though she would cry, and she moved closer to Asphoriel. Lizelle wondered what part she had in all of this.

"Because I'm a better ally than an enemy," Asphoriel answered her. "Because our ends are similar. Because I have done you no harm, nor intend to. Because I could destroy your friends in an instant, if I chose, and you, too, if you ever remove that necklace."

Lizelle nodded and said, "You may leave."

The cat howled its agony or frustration. Asphoriel smiled, then stepped into the Portal and held out his hand for the girl.

Catseye said, "You can't permit—"

"I can, and do," Lizelle said.

Thraas, hearing her words, frowned. Lizelle prayed he would remain quiet for a second longer.

Asphoriel smiled more fully and gestured again for the girl, whose attention had been caught by a purple butterfly. He told Lizelle, "You chose well."

"I think so." She sent the Demon Lord into the heart of the sun and heard his dying shriek as though it sounded in her mind. Beating at the door from which her master had disappeared, the shaven-headed girl screamed wordlessly.

Lizelle fell to the grass, crying and exhausted. She told herself that this time it was truly over, and she felt something deep inside her mind answer that it never would be. So long as she wore the necklace, she knew that she was a part of the God, and the God still loved Asphoriel, though She had left him.

Thraas helped Lizelle stand and embraced her, almost crushing her. He cried, too, gasping something about Ralka and Guire and duty. Catseye watched them without saying anything, though there was something in his gaze that made Lizelle wish she could comfort him. Beside Catseye, the young girl sat hugging herself on the steps of the pavilion. And, near her, the jungle cat nodded its satisfaction and began to wash its fur.

Catseye reached out to put a hand on the girl's shoulder. And then, behind him, by the far wall of the garden where summer gave way to the abyss of winter, Glynaldis, free of her bonds, began to stand. "No!" Lizelle cried, knowing that too much had happened too quickly for her to act again.

Catseye whipped about and brought his hand to his covered eye. As he drew back the green scarf, the world flared, just as it had when the Thief in Shadow had been vanquished in Tyrwilka. Lizelle heard the Empress gasp and saw the woman fling up her arms to protect her sight, and then Lizelle's own sight failed for an instant.

The Empress staggered blindly backward. With her second step, her calves bumped against the low wall, and Lizelle's returning vision caught the Empress's dark silhouette while it seemed to defy gravity for a long moment. Then, with a shriek, Glynaldis flailed for balance and fell. Her scream was immediately lost in the rush of the mountain winds. When the others hurried to peer down the side of the cliff, they saw no more than clouds and rock and snow.

"Gone," growled the jungle cat. "Good."

"It's done?" asked Catseye. Watching him, Lizelle realized without surprise that his strange right eye matched the jungle cat's left, and she saw that where the Cat Lord's

right eye should be there was a small dark hole. "Everything?"

"Yes," said the Cat Lord. "Done."

"Then you owe me."

The Cat Lord continued to lick his paw.

"I wish to be free," Catseye said. "As you are."

"Admirable that is," said the Cat Lord.

"We had an understanding."

"No. An understanding you had."

Catseye glared. He stepped toward the cat as though he
would attack it with his hands, then fell, clutching at his
face and shrieking. Lizelle ran to him, but he pushed her
away. "Cat Lord!" he screamed. "I'm no toy!"

"No?" said the cat. "Not toy, then. But useful you are."

"Because of our link?"

"Yes."

"I wish to be free."

"Who would not?"

"I will be free," Catseye repeated grimly.

Horrified, Lizelle began to understand. Near her, the mad
girl began to whimper, and Thraas put an arm around her
to comfort her.

"Is power not freedom?" the cat asked Catseye.

"No."

The cat turned away.

"Free me!" Catseye cried, almost begging.

"Free yourself," said the cat, as though this were a small
thing.

Catseye's hand darted up to claw at his inhuman eye.
Lizelle gasped and shrieked, "Catseye, no!" Thraas, closer
than she was, leaped forward as if he would stop the Elf.
He was too far away, and too late.

A yellow gem fell into Catseye's palm. He stared at it,
then touched his fingers to his cheek and higher. A second,
human eye filled the socket where the Cat Lord's eye had
been. The gem in Catseye's palm disappeared.

"A joke that was," the Cat Lord said, winking the eye
that had appeared where only darkness had been.

"Some sense of humor," said Thraas, walking back to
stand by the girl.

Catseye laughed. "Cat!" he called. "I'd hug you!"

The cat said, "Heh! Humans! Nothing know they of dignity or gratitude." Two bounds brought him to the edge of the terrace, and he jumped down. Lizelle watched him race from garden to garden and hoped he would not frighten Darkwind. "Free I would be, too!" he called. "Tell none the Cat Lord returns!"

Catseye still grinned foolishly, blinking one eye and then the other. When he saw that Lizelle watched him, he frowned, then laughed again and said, "He wasn't so bad."

"Good cat," Thraas agreed, turning to lead the young girl back toward the ladder. "Thraas will find Merry."

"Wait," Lizelle said. The girl's gaze moved toward her voice, but she did not seem to see her. Lizelle touched the girl's cheek and smiled. "Hello."

"Hello?" the girl said.

"Who are you?"

Without inflection, the girl repeated, "Who are you?"

"I'm Lizelle. I'm a friend."

"I'm Lizelle. I'm—"

"No. Think. Who are you?" It might have been her imagination, but Lizelle thought the necklace gave her words added force.

The girl's eyes flickered, and she said hesitantly, "I'm—Ree? Riawn. Of Oleth-ym-Arion."

Lizelle almost laughed, wanting to hug her. "Greetings, Ree."

In a small child's voice, the girl whispered, "I wet myself," and Lizelle realized that there were things the necklace could not cure. Perhaps time could.

Lizelle said softly, "That's all right, Ree. Don't worry." She glanced at Thraas for support.

The hillman winked at her to show he understood and said, "Yes! Not to worry, Ree! Thraas wets self all the time." The hillman shrugged. "So what?" Taking the girl again by the shoulder, he smiled at Lizelle, then said, "Come. Thraas will help you find dry clothes, Ree. There is priest named Merry who can make you very pretty clothes. Would you like that, Ree?"

"Yes," the girl said shyly.

"Good. Come, then," Thraas said.

Catseye looked at Lizelle. "We'll follow in a minute or two."

"We will wait with Merry." Thraas and Ree began their climb down the golden rungs.

Lizelle stepped close to Catseye to study his face. "You won't be able to do the light-flash trick," she said.

He shrugged. "So? Perhaps I'll never need to."

She placed her hand on his chest and fingered one of the wooden buttons on his jacket. "I've got the strangest bunch of memories from sitting on the Wisest One's chair."

"Yes?"

"Yes. For example, a condiment of tomato paste and vinegar can substitute for brass polish, in an emergency."

Catseye nodded solemnly. "I'll remember that always."

"And someone, somewhere," she said, "thinks a woman who hasn't the least bit of Elvish blood is rather attractive, in spite of being a bit short, a bit thin, and much too dark."

Catseye raised an eyebrow. "Truly?"

Lizelle smiled.

Catseye shook his head. "That's difficult to imagine."

"Oh, I know. What's hardest to imagine is that she thinks—"

He kissed her.

A moment later, she said, "I don't mind letting the others wait, if you don't."

And much later, lying on the grass, Catseye looked across the garden toward The Wall and said, "I don't like to kill."

Lizelle sighed. "You do know how to ruin a mood."

"Sorry."

"No. I agree. I don't like most of this."

"What?" He glanced at her.

"This whole business." She snatched off the necklace and drew back to fling it toward the cliff that dropped into the distant clouds.

Catseye caught her wrist. "You have responsibilities, Lizelle."

"I'm not the Wisest One."

"Then who is?"

Lizelle stared at the gem in her hand and trembled.

epilogue

Setting Out

LIZELLE AND DARKWIND left City Gordia on a grey winter afternoon, but Lizelle felt as happy as if they traveled through the most beautiful day of summer. *What now?* asked Darkwind.

I don't know. Perhaps we'll join Catseye in Tyrwilka. I'd enjoy visiting the Elflands with him. Or maybe we'll see how Merry adapts to life outside his Order. And Thraas has asked us to join him on his travels in the south. Who knows? I just want a vacation from playing adviser to the Empress-to-be. Ree's a sweet girl, but I already tire of court intrigue.

Ah. Does one feel guilt?

For what?

For changing the title of an institution with a history as old as mankind's?

What do you mean?

Nothing. Dumbest one.

Lizelle touched the necklace at her throat and smiled. *That title may be the more accurate one,* she thought. *After all, look whom I chose for a traveling companion.*

Darkwind snorted. *Everyone does something right once.*

About the Author

William Howard Shetterly was born in Columbia, South Carolina, on August 22, 1955. He presently lives in Minneapolis, Minnesota, with his beloved wife, Emma Bull, and his tolerated cats, Chaos and Brain Damage. He has acted Off-Broadway in New York City, but never well. He has played bass for a Minneapolis sort-of-new wave band, but never well. He takes perverse pride in having been expelled from the Choate School.

Along with fellow Ace authors Patricia C. Wrede, Steven Brust, and Pamela C. Dean, Shetterly is a founding member of the Interstate Writers' Workshop, a.k.a. the Scribblies; and he and his wife are coeditors of the shared-world anthology, *Liavek,* to be published by Ace Fantasy in the summer of 1985. Shetterly and Bull are also cofounders of SteelDragon Press.

Other than this, there is nothing he wishes known about himself, except that the rumors are not true, the photos are obvious fakes, the witnesses were paid, and his signature doesn't look anything like that.

AWARD-WINNING
Science Fiction!

The following titles are winners of the prestigious Nebula or Hugo Award for excellence in Science Fiction. A must for lovers of good science fiction everywhere!